Tuesdays with Nester

"What's so hard about it? Stick a gun in someone's face and take what they got."

"There's more to it, boy," Nester growled. "You can't pick a gun 'cause it's pretty. You gotta be ready to use it. You gotta be ready to kill a man just because he got in yer way. And if need be, you gotta be ready to kill anyone else that gets in yer way.

"You know what your problem is? You only wanna hurt them's that has it comin'. I killed men just to clear a path for a getaway. I gunned down plenty of folks that didn't deserve it. I even shot plenty of 'em in the back. You know how much that haunts me to this day?"

Sol shook his head.

"It don't," Nester hissed. "I don't lose one wink o' sleep over none of the widows I made or throats I slit. I don't give a damn whose money I stole. You wanna rob and kill for a livin'? That's the kinda blood that's gotta run through your veins."

Ralph Compton

Death of a Bad Man

A Ralph Compton Novel
by Marcus Galloway

A SIGNET BOOK

SIGNET
Published by New American Library, a division of
Penguin Group (USA) Inc., 375 Hudson Street,
New York, New York 10014, USA
Penguin Group (Canada), 90 Eglinton Avenue East, Suite 700, Toronto,
Ontario M4P 2Y3, Canada (a division of Pearson Penguin Canada Inc.)
Penguin Books Ltd., 80 Strand, London WC2R 0RL, England
Penguin Ireland, 25 St. Stephen's Green, Dublin 2,
Ireland (a division of Penguin Books Ltd.)
Penguin Group (Australia), 250 Camberwell Road, Camberwell, Victoria 3124,
Australia (a division of Pearson Australia Group Pty. Ltd.)
Penguin Books India Pvt. Ltd., 11 Community Centre, Panchsheel Park,
New Delhi - 110 017, India
Penguin Group (NZ), 67 Apollo Drive, Rosedale, North Shore 0632,
New Zealand (a division of Pearson New Zealand Ltd.)
Penguin Books (South Africa) (Pty.) Ltd., 24 Sturdee Avenue,
Rosebank, Johannesburg 2196, South Africa

Penguin Books Ltd., Registered Offices:
80 Strand, London WC2R 0RL, England

First published by Signet, an imprint of New American Library,
a division of Penguin Group (USA) Inc.

First Printing, April 2008
10 9 8 7 6 5 4 3

Printed in the United States of America

THE IMMORTAL COWBOY

This is respectfully dedicated to the "American Cowboy." His was the saga sparked by the turmoil that followed the Civil War, and the passing of more than a century has by no means diminished the flame.

True, the old days and the old ways are but treasured memories, and the old trails have grown dim with the ravages of time, but the spirit of the cowboy lives on.

In my travels—to Texas, Oklahoma, Kansas, Nebraska, Colorado, Wyoming, New Mexico, and Arizona—I always find something that reminds me of the Old West. While I am walking these plains and mountains for the first time, there is this feeling that a part of me is eternal, that I have known these old trails before. I believe it is the undying spirit of the frontier calling, allowing me, through the mind's eye, to step back into time. What is the appeal of the Old West of the American frontier?

It has been epitomized by some as the dark and bloody period in American history. Its heroes—Crockett, Bowie, Hickok, Earp—have been reviled and criticized. Yet the Old West lives on, larger than life.

It has become a symbol of freedom, when there was always another mountain to climb and another river to cross; when a dispute between two men was settled not with expensive lawyers, but with fists, knives, or guns. Barbaric? Maybe. But some things never change. When the cowboy rode into the pages of American history, he left behind a legacy that lives within the hearts of us all.

—Ralph Compton

Chapter 1

Warren, New Mexico, 1883

It was a poor excuse for a mine on the outskirts of a poor excuse for a town. On paper, the mine was originally started up to work a vein of silver found by the uncle of its current boss. Charlie had hired a few men and kept the mine going for just under a year before selling his interests to a larger company based in Albuquerque. That was just enough time for a few shops and even more saloons to open their doors as well.

Actually, it would have been generous to say that any of those businesses had doors to open. All but one building in Warren were actually tents held up by wooden frames that were barely sturdy enough to stand up to the winds that whipped in from the desert.

Every time that wind blew, it kicked up a mess of gritty sand that pelted against the tents like a dry hailstorm. The rocks on the southwestern end of camp loomed over the town like vultures. No matter how much digging was done inside the mine, the shape of those rocks remained unchanged. Charlie, on the other hand, wasn't quite so fortunate.

In Warren's infancy, Charlie had been a slender man with a thick head of hair. Now he was a large man with a thick, rounded head that looked to have been blasted clean by the desert winds. A bristly mustache covered his upper lip but looked more like an old brush that had been glued beneath his nose. Several lines crossed his face, neck and head, but it was impossible to tell which lines were scars and which had simply appeared there over the years.

Charlie's office was one of the only wooden buildings in town, and it also served as his home. Despite the fact that it was one of Warren's most expensive structures, the place wasn't much more than a shack and groaned every time the winds tore past it. Slightly more than half of its windows had glass in their panes, while the rest simply allowed the dust to come and go as it pleased. Considering the state of the house's owner, a few clean rooms wouldn't have made much of a difference anyhow.

As a fairly tame breeze pulled up the top layer of dust from the ground and spat it against the front of Charlie's house, a slightly less tame set of knuckles rapped against the door frame. Charlie didn't twitch at the sound of the knock. Since he'd caught sight of the other man through the narrow front window next to his door, Charlie was content to sit in his chair and pretend he'd gone deaf.

The man outside knocked again. This time, he followed up with a question.

"You got a minute, Charlie?"

Charlie had plenty of minutes, but he still didn't reply.

Before too long, the voice gained a bit of strength

and spoke up again. "Uh, I know you're in there, Charlie. I brought you your lunch, remember?"

Looking down at the mess of bread crumbs and gravy smeared on the plate in front of him, Charlie cursed under his breath and grabbed the napkin that was tucked into the collar of his shirt. "Door's open," he grunted.

Solomon Brakefield stepped inside. He was in his mid-twenties, had a narrow jaw with a clean-shaven face and tussled dark brown hair that was currently filled with enough grit to make it seem as if he'd been deposited by the wind along with the rest of the gravel that was too heavy to fly. Sol gripped his battered hat in one hand out of necessity, but shifted it into two hands out of respect when he stepped into Charlie's home.

"What do you want, Sol?" Charlie asked.

Sol blinked and grinned as if the mere fact that Charlie had remembered his name was a good omen. "I just wanted to talk to you about that percentage we discussed before."

"What percentage?"

"The percentage of profits from that silver I found last week," Sol replied. "You know. The one in that section of collapsing tunnel the rest of the men wanted to seal off?"

Straightening in his chair, Charlie let out a slow breath as he pondered the things he wanted to say. Seeing as how the younger man wasn't affected by the disgusted look upon Charlie's face, the boss took on a distinctly aggressive tone.

"I told you I'd think it over," Charlie said.

Nodding, Sol replied, "Yes, but that was three days

ago. And it was a few days before that when you said any man who found a new vein in that mine would get a cut of the profits."

"Maybe you weren't the one who discovered it. Plenty of men were working on that section of tunnel, you know. My nephew was one of 'em."

Although Sol's brow furrowed a bit, he forced himself to keep his voice calm. "Your nephew barely even steps foot into that mine, sir," he said while tightening his grip upon the brim of his hat. "The moment he heard a rumble, he was the first to leave that tunnel. I was the only one who stayed."

"Ain't that why I pay you?"

After a gesture that was part nod and part wince, Sol told him, "You pay me to dig silver out of those rocks. When your nephew turned tail and . . ." Sol stopped talking when he saw Charlie's upper lip curl into an ugly snarl. "When your nephew decided to leave," Sol amended, "the rest were told to leave as well."

"Then why'd you stay?"

"I had a hunch," Sol said proudly. "And it paid off. I found another vein of silver and you made it known that you'd reward any man who did that. You posted it."

Still scowling, Charlie spat out a grunting laugh and shoved his plate toward the edge of his desk. "I took them notices down."

Sol used one hand to fish something out that had been tucked under his hatband. It was a folded piece of paper. "I saved one, sir," he said. "It's right here."

Staring slack-jawed at the paper in Sol's hand, Charlie let out a noisy breath and climbed out of his chair.

Before he'd even stood fully upright, he was stomping around his desk toward the front door. "I know what I posted! You tryin' to come in here and make demands?"

"No, sir. I only meant to have a word with you about the percentage I'm owed. You said you'd talk to me about it before—"

"And I'm talkin' to you about it now," Charlie cut in. "I don't have everything figured out just yet because you insisted on coming in here and spouting off before I was prepared to tell you what you get."

Sol drew in a breath and took half a step back. His cheeks flushed and he quickly tucked the folded paper back under his hatband. "Oh, I'm sorry. I thought you might've forgotten, is all."

"I've been running this business perfectly well before you showed up," Charlie growled. "If I had a mind to, I could run this whole damn town since the only reason it's here is because of my mine."

"I realize that, sir."

Charlie pressed his advantage like a dog sinking his teeth into a fresh piece of meat. Even though he was roughly the same height as Sol, he stalked forward as if he dwarfed the other man. Reaching out with one arm, Charlie poked Sol's chest with a beefy finger. "Maybe my nephew left that tunnel so he could tell me about that silver. You ever think of that?"

"No, sir."

"Maybe the only reason you were in that tunnel was because I knew there might be silver in there and I needed some men to dig it up. That is what I pay you men for, right?"

"Yes, sir."

Leaning back, Charlie let out another breath. This time, his blubbery lips curled into a grin. The layers under his chin folded one on top of another as he lowered his head in a single nod. "You got some money comin'," he admitted.

Sol's eyebrows rose, but not enough to make him look truly hopeful. "Thank you, sir. That's all I came to—"

"Give me a few days to figure it up."

"I appreciate that, sir, but I was hoping to take a few days for myself. I was gonna get a look at some property a few miles from here."

Those words slid through Charlie's ears like pellets through a greased pig and he barely even gave a sign that he'd heard them at all. "There ain't no way for me to know what anyone's percentage might be until I know how much silver is dug up out of that tunnel. Could be a little, could be a lot. You wouldn't want me to settle for the former when it could be the latter, would ya?"

"Umm, no but . . ."

"Smart man. Just get back to work and I'll get back to you when it's all figured up. Shouldn't be more'n a few days."

"But the fellow who's going to show me that land is expecting me."

Grunting once, Charlie nodded as if his neck had a twitch. "Well, that ain't my concern. You want a few days? It'll be without pay. If I was you, I'd make sure you can afford that before you go skipping about spendin' money you haven't earned yet."

Although Sol's mouth began to form his words, he stopped short of giving them a voice. He gritted his teeth and drew his lips together into a tight line as he slowly pulled his hat down on top of his head. "I suppose I should stay around here while you figure things up."

"Why?" Charlie grunted.

The concern etched into Sol's face and the spark in his eyes made it clear that he had plenty of reasons. No small number of them had to do with the fact that Charlie was infamous for building whatever fortune he had upon the pile of deals he'd broken with his workers.

Then there were the stories about the bounty Charlie had offered for the heads of workers who'd tried to organize and demand a pay raise. Nobody could really say if the workers who'd disappeared had simply moved on to greener pastures or if they were buried somewhere in the desert. In the end, not many folks were anxious to start biting the hand that just barely fed them.

Looking into Charlie's eyes, Sol could tell the other man was about to repeat his question amid another spray from his fat lips. Before he was subjected to that again, Sol said, "I still got some work to do. There may even be another tunnel that has some promise."

The folds of Charlie's brow lifted a bit as he asked, "Really? You found another vein?"

"Maybe."

"Good. Then stay at it and I'll see what I can do to make you happy come payday."

Even though he knew Charlie was lying, Sol turned toward the door. "Thank you, sir."

As he walked outside, Sol kept his steps slow enough to brush against the ground. His ears strained for the first hint that Charlie might pay him some of what he was owed. Perhaps a few dollars would get tossed his way as a show of good faith. Maybe some assurances would be granted to him before he left. If there was any good faith to be shown, it was lost in the sudden slam of door against frame.

Chapter 2

"You should've punched that fat pig right in his snout!"

Even though he'd shouted those words, Matt del Rio wasn't too concerned about anyone but Sol hearing them. In fact, there was so much noise in the Railway Saloon that he could barely hear himself.

Sol chuckled and looked around nervously. Fortunately, there was just as much chance of Matt's words carrying as there was of a railroad actually buying up the land behind the saloon. While either of those things may have been a possibility when the saloon had been built, they weren't any longer. The place was too noisy for much of anything to stand out from the ruckus, and the land turned out to be too rough for tracks to be laid down.

"I wanted to punch him, believe me," Sol replied. "But I wouldn't exactly be able to keep my job afterward. Getting that bonus would be pretty rough, as well."

Matt chuckled and shook his head. "Getting any bonus from that pig is a task in itself. Trust me. Better men than you have tried."

"I heard of men getting their bonuses. If Charlie didn't pay, he wouldn't have so many working for him."

"Sure, he pays," Matt said. "He pays just enough to avoid a riot. But them bonuses are a fool's bet. You're my friend and all, but you're one of them fools if you truly think you'll get that percentage you're after."

Sol had been nursing the same glass of whiskey for nearly the entire length of time he'd been there after his workday was through. He wasn't much of a drinker, but he sure would have liked to toss back the liquor as if it were water. He didn't exactly have the money to do that, so he sipped at his drink and let the firewater trickle down his throat.

The Railway Saloon was a large tent filled with dozens of small round tables that looked more like oversized stools. Because the canvas walls had proven to be too big of a temptation for the local drunks to resist, there were lengths of rope along the top and bottom of each wall. Cowbells were tied to those ropes at odd intervals so they could make enough noise to alert the barkeep and his workers if anyone tried to sneak out before settling their bill. That constant jangle of cowbells gave the saloon its own brand of music that grated men's nerves almost as much as it amused their inebriated minds.

Normally, Sol enjoyed the odd mix of bawdy singing and clattering bells. Now it seemed more like an ache in the back of his head that would follow him no matter where he tried to go. Sol closed his eyes and took another sip of his drink. Since that little bit of whiskey didn't make a dent in his frustration, he drained the rest of it in one more swallow.

"Looks like you're out to raise some hell tonight, huh, Sol?" Matt asked as he raised his glass.

Despite the nod Sol gave the other man, he wasn't able to make the gesture too convincing.

After emptying his own glass, Matt slammed it back onto the bar and wiped his mouth with the back of his hand. "Want another round?"

"I can't afford it," Sol replied.

"This one's on me. After all the rounds you've bought in the months I known you, I'd say I owe you a few."

Sol grinned with genuine surprise. "That'd be great," he said. "Thanks."

Matt smiled even wider as he waved to get the bartender's attention. They were at the end of the bar farthest from the door, simply because they were less likely to be shoved outside from that spot. "Hey!" he shouted. "A couple more drinks over here!" Seeing that he still wasn't getting a response from the wiry man behind the bar, Matt leaned over until he almost slid across the top of the warped wooden boards and onto the floor.

As soon as the bartender felt the tug at his apron, he reflexively swatted at Matt's hand. The barkeep clipped Matt's shoulder, which was just enough to take away the rest of Matt's balance and send him to the floor.

Wincing from a mix of pain and embarrassment, Matt held up two fingers. "Two more whiskeys, please?"

"What in the hell's wrong with you, boy?" the barkeep snapped.

"Me and my friend's glasses are empty," Matt explained sheepishly.

Before the barkeep could respond to that, a shot blasted through the window and cracked one of the rickety supports holding up one end of the tent. That was enough to silence most of the conversations in the saloon as men either drew their own weapons or ducked for cover under the pathetically small tables.

"Holy—" Matt grunted before being cut off by another shot. After that piece of lead had hissed through the saloon to punch through two walls, Matt gasped, "Was that gunfire?"

"Yep," the barkeep replied. "Some fools in the street got guns."

"Who?"

Sitting with his back against his bar and his knees drawn up to his chest, the bartender looked as if he might be sitting alongside a river, skipping stones. He shrugged easily and reached for a shotgun propped against a central spot behind the bar. "Don't know for certain, but I can see 'em through my window," the barkeep replied as he nodded toward the flap that was held open by a crudely stitched hook and eye. "Looks like there's three or four of 'em headed toward Charlie's place."

"Do you think they got Charlie?" Matt asked.

Pausing as another wave of gunshots crackled outside, the bartender grinned and shrugged his shoulders. "You wanna ask 'em, you can be my guest."

When he heard something moving directly behind him, Matt twisted around and cocked his fist up close to his right ear. He almost took a swing at Sol, even after he'd spotted his face.

"What's the matter?" Sol asked. "Were you hit?"

"Hit? No. Those shots are being fired over at Charlie's place."

"The hell they are," Sol replied. "I counted at least five bullets passing through this saloon."

The barkeep winced at the sound of that and muttered, "Aww, damn!"

"What do those men want with Charlie?" Sol asked.

Matt shook his head as if he'd suddenly found himself in a dream. "I don't know what's going on. I just hope I don't get hit by any of that stray lead."

"Hear, hear!" a nearby drunk hollered.

Sitting with his back against the outside of the bar, Sol drew his pistol and checked to make sure it was loaded. His gun belt was old and well worn, but not from excessive use. It had been handed down from one of his cousins right before Sol had struck out for New Mexico. With all the commotion going on around him, Sol couldn't even recall which of his cousins had previously owned that holster.

Sol leaned toward the door and said, "I'm going to see who those men are."

"What?" Matt hissed from the other side of the crack. "Are you loco?"

"Not hardly. I may not be able to trust Charlie farther than I can toss him, but he sure won't be able to pay me if he's killed. He won't be able to pay any of us."

After chewing on that for a few seconds, Matt cursed under his breath. "You're right."

"You want to come with me?"

"No."

Snapping his pistol shut, Sol asked, "Will you come with me anyhow?"

After another pause, Matt replied, "I guess. It sounds like the shooting's about done anyway."

Sol got his feet beneath him while the gunshots tapered off until finally their echoes faded away. Only then did Matt stick his head up from behind the bar.

"Sounds like they're gone," Matt said happily. "That calls for another round."

Although all the drunks within earshot were plenty happy to hear that, Sol wasn't so enthusiastic. Standing up with his gun in hand, he continued toward the front door. "Then stay here where it's safe," he told Matt. Glancing at a set of holes that had been recently blasted through the canvas wall, Sol added, "Or at least where it's kind of safe."

Matt saw those holes and he also saw Sol walking through the door. After letting his eyes bounce back and forth between those two sights, he cursed once more and hopped over the bar. "Not so fast," he hissed as he made it out of the saloon. "If they are still about, you don't want them to see you."

Crouching a bit as he slowly walked down the crooked lane that passed for Warren's Main Street, Sol squinted into the distance. The street ahead of him was littered with water troughs, hitching posts and a boardwalk that looked more like a series of boards that had fallen off the back of a slowly moving wagon. Another saloon was in his line of sight, but that place served up more whores than whiskey. The patrons in there had probably been too busy to even notice any gunfire.

There were also two stores nearby, which were merely

open-backed wagons covered by drooping awnings. The people who ran those stores had most definitely heard the shots, since they were huddled under their wagons.

Sol approached the closest wagon and hunkered down to put his face a bit closer to the old woman hiding beneath it. "Did you see who fired those shots?" he asked.

The woman shook her head. "I didn't see nothin'."

"The barkeep in the Railway says it was some men over at Charlie's place."

Before too long, the old lady nodded. "Yeah. Maybe two or three of 'em."

"I thought you didn't see anything," Matt pointed out.

When the old lady shifted her gaze to Matt, she showed him plenty of fire in her eyes. "And if Charlie is alive and in any condition to ask about it later, that's just what I'll tell him."

"Do you know if those gunmen are still around here?" Sol asked.

The old lady leaned forward just enough to put her nose out slightly past a wagon wheel. She stretched her neck out a bit more so she could look in the direction of Charlie's house. Once she'd seen her fill, she allowed herself to plop back into her original spot. "You're that Brakefield boy who works at the mine?" she asked.

Sol nodded. "Yes, ma'am."

"Maybe you should come under here with me where it's safe."

"I appreciate the offer, but Charlie may need some help."

The old woman scowled and shook her head. Although she clucked her tongue a bit, she didn't say another word.

"She may have a point, you know," Matt told him.

But Sol already had his sights set upon Charlie's house. "Then you can stay here and I'll go."

Matt glanced down at where the old lady was hiding and saw her scoot a bit farther under the wagon. As much as he wanted to join her, he gritted his teeth and took hold of his pistol. "We need to find the law is what we need to do," he said once he'd caught up to Sol.

"The law don't even care enough to post a man in camp," Sol pointed out. "Why would they start to give a damn about some shooting now?"

"We could always let them know what happened. I bet the sheriff will ride out here."

But Sol kept walking. His back was to the Railway Saloon and his eyes were locked upon the house at the end of the crooked street. One hand was wrapped around his old .44 and his free hand was outstretched to brush against each hitching post he passed along the way.

"It might be too late to catch those gunmen now," Sol whispered. "By the time the sheriff comes along, there won't even be any tracks left to follow."

"Really?" Matt asked hopefully. "You think it may already be too late?"

Sol glanced back at the other man and had to smile. Matt looked like he'd just heard the working girls in town had suddenly decided to cut their going rates in half. Before Sol could say anything to dash Matt's hopes, another set of gunshots did the job for him.

The shots came from the vicinity of Charlie's house,

but not from within the house itself. Sol could tell that much, simply because the shots echoed and rolled through the open air like thunder.

Apparently coming to the same conclusion as Sol, Matt whispered, "Those came from outside."

Sol froze in his spot and reflexively thumbed back the hammer of his pistol. "Right there," he said as he pointed toward the left side of Charlie's house. "You see them?"

It would have taken a blind man to miss the sight of those three figures backing away from the house. But even that same blind man would have heard the scrape of boots against the dry ground or the rushed voices of those men growling back and forth amongst themselves.

"Yeah," Matt whispered. "So what are we supposed to do?"

That was a good question.

In fact, Sol felt his teeth grind together as he tried to think of what to say. His eyes twitched in their sockets as he watched the three gunmen move away from the house. It wasn't until one of those gunmen looked directly at him that Sol knew what to do.

"Move," Sol hissed. "Just go."

First, one gunman looked in Sol's direction. Then, after a few quick taps to his partners' shoulders, the rest of them were glaring down the street. One of the men shouted, but those words were swallowed up by the blast of gunfire erupting from all three men's pistols.

"Aw, hell," Sol grumbled as he dove behind the closest water trough. Fortunately, Matt wasn't far behind him.

"What now?" Matt asked.

Sol scrambled to get himself situated so his shoulders were pressed against the trough and the rest of his body was more or less covered by the flimsy wooden box. As the gunmen focused their aim, more and more bullets began drilling through the trough. Before too long, splinters and dirty water were raining down on both of them.

"I'd say it's too late to run," Sol declared. With that, he rolled away from the trough and tucked his legs in beneath him.

As soon as his boots dug into the ground, Sol got his feet beneath him and started running toward another wagon that was parked a few yards in front of the shot-up trough. His initial thought was to keep something solid between himself and the gunmen, but that wasn't going to do the trick as well as he'd hoped. Two of those gunmen were running down the street to shoot from a better angle, while the third had disappeared altogether.

Sol leaned against the wagon, glanced quickly to his right and caught sight of Matt running to try to catch up with him. One of the two closest gunmen fired a round, which caused Sol to reflexively fire back.

It was the first time Sol had ever taken aim at another man.

For that matter, it was one of the few times Sol had even fired his gun. When he felt the pistol buck against his palm and let out its powerful roar, Sol felt every muscle in his body twitch. To his surprise, the gunman at the receiving end of that shot had a very similar reaction.

That gunman tried to jump and duck at the same

time. Not only was the movement awkward, but it almost put him on his backside in the middle of the street. The second gunman hunkered down and sighted along the barrel of his own weapon. By the time he pulled his trigger, his target had already ducked out of his view.

Sol pulled his head behind the wagon and closed his eyes as a pair of bullets whipped past his face. One of those rounds took a bite from the edge of the wagon and the other hissed through empty air. When he opened his eyes again, Sol saw someone looking up at him from beneath the wagon.

Much like the old lady at the first wagon, the owner of this wagon had sought refuge in the first place available to her. Unlike that old woman, however, this one was trapped under her wagon and still in the line of fire. She was also barely in her teens.

Cursing under his breath, Sol waved at the young woman to try and get her to move away from him and toward the farthest end of the wagon. When she wouldn't move, he slammed his fist against the wagon's wheel the way he might stomp his foot to get a stubborn cat to jump. He may have put a heck of a fright into her, but Sol's efforts were successful: The young woman moved farther under the wagon.

"I think one of them's circling around," Matt said as he rushed up to stand beside Sol.

Sol nodded and inched toward the edge. "Fine. You take that one and I'll take these two."

Sol didn't have to wait around to see if Matt would put up a fuss about that arrangement. He didn't even have to look in Matt's direction to know the other man would be squirming and trying to think of something else he would rather do. Since he wasn't about to waste time trying to shove Matt in one direction or another, Sol ran in his direction and hoped Matt would follow suit.

As soon as he jumped out from behind the wagon, Sol raised his gun and was ready to fire. Both of the gunmen had the bottom halves of their faces covered by a bandana. One of the men blinked furiously as he shifted from one foot to another. His breaths were coming so quickly that the front of his bandana expanded and contracted like a bullfrog's neck.

For a moment, all three men stood still and glared at one another. The temporary cease-fire was broken within seconds and lead filled the air once again. Sol did his best to empty his pistol as quickly as possible, while the other two gunmen scattered like birds that had been flushed from a bush. In the space of those few seconds, Sol was all but deafened by the gunfire. As hot lead whipped past him on all sides, he held his ground and kept firing.

His finger was still clamping down upon his trigger when Sol realized his gun was empty.

The other two gunmen had taken cover behind an empty cart on the side of the street less than ten paces in front of him. Both of those men seemed rooted to their spots in much the same way Sol was rooted to his.

"I got him!" a stranger shouted from that direction. "Let's get the hell out of here!"

Hearing that, the two gunmen sidestepped away from the cart and then broke into a run.

Since he'd already emptied his cylinder, Sol could only watch the men go and wonder how he'd managed to survive.

Chapter 3

As much as Sol wanted to chase after those men, he wasn't stupid enough to do it with an empty gun. Most of the loops on his gun belt had been flattened after years of being empty, but there were enough bullets stuck in here and there for him to reload his .44. Once that was done, Sol rushed to the spot where he'd last seen Matt.

The other gunshots he'd heard had come from that same direction, which didn't give Sol much confidence. Even so, he worked his way back to that wagon and held his gun at the ready. Matt wasn't there, but neither were the gunmen. When Sol made it to the spot where those first few bullets had hit the edge of the wagon, he looked down and spotted the face of the young girl who'd been hiding underneath the wagon.

She looked up at him with wide eyes and asked, "Are they gone?"

"I don't know," Sol replied. He looked up and kept shuffling around the wagon. Just as he was approaching the wagon's front end, he heard several horses break into a run.

Sol took a few more hurried steps and immediately

regretted it. The moment he cleared the wagon, two of the three gunmen opened fire. If they weren't also trying to rein their horses in, one of those men might have put Sol down right then and there. As it was, the gunmen seemed more concerned with getting themselves turned toward the edge of town than in lining up a proper shot.

As all three horses found their stride, their riders kept firing behind them. Even amid the gunshots, Sol could hear the other men laughing and shouting to one another before disappearing around a bend.

"Matt?" Sol shouted.

"He's here."

Sol looked around, but couldn't see hide nor hair of Matt or the person who'd just spoken those words. After taking a moment to calm himself, Sol hunkered down to get another look under the wagon. Sure enough, there was someone else under there besides the young woman.

"That you, Matt?" Sol asked.

Although Matt was breathing loudly, he was staring up at the bottom of the wagon as if he were gazing into the heavens.

The young woman was the one to answer Sol's question. "He's been shot," she told him.

Dropping to his hands and knees, Sol tried to crawl under the wagon to get a look at Matt. He was stopped when the top of his head smacked loudly against the wagon's lower edge. When he reflexively reached up to rub his head, Sol nearly cracked his own forehead with the pistol he'd forgotten he was holding. Sol stopped what he was doing before he truly hurt himself and took a measured breath.

Just then, the sound of weak laughter drifted up from the shadows beneath the wagon.

Still rubbing the sore spot on his head, Sol holstered his gun and squinted into the shadows. "You think that's funny?"

Matt was lying on his side and wincing with every chuckle. Even though he grimaced in pain, he still managed to nod. "I sure do."

"Then why don't you come on out from under there and say that to my face?"

"Because I've been shot, Sol."

Those words brought everything back into sharp focus. Sol stood up and took a few steps in the direction the gunmen had gone, but could only see the dust cloud the horses had left behind. Confident the storm had passed, Sol went back to the wagon. "Can he come out from there?" he asked the young woman who had remained within arm's reach of Matt the entire time.

"With your help, maybe," she said.

Looking at the wagon, Sol asked, "Can this be pulled forward a bit?"

"Just give me a hand, Sol," Matt groaned. "No need for all this fuss. I wasn't killed."

"Yeah, but you were shot."

"It's not that bad. Just help me."

Although he would have been much more comfortable with the idea of moving the wagon, it seemed as if Matt was about to start crawling on his own at any second. Sol took hold of the hand Matt extended and asked, "You ready?"

"Come on and do it," Matt snapped.

Sol dug his heels into the dirt and leaned back. The

moment he felt Matt budge, Sol also heard his friend let out a groan that might have come from a wounded animal. Sol immediately eased up and leaned forward again.

"Damn, that hurts!" Matt said through clenched teeth.

The young woman scampered out from under the wagon so quickly that she gave Sol a start. She was a pretty little thing who was small enough to get to her feet almost as soon as she was clear of the wagon. Her dark blue dress was as dirty as someone would expect considering the circumstances and her long braid had several stray strands of light brown hair flying free from the rest. Even so, she managed to look prettier than most of the girls in the camp.

"He was shot in his side," she explained. "I think dragging him like that will only tear the wound open further."

"Oh God," Matt groaned in a voice that had taken a distinctly queasy tone.

Lowering his voice to a whisper, Sol asked the young woman, "How deep is the wound?"

She shrugged and furrowed her brow as if she'd suddenly found herself in water that was several feet over her head.

"Is it more of a scratch or a hole?" Sol asked.

"A scratch," the young woman said gravely. "A big one."

Sol let out a breath and nodded. "That's a good thing." Squatting down to get another look beneath the wagon, Sol asked, "How high up is that wound, Matt?"

After a bit of a pause, Matt replied, "Under my arm. Maybe down a little ways."

"Can you stretch your legs out?"

"I guess."

"Then do it." By the time he'd walked around to the back of the wagon, Sol saw the tip of one of Matt's toes sticking out from the shadows. Sol hunkered down again, grabbed hold of Matt's boots around the ankles and pulled.

Matt let out a few grunts and groans, but didn't holler too badly. After a few more pulls, Sol was able to get Matt most of the way out from under the wagon. "How you doing?" Sol asked.

"Much better if I wasn't shot," Matt replied.

One more pull was all it took to get Matt out from under the wagon. It had seemed like an ordeal, but the process was over before more than a few locals had gathered around the wagon. Several of them whispered to one another before some of the braver souls approached Sol.

"Is he dead?" one of the locals asked.

Now that Matt was more or less in the open, Sol could see the other man's wound. Matt's shirt was ripped to show a bloody gash a couple of inches beneath his right arm. Matt held that arm curled up and clutched to his side as high up as he could manage. A pained grimace seemed to have been permanently stitched onto his face.

"Now that you're done torturing me, how about you get a doctor?" Matt asked.

"Torture?" Sol chuckled. "This doesn't even look as bad as when you twisted your ankle. Remember that? I thought your foot had spun around all the way."

"Yeah, but that happened after I slipped on some loose gravel. This was brought about by a bullet."

Sol reached down to pull aside the ripped flap of Matt's shirt. The skin was shredded along the edges of the wound, but the blood had already slowed to seep into the material rather than pour out of him. "It doesn't look so bad."

"Are you a doctor?"

"No," came a scratchy reply. "But I am."

Both Sol and Matt looked over to find a short old man carrying a large black satchel toward the wagon. The old man's head was pointy as a shovel and had just as much hair.

"Doc Connor!" Matt said with relief. "Great to see you! If it was up to Sol, I might be dead already."

"Not from that wound," Doc Connor barked after taking a quick look. "That's nothing more than a scratch."

"See?" Sol asked smugly. "I told you so."

Matt shook his head and rolled his eyes. His expression brightened when he saw the pretty young woman who'd been under the wagon with him reach out to take his hand. "Are you taking him to your house, Doctor?" she asked. "Because I'll come along with you and help any way I can."

Looking at Sol, Doc Connor said, "Help me get him to his feet."

Matt's eyes widened and he sputtered as Sol and the doctor each took one of his arms and started to lift him to a sitting position. "Ain't this gonna hurt?"

"Yeah," Dr. Connor said as he looped Matt's arm

over his shoulders and straightened up. "It probably will."

Not being one to argue with a doctor, Sol followed the older man's lead and hefted Matt to his feet. Judging by the expression on Matt's face, the doctor truly knew what he was talking about.

Matt groaned and complained all the way to the doctor's house, but all three of them made it without much trouble. Like most of the camp, the house was actually more of a tent built around a wooden frame. Even so, it was one of the cleaner tents. Once Matt was lowered onto a cot, the doctor rolled up his sleeves and started rummaging around for the instruments he was going to need. Already, Sol felt as if he'd been long forgotten. "You need me to stay?" he asked.

"Nope," the doctor replied. "I can handle stitches on my own."

"Stitches?" Matt asked.

Before Sol could give voice to one of the smart-mouth comments that came to mind regarding Matt's whining, he saw the young woman rush past him to sit at Matt's side. She took his hand in hers and patted it as she spoke in a quick, yet soothing tone.

"I'll stay right here," she said. "You want some water?"

Sol grinned at the way Matt tried to make up for the fact that he'd groused like a spoiled child all the way from the wagon to this cot. In fact, the wounded man went so far as to put on a brave face and casually mention the fact that he'd been shot while chasing those killers out of town.

Waving once to Matt, Sol left the small house so

the doctor could do whatever needed to be done. Even after he was making his way to the street, Sol could hear Matt talking up his end of the fight to the wide-eyed girl who'd dragged him to safety. Judging by the smirk on her face, she wasn't buying the entire story Matt was feeding her, but she let him tell it all the same.

Now that Matt had been delivered to the proper spot and the gunmen were no longer firing their shots, the town seemed more like its normal self. In fact, the place seemed a bit too normal for Sol's liking. There wasn't anything else to see, so the locals had all gotten back to their own affairs whether that involved working in one of the businesses or filling their gullets with liquor. Glancing at the men and women who wandered up and down the misaligned streets, Sol couldn't help but wonder what it would take to hold their interest for more than a few seconds.

Rather than try to figure out what made those folks tick, Sol walked to Charlie's house. Charlie stood in front of his place with his thumbs hooked around the black suspenders that were buttoned into the waistband of his pants. When he saw Sol coming, Charlie began to stalk toward him as if he meant to pounce the moment he was close enough to do so. Even from where he was standing, Sol could see the front door had been kicked in and even more of the windows had been broken.

"What happened here?" Sol asked.

"You want to know what happened?" Charlie snapped. "All three of them bust into my home, waving their guns around and screaming like a bunch of wild men. They told me to hand over my money. I told 'em to get stuffed and they started shooting. One of 'em jammed his gun in my face and said I was dead if I didn't change my mind. Since they would've gotten to the money after a bit more searching anyway, I told 'em where to look."

"Then they left?" Sol asked.

"Yeah. They got mad as hell and started shooting even more. After that," Charlie sighed, "you know the rest. If you want to hear more stories, go ask someone else. Did you at least get a look at which way they took off to?"

Sol pointed toward the last direction he'd seen the three gunmen ride. "That way," he replied. "How much money did they get?"

"All of it," Charlie grunted. "They got damn near all of it."

"You mean the payroll?"

Charlie nodded. "Yeah. That, as well as a good portion of some funds that were necessary to keep this operation up and running." Although he'd cast his eyes downward, Charlie glimpsed up quickly to watch Sol's face as he added, "They even got the money I was gonna use to pay out my bonuses. Sorry about that, Sol. I know that percentage was important to you."

"It was all important, sir."

"Yeah," Charlie grunted. "I suppose it was. Not that it matters anyhow. It's all gone and there ain't none of it that's coming back."

"Not on its own," Sol pointed out. "But it might come back if it had a little help."

Blinking furiously, Charlie stared into Sol's eyes. It was all Sol could do to keep his chin up and his eyes focused upon Charlie. Sol's next words came out of him like a flock of doves exploding from a magician's hat. They came from nowhere and were impossible to catch once they'd been set free.

"I can bring it back for you," Sol said.

"What?" Charlie asked as he continued to blink and twist his head like a dog that had been subjected to a bad opera. "You want to fetch my money and bring it back?"

"Yes, sir."

"But you're just a miner. If I needed something dug or sifted, I'd let you know. Otherwise, just head home and thank your lucky stars you didn't get killed."

As Charlie started to turn his back on him, Sol stood up straight and spoke to his boss in a confident tone. It may have been the longest that Sol had locked eyes with Charlie since he'd first been hired on to work the silver mine.

"I can find them, sir," Sol said.

Charlie looked as if he was about to dismiss that statement without another thought, but couldn't take his eyes from the other man's steely glare. "You can, huh?"

"Yes, sir. I know this area pretty well and there's not a lot of places for them to hide. It's also not too hard to track them, but I'd have to get started before the wind's had enough time to clear everything away."

Lifting his face into one of the passing breezes, Charlie narrowed his eyes and leaned forward. "You were out here shooting back at those robbers, weren't you?"

"Yes, sir."

"Did you hit any of 'em?"

Sol thought for a moment before shrugging. "Maybe, but it's hard to say. I got a good feel for how they work, though."

"Yeah?" Charlie grunted. "What's that supposed to mean?"

"They're cowards because they had to rush in on one man all at once. They're stupid because they made so much noise in doing it. And, since I'm standing here without a scratch and my friend only needs a few stitches, they're not very good with those guns they like to wave around so much."

"And what would you do if you did catch up to them?"

"Take your money back," Sol replied.

"Why concern yourself over something like that?"

"Because some of that's my money too."

Although Charlie had been scowling at first, his expression slowly shifted to one of curious disbelief. Now his thick lips curled to reveal an incomplete set of crooked, slightly brown teeth. "I suppose you're right about that. If you can get my money back for me, I'll make sure you'll get what's coming to you."

"Plus a bonus."

"Bonus?"

Sol nodded. "Isn't that fair? I mean, I would be putting myself at risk when I could just sit back and have another couple of drinks at the Railway."

"The law works for free," Charlie pointed out.

"Sure, when the law works at all. You and I both know it could be a day or two before the sheriff even hears about this. Even if he hears about it tomorrow, it'll be another day or two before he gets out here. It could take longer depending on what town he's in or where else he may be riding. After that, how long do you think it'll take for him to raise a posse?"

Charlie patted the air and nodded. "All right, all right, you made your point. How much of a bonus are you talking about?"

Impressed that the negotiations had gotten this far, Sol did some quick figuring in his head. "How about a hundred dollars?" he offered once he thought he'd come up with a fairly good idea of how much Charlie could have lost.

"Fine," Charlie replied as he quickly stuck out his hand. "It's a deal."

Apparently, Sol had guessed a bit on the low side where Charlie's losses were concerned. Even so, Sol grasped Charlie's hand and shook it.

Rather than release his grip, Charlie tightened it and pulled Sol close enough to impose his onion-tainted breath upon him. "You're a good worker, so I hope you don't get yerself killed. But, good worker or not, you should know that I know exactly how much money was taken from me. I know it right down to the penny."

"I thought you would, sir," Sol replied.

"And if there's one cent of it missing, I'll take it out of yer hide."

Sol nodded, doing his level best to keep his gaze steady and his grip strong.

"Just to prove that you do find 'em," Charlie continued, "you'd better bring me the gun of the man who messed up my face. It was a real fancy number with pearl handles and all."

Although it was difficult to pick out which part of the many scars, bumps, wrinkles or cuts Charlie was referring to, Sol guessed the freshest of those eyesores was the gash on Charlie's lip.

"I'll see what I can do," Sol told him.

Nodding, Charlie let go of Sol's hand as if he'd been tricked into sticking his fingers into a freshly gutted fish. "I'll need my money and proof that you got them robbers if you're to get your bonus. If you take too long, the deal's off."

Chapter 4

Sol was in such a hurry to get back to the doctor's tent that he nearly smacked his head against the wooden post holding the front flap open. When he got inside, Sol smiled widely when he found Matt sitting on the edge of a chair. The young woman who'd hidden with him under her wagon was wringing out a cloth over a basin of water.

"What's got you so cheery?" Matt asked. His shirt was gone, but his torso was mostly covered by the layers of bandages that wrapped around his rib cage.

"Just glad to see you're still alive and kicking," Sol replied. "How's the wound?"

"Don't come in here talking like that." The young woman shuddered. "He needs peace and quiet."

Matt smiled up at her and said, "Mind if I have a word with my friend here, sweet thing?"

She grinned and averted her eyes. "All right, but don't try to get up. Remember what the doctor said."

"I remember."

She nodded and handed him the wet cloth. When she looked over to Sol, her smile lost just a bit of its sparkle. "Don't upset him," was all she said before leaving the tent.

Sol winced and pulled up one of the nearby stools. "What'd I do to her?" he asked.

"Nothing. She's just a bit anxious. You should have seen her pestering Doc Connors when he worked on my stitches. He went off to get a drink as soon as he was done rather than stay around here." Still looking at the front of the tent as if the woman were standing in the doorway, Matt said, "Her name's Patricia."

"I think I may have seen her around the camp before."

"Could be. She sells fancy suits and dresses from the back of that wagon."

"I guess that would explain why I haven't done more than seen her about," Sol said. "It's a wonder she makes any profit selling fancy clothes in a mining camp."

"She's a nice girl," Matt insisted.

Sol grinned and added, "A real sweet thing, huh?"

Matt blushed. It was an odd addition to his dirty face and tired eyes. "I suppose we have kind of taken a shine to each other. I just hope she doesn't fuss this much about everyone who gets hurt around here."

"Speaking of getting hurt, how serious is that?" Sol asked as he pointed toward Matt's cotton casing.

"Oh . . . uh . . . it's just a cut. A real big cut, to be sure, but still just a cut. Doc Connors says the bullet just caught me as it passed on by. It sounds about right to me, but I don't have a lot of experience in such things."

"Good," Sol said. "Then maybe you'll be well enough

to come with me when I track down the men who shot you."

Matt stared blankly back at him for a few moments. Then he blinked, took a breath and blinked some more. Finally, Matt chuckled and then winced as he pressed a hand to his side. "I said I wasn't experienced in such things as gunfights, Sol, not that I wanted to earn some experience in that area."

"It shouldn't be too hard. That is, if we don't wait around too long. I saw which direction they were headed and there's not much of anything out that way for miles. Hell, there's barely anything around here in any direction. I've done some tracking and this sort of ground is perfect for—"

"What on earth are you talking about?" Matt asked.

Now it was Sol's turn to stare in disbelief. "What do you mean?" he asked. "Haven't you been listening?"

"Yeah, and you sound like you're going crazier by the moment. I mean . . ." Glancing toward the door and then shooting another glance toward the back of the tent, Matt lowered his voice as if the whole world were trying to listen in. "I mean, you're talking about hunting down armed men?"

Sol nodded. "They barely got out of here when they tried to take on one ugly fool like Charlie. When we stood up to them, they ran away!"

"After they shot me!"

"It's just a scratch, Matt."

"Not so you'd know. You barely even asked how I got hurt."

Settling onto his stool, Sol took a deep breath and placed his hands upon his knees. "Tell me what happened."

After a few stuttering starts, Matt grimaced and shook his head. "I thought I had the drop on him, but the fellow turned and fired."

"And then?"

"Then I fell down."

"And then?" Sol asked patiently.

Giving in with a tired sigh, Matt said, "And then he ran away."

Sol nodded smugly. "How close was he?"

"Maybe a bit farther than you are to me."

Standing up, Sol took a few steps back and then pointed a finger at Matt. "He was right about here, pulled his trigger and barely managed to scratch you."

"It's a pretty bad scratch," Matt grumbled.

"I think I may be able to kill you from here," Sol said.

"Is that supposed to make me feel better or worse?"

"It should make you feel like these gunmen were just as scared of us as we were of them. Probably more so," Sol explained. "If I didn't need to tend to you, we could probably have chased them down before they got too far away from camp."

"Sorry to hear I weighed you down," Matt chided.

"You know what I'm trying to say. We can do this."

"Why should we?"

"First of all, we'd be paid," Sol pointed out.

"Money don't spend when you're dead." Matt shifted in his spot, but seemed to be more uncomfortable with the conversation than he was with his wound or the bandages wrapped around his torso. "This ain't our job to do. We're miners, not bounty hunters."

"There's a hundred dollars for us if we get this job

done right. Seeing as how anxious Charlie was to get his property back, I'm sure he'd pay more if we play our cards right after the job's done."

"I almost got killed," Matt whined. "If that man's aim was a few inches different, I could have gotten a hell of a lot more than a scratch. What would you do even if you did find those men? Fight them? All three of them? They won't be running away then. Have you thought about that? They'll be out in the open and may even shoot us from our saddles if they see us coming."

Sol was already shaking his head. "It won't be like that. They were scared, Matt. I could tell. They're not killers. They might have been out to steal some money, but they're not real bad men."

"How do you know that?"

Sol could feel his heart slamming against the inside of his ribs. He pulled each breath in through a quick gulp and gritted his teeth as if those breaths were threatening to escape. "I wouldn't ask you to come along with me if I thought we couldn't do this."

"Have you ever even shot a man?"

"No," Sol quickly replied. "But I could."

And there it was.

Sol could feel the air become a thick, uncomfortable stew. For the next few moments, both men stared back at each other in silence. Then Matt shifted his gaze toward the front of the tent.

"I haven't known you for long," Matt said, "but I didn't imagine you'd say something like that."

Lacing his fingers together, Sol bowed his head and said, "You carry a gun just like I do. Just like nearly everyone in this camp does. You drew your gun when we went after those fellows running out of Charlie's house. What did you expect to do once we got there?"

"I don't know, Sol."

"I'm not the only one who's pulled a trigger," Sol said as he got to his feet and turned his back to Matt. "I hear shots fired from the saloons around here every night."

"Those are drunks or men getting into fights. That's different."

"How?"

"I don't know," Matt said in a voice that had suddenly become tired and heavy. "I don't even want to think about shooting someone."

"What if they hurt that pretty little thing you've suddenly taken a shine to?" Sol asked. "What would you do then?"

"I'd think of something, I guess," Matt replied defensively. "But you're just spouting off. You and I break apart rocks and sift dirt for a living and now you want to take your chances against outlaws? That's crazy talk, Sol!"

Suddenly, Sol snapped forward like a rattler with its fangs bared. Matt recoiled as if that were exactly what he was facing.

"I broke my back to earn my money and that fat pig sitting in that nice house seems content to let it ride away," Sol hissed. "He's probably got plenty of cash somewhere else, but do you think he'll give that to us or any of the other workers?"

"No," Matt replied.

"Maybe if we pull this job off, we can get into another line of work. There's plenty of rewards posted for plenty of other men and they're a whole lot more than a hundred dollars. Most of the fools on those posters are on the run after killing someone with a lucky shot. I've known of bad men and they put these idiots to shame. We're not going after that sort, Matt. We're going after robbers who can't shoot straight."

Matt shook his head slowly. "I . . . don't want to take that chance. I just found this pretty little girl here and in some strange way it's because of you. Thanks for that, Sol, but I ain't about to make Patricia a widow after I just found her."

"Widow? Don't you have to marry her before she can be your widow?"

"I got a good feeling about her," Matt replied with a twinkle in his eye. "You saw the way she looked at me."

In fact, Sol didn't have to think back to when the young woman had been looking at Matt. All Sol needed to do was turn and look outside the tent to find her keeping busy while also watching over the tent like a guardian angel. Turning back to Matt, Sol said, "She is pretty and she does seem to like you."

"There's plenty of ladies in camp, Sol. I know plenty of 'em's been giving you the eye."

"I suppose so."

Matt let out a breath that he seemed to have been holding ever since Sol had walked into the tent. He winced and squirmed, but was soon able to get to his feet. Once he was standing, Matt walked over to the tent's flap and waved to Patricia. "There's plenty of silver to be had in those mines, Sol. If you were like the rest of us, you'd stuff a few of them little nuggets into your pockets while you're working. Everybody does that every now and then. I think Charlie even knows about it."

"I don't see how he wouldn't know," Sol said with a laugh. "It's not like you and them others are very swift about it."

"I'm just saying that there's plenty of ways to make money. You do it right and you may just wind up with a sweet little lady of your own and a house to go along with her."

Even though Sol couldn't miss the grin that had staked its claim upon Matt's face, his own smile seemed to have melted away like the top of a frozen lake in the first weeks of spring. And, like that frozen layer of ice, Sol's grin wasn't so quick to return.

"So," Matt sighed, "are you going to join me for a drink? I'd like to give you and Patricia a proper introduction."

Sol shook his head. "Nah. I don't think she likes me very much."

"That's nonsense. I think she's just scared because the last time she saw you, you had a smoking gun in your hand."

"Could be."

"She'll change her mind when we all sit down over supper," Matt said. "How about this Sunday?"

Sol nodded without putting much of anything behind it. "If I'm back by then."

"What do you mean? Where are you going?"

"I told you where I'm going," Sol replied.

"Alone? You're going after those killers alone?"

"Yes. I think I can manage it."

Matt grunted and groaned as he picked up his shirt

and stuck his arms through the sleeves. With all the fussing he was doing, he looked more like a boy wriggling into a freshly starched Sunday suit. "Fine. I'll come with you."

"No," Sol said. "You won't." This time, he put enough steam into his words that they stopped Matt in his tracks.

"But . . . you could get hurt," Matt said. "Or worse."

"I could get hurt in a silver mine."

"It's not gonna do you any good to go around and around like this, Sol."

Nodding solemnly, Sol replied, "I know. That's why I'll take this job on my own and you can have supper with your new sweetheart. She seems very nice and I can tell she thinks the world of you."

"Yeah . . . but . . . you could . . ." Despite all of Matt's sputtering, he was unable to say much of anything else. Finally, he wound up shaking his head and grabbing hold of Sol by his shoulders. "I owe you everything. Those men might have killed me if you weren't there."

Sol laughed and shook his head. "You wouldn't have been anywhere near those robbers if not for me. It's best that I get going before I get you into any more trouble."

"Are you sure you won't—"

"Yes," Sol interrupted. "I'm sure. Thanks anyway."

There wasn't much else to say after that. Sol shook Matt's hand and left the tent. He passed Patricia along the way and showed her a small yet genuine smile.

She smiled right back at him.

Chapter 5

During his time in Warren, Sol had grown accustomed to the winds that periodically ripped through town like a band of raiders. Anyone who'd lived there for more than a week needed to learn to live with those winds or be driven crazy by them. Sol had never cursed a simple thing like the wind until he'd decided to try and track down those three men who'd robbed Charlie.

A few of the locals in town were more than willing to point in the direction they'd seen the robbers go after making their escape. There had been some tracks beaten into the ground by frantic hooves to lead Sol a bit farther, but there wasn't much to see after that. The wind had wiped that slate clean like an unseen broom spreading all the sand perfectly over the ground until the terrain was as smooth as the bottom of a lake.

Sol rode in circles for the better part of a day until he finally picked up on a set of tracks that were just big enough to have possibly been laid down by three men. Unfortunately, the tracks were headed toward Warren and not away from it. They could have been put there when the robbers were on their way to visit

Charlie, but Sol was fairly certain they'd been left behind by someone else altogether. When he came to that conclusion, Sol entertained the notion of admitting defeat and heading back into town so he could take Matt up on his offer of supper with Patricia.

After letting that thought slide around in his head for a few seconds, Sol knew that simply wasn't going to happen.

Matt was a good fellow and a good friend.

Patricia seemed like a nice young woman and might warm up to him if given some time.

The only problem was that Sol didn't want to wait around for some woman to shuffle her feet until she decided to grace him with a favorable glance. In fact, Sol wasn't about to vie for anyone else's favor. He wasn't about to fight for the chance to work in a mine and he wasn't going to bleed just to put himself in the good graces of a man like Charlie. Sol had taken a job and he wanted to see it through. Riding on his own to track down these robbers may have been a few paces south of reasonable, but it just felt right.

As soon as he thought that, Sol nodded solemnly.

It felt right.

He didn't know if he was going to get himself killed along the way, but what he was doing now sure suited him more than swinging a pickax in the dark.

Instinctively, Sol got his bearings and rode to a spot that would put him along the path he'd taken when he'd first left town. Warren was behind him and he was headed in the same direction the robbers had gone when they'd charged out with Charlie's money. After all the talk he'd given to Matt about being able to find someone in such open terrain, Sol figured it was time to put that theory to work.

Sol believed every word he'd said about the robbers being stupid and cowardly. It stood to reason that it shouldn't be too difficult to track down a bunch of stupid cowards. After all, as long as a man knew what sort of animal he was hunting, it should be fairly easy to guess what it would do and where it would go.

When he hadn't caught sight of his prey or even a hint of where they might have gone, Sol began to think he'd bitten off a bit too much with this task. But there was no turning back. In his mind, the man he'd been when picking silver off the ground was dead and buried in that mine. He could always go back, but he knew he'd have to swallow enough of his self-respect to choke him for years to come.

And, like a sign from some wayward angel, the abandoned campsite came into Sol's view.

When he saw it, he thought his eyes were deceiving him. There was no way he could seriously stumble upon something like that so easily. And there couldn't be a chance that this spot was actually the one he'd been looking for. That would be akin to sticking his hand into a haystack and digging out that needle everyone had been talking so much about.

Sol snapped his reins to close the distance between himself and that campsite even faster. The closer he got, the more he realized he hadn't just stumbled upon the spot out of sheer happenstance. Smoke from the cooking fire still hung in the air like a faint smudge. Whoever had been responsible for putting out those flames hadn't done a very good job, since there were still a few wisps of smoke curling up from a pile of wood that had been hastily stamped into a mess of splinters and ash.

Although there wasn't another soul in sight, Sol drew his gun as soon as he climbed down from his saddle. The remains of the campsite were a few paces in front of him and Sol took every step as though he was expecting to be attacked at any second.

His eyes darted back and forth in search of any trace of movement.

His gun hand remained at hip level and tensed in expectation of a fight.

When he finally got close enough to smell the smoldering wood, Sol stopped and kept still just in case a trap was about to be sprung.

The only thing that moved was the smoke that rose up from the broken sticks and was swept up into the air.

Sol kept his gun in hand as he hunkered down to get a closer look at the ground surrounding the fire. Although he couldn't be absolutely certain, there could have been three men at that camp. There were too many tracks for it to be just one or two, but there weren't enough for that number to be much higher than that. They'd also been in a rush and had done a piss-poor job of cleaning up after themselves. All in all, they sounded like the very idiots Sol was looking for.

Grinning to himself, Sol holstered his pistol and took another look around. Since any killer would have made his presence known by now, he wasn't concerned with being ambushed. Instead, he was looking for the next marker to point him in the right direction.

Before searching too hard, he reminded himself of the caliber of men he was after. If they hadn't thought ahead enough to properly douse their fire, they probably weren't bright enough to cover their tracks any other way. Being careful not to disturb the ground upon which he walked, Sol kept his eyes focused on the dirt and moved slowly around the campfire.

When he made it to the side that was pointing away from Warren, Sol saw plenty of freshly laid tracks in the gritty dirt. While he knew some trackers might have been able to tell what kind of horses were being ridden and how fast they were going, Sol wasn't nearly that skilled. He had eyes in his head, though, which was enough to let him know which direction these horses had gone.

"I'll be damned," Sol whispered to himself. "I might just be able to pull this off."

He straightened up and looked around proudly, but there wasn't anyone else to pat him on the back. Keeping his smile in place all the way back to his horse, Sol flicked his reins and got moving along a path that ran next to the tracks he'd spotted.

He kept following those tracks until the sun began to dip below the horizon. Within the next several minutes, the sky took on several different shades of orange and yellow. The sandy terrain was rough and jagged, but Sol felt oddly at home amid all of that wildness.

Without the rumble of wagons or the sound of other folks' voices ringing in his ears, Sol was able to hear himself think. In this case, that was all he needed to find the tracks he'd been after and follow them to a cluster of rocks that rose from the ground like an old giant's backbone. There were a few trees scattered along those rocks, hanging on to the sides as if they were just too stubborn to die. Unlike most trees, which seemed to blossom toward the heavens, these had a few thorny branches reaching out as if to scratch the sky out of spite.

If he'd listened to the common sense spouted by Matt, Sol would have been in a room somewhere waiting for supper to be brought to him on a plate. His back, shoulders and neck would have been aching after a long day's work and he would be looking forward to laying his head down and closing his eyes. Instead, Sol felt like he could jump down from his horse's back and run the rest of the way to those rocks.

More than that, Sol knew he would see one of those robbers any moment now. In fact, this was the first time he could put himself in the shoes of the men he'd seen gathered around the faro tables night after night. Those fellows always went on about how their numbers were bound to come up. Sol knew his own number was going to come up as well. As he got closer to those rocks, he could taste victory on the back of his throat. It was sweet. So that was why those fools kept playing faro.

Sol glanced down and behind him to double-check the tracks. The sun was continuing its slow fall, which now put a deep red hue into the sky that bled down into the sandy dirt. After a bit of squinting, Sol was able to pick out the tracks. He had to shake his head because the only reason there was so much dirt to be pushed around by those horses was that it had been blown away from a flat plane of rock less than a quarter mile to the north. If those riders had been smart enough to steer toward that barren plane, nobody would have been able to track them. If they were the right tracks, he would know soon enough. If they weren't, he wouldn't have had much of a shot at finding the gunmen anyhow.

But Sol didn't spend too much time fretting about that second possibility. Something in his gut told him those riders didn't have the sense to scout this country out enough to know about that rocky plane. That same sort of rushed thinking would lead them to the first refuge they could see, which was the spiny ridge in Sol's sight at the moment.

Before taking another step in that direction, Sol pulled back on his reins until his horse had come to a stop. The gray gelding chomped on his bit and shifted anxiously from one leg to another. Sol knew just how he felt.

After taking a moment to survey the land, Sol decided to cut to the left and ride around that side of the ridge. It was the lower side of the rocks, which meant it should be easier for him to get closer to anyone who might be watching from a higher vantage point at the opposite end. Then again, he guessed he could also see the sense in heading for the higher end of the ridge; the rocks themselves would provide more cover.

Like one of those gamblers who had a wad of cash burning a hole in their pockets, Sol couldn't hold himself back one more second. The sun was still dropping and the sky was shifting from shades of red to the purple end of the spectrum. Before long, those purples would fade into black and then Sol would be riding in the dark.

Following his gut, Sol snapped his reins and steered his gelding to the left. For all he knew, those gunmen could have approached those rocks hours ago and kept on riding. One thing that Sol did know was that there wasn't another town close enough to be reached from that spot unless the gunmen were willing to whip their horses within an inch of their lives.

Sol's thought flowed through his mind in a rush as he rode toward that ridge. Perhaps because he was so preoccupied, he reached the ridge a lot quicker than he'd anticipated. There were still a few streaks of color in the sky, which made it that much easier for him to make certain his pistol was loaded. He also kept a Winchester rifle in the boot on his saddle, which he'd mostly used for hunting. He checked that weapon as well before sliding it back into its well-worn leather home.

Doing his best to approach the ridge without being too noisy about it, Sol could feel the muscles in his stomach clenching with anticipation. More than anything, he wanted to dig his heels into his horse's sides so he could get around the rocks as quickly as possible. Seeing the vague smudge of black smoke rising from somewhere behind that ridge made his anxiousness even harder to bear.

The moment he'd gotten close enough to the ridge, Sol brought his horse to a stop and climbed down from his saddle. One hand came to a rest upon the gun at his side and the other reached out to take the

Winchester from its boot. Once he heard the crackle of a fire and a few muted voices, Sol smiled.

Working his way to the rocks, Sol leaned against them and poked his head over to get a look around them. Only then did he truly get a taste of what those men at the faro tables had felt.

Sol's number had hit.

Chapter 6

The first face Sol could see belonged to one of the men who'd traded lead with him back in Warren. There was another man sitting with his back to the ridge, but that didn't worry Sol. What did worry him was the fact that he could see only two of the gunmen when he knew there were at least three.

Since trying to find the other man would have required Sol to move around and possibly draw attention to himself, he stayed put. Besides, he figured the third man was probably just off somewhere relieving himself or tending to one of the horses.

"What the hell are you doin' there?" someone asked from a spot that was high and to Sol's right.

The tension in Sol's belly suddenly felt more like an iron fist gripping his innards. When he started to turn to get a look at the man who'd spoken, Sol heard boots scrambling against the nearby rocks.

"Not so fast," the man snarled as he closed in on Sol. "You didn't answer my question."

Gritting his teeth so hard that he nearly cracked them, Sol forced himself to turn toward the man. In much the same way that he'd known these were the men he was after, Sol knew the man approaching him already had his gun drawn and aimed directly at him. Sure enough, once he turned enough to get the look he was after, Sol found himself staring down the barrel of a pistol.

"Who the hell are you, mister?" the other man asked.

Sol couldn't reply. It was all he could do to keep himself from shaking like one of the barren branches scratching at the sky.

From the small fire that had been built on the other side of the ridge, one of the men asked, "That you, Bill?"

The man pointing his gun at Sol nodded and shouted, "Yeah, it's me. Looks like we got some company."

"How many?"

Bill was a big fellow with an ample belly. A bowler hat was pulled down low onto his head and had a rim that was just wide enough to cast a shadow over his face. A wide mouth hung open so loosely that it seemed doubtful it could shut. When he spoke again, his words came out in a slobbering whisper. "Who else is with you, boy?"

Like any man over the age of twenty, Sol didn't appreciate being called boy. He used that spark to rebuild the fire inside that had gotten him this far.

Bill leaned forward and extended his arm to shove the pistol into Sol's face. "If you ain't hearin' me so good, maybe you could use another hole in yer head."

Sol forced himself to look over the gun being pointed at him and into the eyes of the man holding it. "You're one of the men who robbed Charlie," he said.

"Who?"

"The owner of that mine in Warren," Sol explained. "Charlie. You robbed him."

"You mean Mr. Lowell? What the hell do you know about that?"

There were footsteps coming from the direction of the campfire, but Sol wasn't about to look that way. He had more than enough on his plate dealing with Bill.

"Who is it, damn it?" one of the other men shouted.

"I don't know for certain, but I think he's the law," Bill hollered back.

"Is there more than one?"

Bill let out a bellowing reply as he turned to look at his partners. "Give me a second without you chewin' my ear and I can—"

Before Bill had a chance to say another word, Sol made his move. After pulling his knees up toward his chest, he sprang forward and reached for his holstered pistol.

Bill snapped his head around and let out a surprised grunt when he saw Sol coming at him. He had to move his aim an inch or so to the side, which was just enough to give Sol a fighting chance. Before Bill could adjust his aim, Sol reached out to slap away Bill's gun. The pistol barked once and sent a round sparking against a nearby rock.

Sol's gun let out a quick, sharp roar and jumped within his grasp. That brief explosion was enough to illuminate Bill's face like a photographer's flash powder. The expression on Bill's face showed equal measures of pain and surprise. His mouth still hung agape, but Bill's eyes were now just as wide.

When Bill clenched his finger around his trigger, it

was more out of reflex than anything else. Even so, he was close enough to Sol to draw blood with that single shot.

When he felt the touch of hot lead nipping at his ankle, Sol jumped back and fired his own gun again. His arm was held out rigidly in front of him, so his bullet wound up drilling a hole into Bill's chest and dropping the other man like a sack of rocks.

Scrambling on the rocks, Sol fought to maintain his balance while getting away from the other two men. All the while, he couldn't help but stare at Bill's face. The bigger man's natural ugliness was made worse by the random twitches and clenching that came as he spat out his final breath.

"Bill?" one of the other men shouted.

Sol couldn't take his eyes off of Bill. In the space of a few seconds, the man on the ground let one more breath slip away from him and gave up whatever it was that separated a man from a pile of bones. After that, he was nothing but a fleshy husk.

"Hold on, Bill! We're comin'!"

Sol looked toward the campfire and saw the other two men running toward him. Just then, it seemed like years since he'd taken his first step onto that ridge. Whatever plan he may have had was gone. All that remained was the desperate struggle to keep from winding up like Bill.

"He shot Bill!" one of the other men hollered. He was a young fellow who seemed vaguely familiar from the robbery back in town. With fear etched into his face, he looked more like a kid than anyone capable of doing any harm. Snapping his head back and forth between Sol and the other man closest to him, the kid shouted, "The law found us! I told you, Garver! I told you we wouldn't get away with this!"

Garver was on one knee with a rifle in his hands. He'd positioned himself at the edge of the flickering light being cast by the campfire. While his young partner stumbled around like a drunk, Garver remained still. "Shut up!" he snapped as he brought the rifle to his shoulder. "It's just one of them up there."

"How the hell do you know?"

"Because we would'a seen the rest by now. Just step aside so I can take my shot!"

Once the kid stepped aside, Sol knew what would come next. Sure enough, Garver aimed and fired in short order. His rifle sent a round toward the ridge that sent a brief shower of sparks down upon Sol's back.

Sol's ribs still hurt from dropping and slamming himself against the rock just before Garver had taken his shot. Now that he'd heard Garver's rifle, Sol wondered what had happened to his own Winchester. Before Sol could answer that question, Garver fired at him again.

"Did you hit him?" the kid asked.

Garver didn't move except to lever in a fresh round. "Why don't you go see for yourself, 'stead of flapping your lips?"

Although the kid did start working his way toward the ridge, he wasn't quick about it.

Lying on his belly, Sol could see his Winchester lying within arm's reach. When he started to extend his arm to retrieve the rifle, another bullet from Garver hissed close enough to make Sol reflexively swear under his breath as he pulled his hand back.

"He's still up there!" Garver said. "Go finish him off!"

"You still alive up there, Bill?" the kid asked.

Since Garver and Sol both chose to keep quiet, the kid didn't get a reply. His footsteps echoed nicely against the rocks, however, as if the campfire were a stage and the ridge held the tiered seats at the edge of the theater.

Sol could feel his heart thumping within his chest. He swore he could even hear it slapping against the ground as he wriggled his way toward the rifle without lifting his chest from the dirt. Along the way, Sol's foot nudged Bill's body as if to remind him of what might await him if he didn't get a move on. Steeling himself for the worst, Sol reached out for his rifle. Garver fired at him almost exactly when Sol had figured he would. Although he pulled back his arm out of reflex, Sol quickly reached forward again while Garver was working the lever on his own rifle.

There was no time to savor the victory when Sol finally did close his fingers around his Winchester. The kid had scampered up the rocks and was racing toward him like a runaway train. When he saw the body lying nearby, the kid got even more steam in his strides.

Now that he was closer, Sol could recognize the kid from the robbery. It wasn't so much the kid's face that jogged Sol's memory, but the way he stood with his feet splayed and the way he held his gun in a tight, trembling fist. The kid had done some yelling back in town and he kept on hollering now that one of his partners had been dropped.

That kid took aim as Sol lifted his rifle and pulled his trigger. Both men fired and both of them missed.

Although the kid was rattled by the lead that whipped past him, Sol took the opportunity to scramble back to his feet and rush toward the kid. Pushing through the biting pain in his ankle, Sol lowered his head and drove his shoulder into the kid's midsection. Surprised by the impact, the kid pulled his trigger again. Sol didn't feel a bullet hit him anywhere, but his ears definitely took some punishment from the close proximity of the shot.

Sol's feet kept churning against the rock and he continued to drive the kid backward. As the kid lost more of his balance, both of them gained momentum and they rushed toward the edge of the ridge. After a brief fall, they landed a few yards away from the campfire. The kid landed with both of his shoulders hitting the ground at the same time. Sol had most of his fall broken by the kid and absorbed the rest upon his knees and one outstretched arm. It turned out that didn't help Sol very much as pain shot through all of his extremities and rippled throughout his body. At least that put the nick on his ankle out of his mind.

Sol caught a glimpse of the kid's pained expression and took that opportunity to deliver a chopping blow to the kid's jaw. The stock of Sol's rifle snapped forward and caught the kid in the face with a loud crunch. Even as blood sprayed from his mouth, however, the kid grabbed hold of the rifle just in front of the trigger guard. Youthful strength and desperation kept Sol from moving the Winchester much more than an inch or so in any direction.

In the midst of struggling to reclaim his rifle, Sol caught a hint of movement in the corner of his eye.

He turned to look toward the campfire and saw Garver sighting along the top of his own rifle.

Without wasting another moment, Sol drew upon every ounce of strength he had to twist the rifle toward Garver. He pulled his trigger the moment he had it pointed in the proper direction. Not only did the shot startle the kid, but the heat from the barrel was enough to make him immediately release his grip.

Garver flinched as the shot was fired at him. Although he wasn't hit by the hastily fired round, his aim was knocked well off of center and he fired several feet to Sol's left. Snarling an obscenity through gritted teeth, Garver worked the lever of his rifle and fixed his eyes upon his target.

As he watched the rifleman, Sol hoped the other man would just turn tail and run. After all, he was a cowardly idiot, wasn't he? Cowards ran. That's what they did.

This one didn't.

Garver held his ground and prepared to fire another shot.

A gun did go off, but it wasn't the rifle in Garver's hands. Instead, Sol had rolled away from the kid and pulled his trigger to knock Garver onto his back like he was a target in a shooting gallery. Sol fired again out of blind reflex, but that bullet hissed through the air over Garver's squirming body.

"Jesus!" the kid hollered through a bloody mouth.

When Sol looked down at him, the kid still had a pistol gripped in his hand. Even with that gun in his possession, the kid was more concerned with digging his heels into the dirt beneath him and pushing away.

"Don't kill me!" the kid begged. "Please don't kill me."

Sol could hear Garver moaning in pain, but that man didn't look like he would be quick to sit up any time soon. Getting to his feet, Sol kept his rifle aimed at the kid until he could reach down and take away his gun. The kid gave it up as if the pistol had been burning his hands.

"Where's the money you stole?" Sol asked.

The kid kept shuffling away upon his back. When he started to push himself upright using both hands, the kid was stopped by the sight of Sol aiming his rifle directly at him. The kid clenched his eyes shut and rolled onto his side.

"Don't shoot me. Please," the kid whined.

The thing that struck Sol as so peculiar was how calm he felt at that moment. His thoughts were collected enough for him to take a moment and look around. He assessed the situation as though he was deciding where he should pound the first nail when mending a fence.

Since the kid wasn't even looking at him, Sol shifted his attention over to Garver. He'd been hit in the left side, somewhere toward the bottom of his ribs or possibly just beneath his rib cage. Even though he writhed in pain, Garver still fought to keep possession of his rifle. He didn't have enough strength to maintain his grip upon the weapon, however, once Sol scooped his toe beneath the rifle and snapped his leg to send the rifle flying through the air.

"Where's the money?" Sol asked.

"We were . . . just making the delivery," Garver grunted.

"Tell me where it is."

Pulling in a deep breath, Garver forced his eyes to open all the way so he could get a clear look at Sol. Grinning, he said, "You're that fella who tried to chase us out of town."

"I did chase you out of town. Where's the money?"

"So you aim to shoot us for it?"

Now that he'd had a better chance to look at Garver's wounded side, Sol could see some striking similarities between that wound and Matt's wound. Both were fairly bloody, but didn't seem to affect either man's ability to talk. Since Garver was already trying to sit up, it seemed the wound was far from lethal.

"What's Charlie paying you?" Garver asked. "Probably three or four hundred?"

"Where is it?"

Garver glared up at Sol with the grin still smeared across his face.

Hearing a few sharp breaths coming from the kid, Sol caught sight of him crawling toward the gun he'd dropped before. Sol shifted his aim toward the kid and pulled his trigger. The Winchester bucked against his shoulder, but put a round into the dirt rather than into the kid. Fortunately, that dirt had only been an inch or two from the kid's knee and that was plenty close enough to drop the kid right back onto his side and curl him up like a dying caterpillar.

Sol looked back to Garver as soon as the shot was fired. The fire in his eyes was more than enough to wipe the grin off of Garver's face.

"Who the hell are you?" Garver asked.

"That doesn't matter."

"Are you a hired gun?"

Sol didn't reply.

Letting out a sigh, Garver shook his head and grumbled, "You either got some real sand or you ain't got a brain in your head to come after us all alone like this."

"Don't make me ask you again," Sol said as he sighted along the top of the Winchester.

"The money's in those saddlebags," Garver replied as he waved toward a pile that looked to be all of the men's combined belongings.

"Which ones?"

After scowling a bit, Garver said, "All three of them."

"All right, then. What about some rope?" Hearing some more commotion coming from the kid, Sol stepped back so he could keep an eye on both of the men at the same time. "Get some rope, kid."

The youngest of the robbers twitched at the sound of Sol's voice. Before Sol had to repeat himself, the kid crawled over to one of the horses and reached up toward the saddle.

"Just the rope," Sol warned. "Don't be stupid."

Freezing with his arms extended toward the saddle, the kid barely seemed to have realized that he'd also been reaching toward the boot hanging from that saddle. He moved especially slow as he carefully took the coiled rope hanging from the saddle and walked toward Sol.

Within minutes, Sol had the kid tie Garver up. Sol then pressed the Winchester's barrel into the small of the kid's back and quickly tied up that one's wrists and ankles. When he stepped back to admire what he'd done, Sol could scarcely believe he'd pulled it off. Rather than strand the men at the camp without a horse, Sol left one animal behind and gathered up the other two.

Sol half expected one of the robbers to surprise him by breaking loose and taking another shot at him. The knots held just fine, however, allowing Sol to get the horses and load the saddlebags onto their backs. Just to be certain, he flipped a few of those bags open to get a look inside. Although one of them wasn't even half-full, the rest were stuffed with wads of bundled cash. When he walked back to the campfire, Sol could hear one of the men making a noise. It was the kid. He was crying.

"I told you," the kid whimpered. "I told you he'd kill us. I should'a never agreed to help you."

"Just shut up, will you?" Garver grunted.

Sol collected all the pistols he could find and then led the horses toward the ridge.

"What about us?" Garver asked. "You just gonna leave us here?"

Sol kept walking.

"We can split the money," Garver shouted. "Forget about this little baby with me, we can work real good together! I can make you rich!"

Sol walked around the ridge to where his gray gelding was waiting.

"We could be partners!" Garver hollered. "That way I won't have to hunt you down to get that money back!" Although Sol didn't respond to that, the kid must have had something to say because Garver quickly followed up with "Aw, good Lord, stop yer blubbering!"

Chapter 7

The ride back into Warren was a slow one. Night had fallen and most anyone would have known better than to keep moving when their horse could barely see where its next step was going to land. There was half a moon hanging in the sky, which gave Sol something to go by. Once his eyes had adjusted, the glow from all the stars overhead seemed to add a dim shine to the moon's pale luminescence.

Critters were out and about, sniffing at Sol as if they knew for certain the man's eyes weren't sharp enough to see them. It felt as if the whole world was slowing down and taking a rest. Sol lifted his chin to the shifting winds and closed his eyes. Rather than take a breath, he merely allowed the night air to fill his lungs. It was cool and left the taste of the desert in the back of his throat. When he opened his eyes again, he looked up at what could have been hundreds of little holes that had been shot into the roof overhead. The more he looked at all those points of light, he thought there could be thousands of them. Truth be told, he'd never really put much thought into counting them. Sol had always wondered what became of those rounds that were fired up into the air on New Year's Day or any other time when folks wanted to make noise. He chuckled before allowing his thoughts drift back to things he knew more about.

One thing he knew for certain was that he was carrying an awful lot of money. The saddlebags had been heavy when he'd loaded them onto the horses, and a few of them were even bulging at their seams. Another thing he knew was that he was lucky to be alive. That little bit of certainty made Sol look up again at the sky and drink in the sight of it.

His heart raced in his chest, making the blood rush through his veins like a whitewater current. Because of that, Sol couldn't just pick a spot and make camp. He was too excited after his fight with those robbers and the night was too beautiful for him to let it slip by while his eyes were closed.

Sol decided to keep riding into town. He would take it slow and easy so the horses wouldn't get tripped up in the dark. Now that the ridge was behind him and he knew where he was headed, the mostly flat terrain didn't have much to throw at him. Still, Sol didn't pretend to know every crack in the ground or every spot that might pose a threat. The simple fact of the matter was that he wouldn't have been able to sit still if his life depended on it.

When he got back to town, Sol decided he would buy himself a drink.

He'd earned it.

It turned out that Sol bought himself a few drinks. Rather than go to the Railway Saloon, he stumbled into a place on the edge of town that had been there since before Warren had even tried to call itself a town. The only marking the old tent had was the word SALOON painted across the front. A good portion of those letters had faded from the sun or been washed away by the wind, but everyone in town knew the place served whiskey. Few locals went there anymore now that they had other saloons like the Railway to fill that need, but Sol was too tired to go any farther.

After his first drink, he bought another. Before he knew it, he'd polished off the better portion of a bottle and still hadn't felt more than a slight spinning behind his eyes. When he was finally too tired to stand up, Sol slapped down enough money to pay for his bottle and then walked to one of the tables in the back.

To be fair, calling the crooked collection of planks "tables" was being generous. Even calling the splintered old door lying flat on its side "a bar" was stretching things awfully thin. Sol got to his table, laid his head down and drifted to sleep.

He awoke with a start and jumped to his feet. The sky outside had taken on a fuzzy shade of red and, rather than check the time, Sol rushed outside to where he'd left his horse and the two he'd taken from the robbers. There were a few kids poking around the animals. One of them was a teen with a rough face and angry eyes.

"Get away from there!" Sol snapped.

The teen still had one hand upon one of the robbers' horses' flank and kept it there. "We ain't doin' nothin'," he grunted.

As Sol took another couple of steps forward, he snarled at the kids before he realized what he was doing. "I said back away."

The younger kids scattered and the teen took a few steps back.

"Sorry, mister," the teen said as he tried to keep his composure. "Honest mistake is all it was." With that minimal effort to show he wasn't scared, he turned and bolted.

Sol relaxed a bit and examined the horses. All the saddlebags were in place and none of them appeared to have been opened. Just to be certain, he reached out to take a look inside them for himself. It wasn't until then that he realized his right hand had come to a rest upon his holstered pistol sometime while he'd been approaching the kids.

No wonder those young ones had changed their tune so quickly.

Although Sol had been amazed that he could leave all that money sitting outside like that, he was even more surprised that he'd reached for his gun when addressing a bunch of children and one smart-mouthed boy.

He certainly wasn't accustomed to hauling around so much money. As for the second half of his quandary, Sol had no explanation.

All the money seemed to be there. Since the kids hadn't been nearly slick enough to pocket a few bills before scattering, Sol figured he had an angel looking out for him. The sky was growing brighter and the watch in Sol's pocket told him it was coming up to seven o'clock in the morning. Rather than go back into the filthy little saloon, he gathered up all the horses' reins and led them farther into town.

A couple folks looked Sol's way, but they tipped their hats as if nothing had transpired since the last time they'd crossed paths. Sol didn't feel like playing along with the usual niceties, so he kept his head down and his mouth shut until he reached Charlie's house.

Sol knocked on the door out of reflex and suddenly felt foolish for doing so. Rather than wait to be beckoned, he pushed the door open and walked inside. Charlie was pulling his belt tight around his thick waist and waddling toward the door.

"Hey!" Charlie grunted. "This is my home! You'll knock if you wanna see me 'fore business hours."

"This is business," Sol replied. "And I didn't think you'd want me to wait."

"You find my money?"

Sol nodded.

Seeing that was enough to bring a smile to Charlie's face. "Well, that's a different story. Where is it?"

Pushing the door all the way open, Sol turned and walked toward the horses. When he saw Charlie step up next to him, Sol waved toward the animals and the bags that were hung across their backs.

"It's in those saddlebags," Sol said.

Charlie rushed to the horses like a child running toward a stack of Christmas presents. He tried to lift the first bag, but grunted and had to let it go so he could collect his strength. "This is heavy. You wanna give me a hand?"

Sol draped one set of saddlebags over his shoulder and carried another. Charlie rushed back out to make a second trip so he could get the rest of the money inside his house. Once that was done, he slammed the door shut and locked it.

"Take a seat," Charlie said. "I need to count it up."

Sol didn't make a move toward any of the chairs and

Charlie was too preoccupied to notice. He pulled open the first bag and shoved his hands inside. It was odd to see a man who looked as rough as a piece of dried leather handle something as delicately as Charlie handled that money. Judging by the expression on Charlie's face, the mine's boss might have thought he'd break those bills if he didn't show them the proper respect.

"You didn't tell me there would be so much," Sol said.

"Hush up," Charlie grunted. "You'll make me lose count."

Waiting until Charlie was focused once more upon his task, Sol added, "It would have been good to know what I was after."

"Why? So you could gouge me for a bigger fee?"

"Don't you think I deserve it?"

Although Charlie had to stop what he was doing, he didn't seem to mind sitting behind his desk with his hands buried in the money. The saddlebags were stacked beside him and he hunched over like a hawk guarding a fresh kill. "If all my money's here, you'll get your fee. What about the bonus?"

Sol pulled aside his jacket to display the kid's pistol tucked beneath his gun belt. "Is that good enough?"

"Took that right off of them yellow thieves?"

"Yes."

"That mean they're dead?" Charlie asked. When he didn't get a reply, he grunted, "I reckon that'll do."

Sol's jacket snagged upon the gun handle, so both his gun and the kid's were in plain sight.

Charlie waved at Sol as if he was shooing away a fly. "Hell, I barely thought you'd go out there after those thieves."

"I told you I would."

"Yeah, but . . . I guessed you'd never make it back alive if you tried something as foolish as that."

Nodding slowly, Sol glared at Charlie and asked, "Really? Is that what you thought?"

Although Charlie was smirking when he looked up from his money, that glib expression didn't last too long when he saw the look in Sol's eyes. Charlie glanced down toward Sol's right hand, which was hanging a bit too close to his holster. "Well, not that I wanted you dead. Aww, you know what I mean."

"Yes. I know exactly what you mean."

Charlie nodded in what he thought was a shared joke and continued counting his money. It didn't take him long to get through the first set of saddlebags, so he hefted the next one onto his desk and repeated the process.

Sol stood by the door and watched. Every so often, he glanced out the window, but didn't see much of anything outside to hold his interest. As much as it turned his stomach to do so, Sol looked back at Charlie. "So you just thought I was going to run out there and die?" he asked.

Charlie didn't look up from his counting, but his hands stopped. In fact, for a couple of seconds, Charlie looked like a big, poorly carved statue propped up behind an old desk. "No," he muttered. "I said I'd pay you, didn't I?"

"Sure. A hundred dollars. Even those robbers guessed you'd pay a whole lot more than that."

"So you're after my money, is that it?"

Sol shook his head. "I just don't see why you'd

let me go riding off without knowing what I needed to know."

"I was robbed," Charlie snarled. "What could I have told you?"

"What they looked like, for one thing. Also, how you knew them."

Charlie's hand twitched so hard when he heard those words that he dropped the bills he'd been holding.

"Those men knew you by name. They also got away with so much money that they had to have known when you'd have that much on you. I know for a fact you send a good portion of your money into Albuquerque every week on the Wednesday stage that passes through here."

"Oh, you know all that, do you?"

"Yes," Sol replied with a nod. "I've helped load those stages for you because you're too lazy to get up off your own fat ass and do it yourself."

That brought Charlie to his feet real quick. "What did you just say to me?"

Sol wanted to step back. Part of him even wanted to take back what he'd just said. Maybe it was the whiskey or the lack of sleep or the excitement from the night before, but he held his ground and said, "You heard me, Charlie. I've done plenty of work for you, just like all the others who work that mine. We don't get raises because you've always got a sad story about how you're barely keeping your head above water. Turns out that you're so tight with your money that you'd rather arrange for it to be stolen just so you can keep telling your sad stories to the rest of us."

"I pay men when they earn it."

"What did you pay those robbers?" Sol asked. "One of them dropped your name right before he claimed to be following orders. Were those your orders, Charlie?"

"That's crazy talk!"

"I'm pretty certain it wasn't anyone who worked at the mine, so maybe it was someone who takes the money into Albuquerque." Seeing the twitch in the corner of Charlie's eye, Sol nodded. "That's it, isn't it? That also explains how they got all that money packed up and loaded onto their horses before a shot was fired or anyone heard you raise your voice."

"I was robbed, damn it," Charlie snapped. "If you don't believe me, then go to hell!"

"You see?" Sol asked. "I haven't even touched your money yet and you're screaming loud enough to be heard outside. You still expect me to believe you'd keep quiet long enough for those three men to take that small fortune you got there?"

"They had guns."

"Come to think of it," Sol replied as he reached for his holster, "so do I."

Charlie's eyes went wide as he reached for the drawer on the right side of his desk. His eyes somehow grew wider when he saw that Sol had already beaten him to the draw. Charlie's jaw went slack for a moment, but he recovered before he started trapping any flies.

"Wh-what's the meaning of this?" Charlie stammered.

Although Sol felt his fingers snagging upon the edge of his holster and even tripping up along the side of his pistol, he'd managed to clear leather at a fairly decent pace. Now that he'd already stopped Charlie from moving any farther, Sol had a few seconds to adjust his grip on the pistol and get his finger on the trigger.

Sweat broke out upon Charlie's forehead. He nervously licked his lips as if all of the desert's heat had suddenly caught up to him. Watching as Charlie began to squirm, Sol felt something settle into the back of his mind. "You weren't robbed at all," he declared. "That's why you didn't make enough commotion until there was no other choice," Sol said as a way to air his thoughts out. "That's why you didn't start shooting with one of those guns you got stashed in your desk. And that's why you didn't take so much as a scratch when the shooting did start."

"I got lucky, is all," Charlie grunted. "You were there."

"Yes, I was. I saw those men come out with guns drawn and I heard shots being fired before that." Glancing toward the door, Sol went through everything he could remember about that robbery. "You wanted those robbers to be seen. It was all a big show. That's why they fired at the Railway so much. They wanted to draw as many folks out as they could. That's why you were content to sit back and wait instead of doing whatever it took to hunt those men down. Seeing as how you practically roll around in your money like a pig in mud, I can't believe this didn't seem obvious before."

"All right," Charlie said as he raised his hands away from the desk drawer. "Maybe it wasn't a robbery."

"Then what was it?"

"Those men are couriers who haul the second shipments into Old Mexico."

"Old Mexico? What second shipments? How many shipments are there?"

"Only two," Charlie replied. "I swear. One goes to Albuquerque and the other goes south across the border."

"Why?"

The sweat was running in small rivers down Charlie's face by now. His lips even started to tremble as he kept thinking of what he should say and then rejected it before he could get a word out. All of that only served to make things clearer for Sol.

Charlie let out a nervous laugh. "Does it really matter why? I mean, there's plenty of money here. You wanted a bigger bonus, so you can have one."

"What's the second shipment?" Sol asked

Although Charlie's face had lost all its color, he'd taken on a peculiar sort of calm that was usually reserved for men whose neck was already in the noose. "You don't know what you're gettin' into here. I swear you don't."

"I'll take my chances. Tell me what's going on here or I'll take a chance on shooting you before anyone thinks to open that door."

Charlie paused and pulled in a long, noisy breath. "I got partners. They got partners of their own in California. You know what it's like, Sol. I know you men help yourselves to some of them loose bits of silver. Well, I scrape off some loose bits of the profits for myself and send the rest to Albuquerque, which gets split up so they can shave off their own piece and send it to Old Mexico. I'd wager even the bigwigs in California shave off some more before they declare their earnings to the government, who shave off their own piece and call it taxes. Hell, it's the same bit of stealing all around and it's probably been going on since money was invented."

"All part of the natural order of things, huh?" Sol asked. "Then why are you sweating so badly?"

Charlie reached up to wipe away the sweat that had trickled into his eyes. "I can cut you in. I always knew you was a good worker."

"You did, huh? What's my Christian name?"

"What?"

"My Christian name," Sol repeated. "First and last. What is it?" After a few quiet seconds, Sol shook his head. "You don't even know who I am apart from just another back to break down in that mine."

"I'll pay you to forget all about this."

"You won't have to worry about that," Sol said. "For the first time in a while, you're going to tell your partners the truth."

"What truth?"

"That you were robbed."

Those words came out of Sol's mouth almost as if he hadn't known they were in there. However big of a surprise those words may have been, there was no denying how good it felt to say them. Seeing the newest expression to twist Charlie's features, however, felt even better.

"Robbed?" Charlie grunted. "By you? That's a hoot."

Sol could hardly believe it when he saw Charlie

smirk at him. When he extended his arm to point his pistol directly at Charlie's face, Sol's only intention was to wipe that smirk away.

It worked.

"You ain't a robber," Charlie said. "You just don't have it in you."

"Why don't you put me to the test and we can both find that out for certain?"

Charlie wasn't about to take him up on that offer. Instead, he raised his hands a bit higher and stared directly at Sol. His breaths became heavier until they sounded more like pants from a tired dog.

"What are you gonna do?" Charlie wheezed. "Kill me?"

"Not if you do what I tell you."

Nodding quickly enough to send sweat flying into the air, Charlie said, "I'll do what you ask. We can work something—"

"Too late for that," Sol snapped in a voice that was so sharp that he barely even recognized it. "No more deals. I don't want to hear another word from you."

Charlie did what he was told. In fact, he did it so quickly that it struck Sol as downright peculiar.

"Where's a closet in this house? Point to it."

Charlie pointed toward the next room with a trembling hand.

"Walk around that desk and go to the closet."

"But I—"

"I told you to shut your mouth!" Sol snapped.

For a moment, Sol thought the bigger man was going to cry. Considering all the strutting and barking Charlie did on a daily basis, the sight of him now was more than a little funny. It went from funny to pathetic when Charlie walked around from behind his desk. He'd soiled his trousers.

Sol didn't say a word about Charlie's condition and he didn't laugh. "Go to the closet," he said calmly.

Charlie took him to a smaller room that was lined with dusty shelves containing everything from books to moldy loaves of bread. There was a cot in there as well, which was situated next to a short, narrow door. Charlie walked over to that door and stood there with his back to Sol as if he were looking forward to taking a bullet.

"Get in," Sol commanded.

Charlie got into the closet and sat huddled against the far wall.

Closing the door partway, Sol kept his gun aimed at Charlie as he said, "I'm going to search your house for the money you got stashed."

"There isn't any—"

This time, all it took was a glare and a subtle, sideways tilt of Sol's head to shut the big man up.

"I'll search on my own," Sol said after Charlie had clamped his mouth shut and lowered his head. "If I hear so much as a creak from this room or see the door so much as budge, I'll empty every bullet I have into this closet. You understand?"

Charlie nodded and his shoulders began to shake.

When Sol closed the door, he did so as if there were a sleeping baby in there that he didn't want to awaken. Sol backed away from the closet and started looking out all the windows in the house. Folks weren't usually anxious to pay Charlie a visit and today was no exception. Since it was also a bit early to conduct business, the rest of the town went about its own affairs as if the house didn't even exist.

Sol was careful not to make any noise as he gathered up the money and left through the front door. It took a few trips back and forth, but nobody was outside waiting for him. When he was finished, Sol holstered his gun and calmly walked over to the horses and led them away.

Nobody seemed interested in stopping him and Charlie was being as quiet as a church mouse. Sol had done it. Somehow, he'd gotten away with more money than he could have earned in a lifetime. Not only that, but it was easy.

So easy.

Chapter 8

Sol didn't charge from town like the other robbers had. In fact, he moved only slightly faster than if he were about to report to work in the next couple of hours. That way, he only got a few glances from a few folks on his way out. The rest of the world, as it was known to do, ignored him.

As the sun climbed its way up into the sky and the light became brighter, the entire town seemed to wake up like a single living thing. The folks filling the streets were that thing's blood and the mine was its heart. Sol looked toward that all-too-familiar hole in the ground and then was all too happy to dismiss it.

When he got to Doc Connor's office, Sol looked inside the tent without wasting a thought on the money carried by his and the other two horses. In an odd sort of way, Sol was calmer than he'd ever been. He'd done the unthinkable and the world hadn't fallen down around his ears. Once that was behind him, Sol felt like he could walk through fire.

"He ain't here," came a gruff voice from within the tent.

Sol waited for the doctor to step outside.

"You're looking for Matt, right?" the doctor asked.

"Yes. Do you know where I can find him?"

"Wherever that little lady is, that's where you'll find him."

"Was he fit for work?" Sol asked.

"I recommended he take a day or two to rest, but he seemed pretty anxious to get out of here. If he pops his stitches, it'll be his own damn fault."

"Thanks." With that, Sol tipped his hat and climbed into his saddle.

"Where you going with all them horses?"

Although the question may have been innocent enough under normal circumstances, Sol didn't treat it as such. Instead, he turned to fix a hard stare upon the doctor.

Doc Connor recoiled a bit and quickly added, "Just making conversation, son. I didn't know you owned one horse and now you're leading a whole team."

"Did Matt settle up his bill?" Sol asked.

Obviously thrown off by the sudden change in topic, the doctor took a moment to reply. When he did, he shook his head and said, "Not just yet, but he's good for it. I was just fooling when I said that about his stitches. If he tears them, I'll sew him up again."

"That's not what I meant," Sol said. Leaning to one side, he reached into his saddlebag and grabbed one of the bundles of cash that Charlie hadn't pulled apart. Without bothering to look at the bundle, Sol removed it from the bag and tossed it to the doctor.

"Wh-what's this?" Connor sputtered as he clumsily caught the money.

"Your payment. Is it enough?"

Connor chuckled and said, "Yes, as well as whatever else Matt may need by way of medical services for a few years. In fact, you'd probably still have some change coming."

"Keep it," Sol said as he brought his horse around. "I've got to go."

"Where are you going?" Before he got another glare from Sol, Connor added, "Will you be coming back? I mean, I thought you worked at the mine."

"I tendered my resignation."

"Oh, well . . . if you don't mind me asking . . . are you . . . all right?"

Sol looked back at the doctor, but this time Connor didn't look away. In fact, Sol could see some genuine concern in the other man's eyes. Slowly, Sol nodded. "Just a bit rattled, I guess."

"I can smell the whiskey on your breath from here, son," Connor added in a tactfully quiet tone. "Used to have my bouts with the bottle myself, so I know a late night when I catch a whiff of one."

Sol nodded. "Promise me something, Doc."

"What is it?"

"You won't tell anyone where you got that money."

Dr. Connor looked down at the money in his hand and promptly tucked it under his coat. "Should I bother asking where you got it?"

Sol chuckled and shook his head. "Let's just say you'll probably find out soon. And when you do, I doubt you'll want to give it back. So long, now."

The next place Sol visited was the wagon where he and Matt had hidden from those robbers. Sure enough, Patricia was there and she looked even prettier than Sol had remembered. When she caught sight of him, however, the shine in her eyes dimmed and she turned away. Sol rode up to her anyway.

"Sounds like you and Matt are quite the pair," Sol said.

She looked up at him as if she were defending Matt's memory. "I think you should stay away from him," she said.

"I agree."

She winced out of surprise and then focused her eyes upon him. "He's working, if you insist on finding him."

"I only came by to give you this." With that, Sol handed over the reins to one of the spare horses he'd taken from the robbers. That horse was also carrying one of the sets of saddlebags filled with Charlie's money.

"What's this?" Patricia asked.

"A horse. It belongs to Matt. Be sure to take the saddlebags off and hide them until he can get to them. They've got some valuables inside."

Although she clearly didn't like talking to him, Patricia seemed to hate agreeing with him even more. "All right," she said reluctantly. "I'll make sure he gets it."

"And if anyone else comes around asking about it, don't tell them I was even here. In fact, you should hide these bags somewhere safe."

"What have you done?"

Sol's eyes narrowed to intense slits. Although he didn't feel the urge to draw his gun, he did want to reach to his holster just to make sure he could get to his weapon. "What kind of question is that?" he asked.

"I don't know much about you, but you're the one who got Matt shot. Now you come around here dropping off his things on a stolen horse. That's it, isn't it? Those horses are stolen. Nobody who earns what Matt earns can just ride around with all those horses."

"You don't know a thing about me, lady," Sol said. "And you barely know Matt."

"But I care about him."

"Care about him?" Sol scoffed. "Love at first sight, huh? I don't suppose it's an accident that a pretty little thing like yourself is running this store. I'll bet you're real good at smiling at the right men to bring them close and then bat your eyelashes so you can get them to buy a bunch of fancy suits they hardly need."

Patricia looked at him without batting an eye. "Matt's come around here for weeks. He's tried talking to me plenty of times before that. He gets nervous and I didn't want to scare him away. When I saw him bleeding, I thought I might lose something wonderful before I ever got a chance to let it happen."

As much as he wanted to hang on to the anger that had flared up when Patricia had looked at him like he was trash, Sol couldn't manage it. In fact, he recalled Matt mentioning a certain lady he'd had his eye on that vaguely matched Patricia's description. The subject had come up a few times, but had always been quickly changed.

"Matt's a good man," she said. "He's said some good things about you and you did help get him to the doctor. But I saw when you had that gun in your hand that day. You liked it. Now you come around like you're trying to hide something. Well, if those horses are . . ." She let her sentence trail off as if she didn't even want to follow her line of thought to its conclusion.

Sol didn't take one bit of comfort from the fact that Patricia had her facts a bit tangled. The way her body was tensed reminded him of a deer that had caught scent of a predator, but couldn't quite see it yet. "Fine. I'll keep the horses. Will you at least hold on to this bag and give it to Matt?" he asked.

"Why don't you give it to him yourself?"

"Because I'm leaving town and don't have the time to track him down."

When Patricia heard that, she had enough courtesy to keep from smiling. It was plain to see, however, that she liked the sound of it just fine. "Should I tell him when you'll be back?"

Sol shook his head. "I don't even know that."

"All right, then." Patricia turned around to her wagon. The canvas cover was separated from the base and held up by two poles to form an awning. Beneath the awning, there were several shelves of various trinkets ranging from pocket watches and tie tacks to handkerchiefs and satin gloves. The shelves were actually drawers that had been pulled out and left open to display the merchandise.

As Patricia pulled some of the lower drawers completely out, Sol looked around to make sure nobody else was watching. There were plenty of folks passing by on the street and a few glanced over to the wagon. Those few looked away again when they caught an eyeful of Sol instead of the pretty face they'd been expecting.

When Sol looked back at what Patricia was doing,

he discovered she'd pulled out all the shelves in the bottom half of her display. The hole that left was big enough for him to see stacks of folded waistcoats behind the wooden case that held the drawers.

"Put the bags in there," Patricia said as she stepped aside to allow Sol to get to the opening.

Sol took the bags off one horse's back and folded them as flat as he could manage. Once he got the bags through the opening, he felt around for a good place to leave them.

"Go on," Patricia urged him. "There's nothing to break in there."

Dropping the set of saddlebags behind the rack, Sol heard a heavy thump. As soon as he pulled his hands free, Patricia busied herself by sliding the drawers back into place.

"I appreciate this," Sol said.

She nodded and finished straightening her display. When she turned around again, Patricia sighed and put on a smile that seemed more like a layer of frosting that wasn't quite thick enough to cover the cake. "You want me to tell Matt anything when I see him? Besides to pick up these bags, I mean."

"Actually," Sol replied with a slight wince, "could you deliver a message to him?"

"Sure."

"Do you have any paper?"

Patricia sighed again as she dug into the pocket of her skirt to remove a small journal and a pencil. The pages of the journal were covered in figures and receipts that had been hastily scribbled in no particular order. "Tear out a page and write what you want," she said. "I promise I won't read it."

Sol didn't take much more of her time. He could already hear some commotion coming from the direction of Charlie's house, so he scratched out a note that was even messier than Patricia's receipts. It read:

> *Take the bags and put them to use*
> *Don't tell anyone about them*
> *Forget you ever knew me*
> *Your friend, Sol*

After folding the note in half, Sol handed it to Patricia. She accepted it, tucked it into another pocket and then cocked her head to one side. "You should go now," she said.

"Yeah. I know."

Sol turned to leave, but was stopped by a gentle hand upon his shoulder. Even though there wasn't anyone else within arm's reach, he was still surprised to see that Patricia had been the one to stop him.

"Thank you," she said.

The words were heartfelt, but cut deeply as well. Since she couldn't know what was in those bags, there was only one thing she could be thanking him for. Sol nodded to her, climbed into his saddle and rode away.

Chapter 9

The moment that place was behind him, the weight that Sol had felt upon his shoulders was lifted. He forgot about what his friend Matt might have said to him. He forgot about the nervous fear that had been in Patricia's eyes. Sol even forgot about Charlie being shut up in that closet. Judging by the men on horseback who bolted from town not too far behind him, Sol guessed that Charlie had gotten himself out of that closet just fine.

Sol didn't know those riders were behind him right away. Still leading the other horses, he'd been too busy enjoying the feel of the wind in his face as he raced away from Warren. Sol couldn't hear much of anything else through the stomping of those hooves, and when he'd taken a few glances behind him, he couldn't see through the gritty dust cloud those hooves were kicking up. Before too long, Sol could hear gunshots without much problem at all.

The first shot had been just a pop in the distance behind him. Sol turned in his saddle and steered his gray gelding to one side so he could at least get a look through the thinner edge of the dust cloud. It took a couple of seconds and a whole lot of squinting, but Sol eventually caught sight of the men that were riding out of town. They weren't nearly as close as he'd been expecting, but were making plenty of noise as they charged into the open terrain surrounding Warren.

Sol came up with an idea and didn't waste a second before putting it into motion. He pulled back on his reins hard enough to bring his horse to a noisy stop. The gelding let out a few whinnies in protest and even stomped the ground a bit, but slowed to a halt. The other two horses quickly followed suit.

Before the trailing horses had come to a full stop, Sol jumped from the saddle. He kept his eyes on the approaching riders as he quickly unbuckled the set of saddlebags from one of the other horses' back. Since the second spare horse had already been stripped of his bags, Sol didn't have to worry too much about that one.

There were at least two or three other riders leaving Warren. Every so often, they would fire a shot or two, but they were still well outside pistol range. He guessed they were on the outer edge of a rifle's range, but Sol didn't hear any lead coming close enough to be a concern just yet. Sol got the second set of saddlebags across the back of his own gray gelding. After climbing back into his saddle, he looked behind him and saw the other riders had closed a good amount of distance.

Sol had no way of knowing for certain who those riders were. He did know that Charlie had had more than enough time to gather his courage and open that closet door. It only made sense that the big fellow would be out for blood as soon as he threw on a fresh pair of britches.

Since Sol wasn't wild about the idea of staying put to get a better look at those men, he tapped his heels against his gelding's side and tugged the reins connected to the other two horses. All three of the horses lurched forward and quickly fell into step with one another.

As the horsemen behind Sol got closer, one of the riders shouted, "That you, Brakefield?"

Seeing as how the man knew Sol's last name, that meant he had to be one of the overseers who actually got their hands dirty in the mine on a day-to-day basis. Of course, that didn't make Sol want to turn around and chat with the man. If they worked for Charlie in any way, they had to be counted as a threat.

Unlike the last time he'd been shot at, Sol didn't feel his thoughts swirl inside him like a dust devil. He kept his head down and steered toward a patch of trees that sprouted up to the left of the trail. Those trees were only a little ways ahead, but Sol knew he could use every bit of space he could get. Drawing his pistol, he shifted in his saddle and looked behind him.

The other riders were still about a couple hundred yards behind him and gaining slowly. More shots cracked through the air, but Sol didn't pay them any mind. Instead, he fired a couple shots of his own until he saw the other riders break apart from one another. Once that bit of panic had been sewn, Sol snapped the reins of the other two horses he'd been leading and then released the leather straps completely.

For the next several paces, the other two horses kept following Sol. Once Sol broke to the north, however, one of the horses continued along its original path while the second one did its best to run alongside Sol's gray gelding.

"Go on!" Sol yelled at the vigilant horse.

The other animal wouldn't give up. In fact, it churned its legs even harder as it struggled to keep up with Sol.

"I said git!"

The other horse was still following him better than those other ones with riders in their saddles.

Sol lowered his pistol and fired a few shots into the ground between him and the nearby horse. Not only did that shot cause the other horse to veer away, but it also added some steam into the stride of his own gray gelding. Both horses took off even faster in different directions. Better yet, the additional shots made the pursuing riders pull back a bit more. It seemed Charlie wasn't paying them enough to charge into hot lead.

Keeping his head down, Sol glanced behind him and saw the dust cloud thinning out as the other two horses bolted along their own path. Sol snapped his reins to get to those trees as quickly as he could. Once there, he steered around them and then snapped his reins again. The gray gelding surprised him with how fast it could move. Sol held on to his reins tightly and focused all of his attention in riding out the storm he'd caused. When he looked around again, the other riders had split up to follow the other horses that weren't shooting back at them.

More shots were fired, but Sol didn't hear any bullets hissing anywhere close to him. For the next several minutes, the only thing he concerned himself with was the rush of wind against his face and the rumble of his gelding's hooves against the earth. Leaning down over his horse's neck, Sol felt as if he could make it all the way to Canada before sundown. Warren was nothing but a distant memory and his new life stretched out before him like a newly discovered land.

After some time had passed, it was clear that Sol wasn't being followed. As an afterthought, he glanced over his shoulder and wasn't at all surprised to find that he was on his own. He'd covered a mile or maybe two and there had been plenty of hills, rocks and trees along the way. Straightening up in the saddle, Sol pulled back on the reins and allowed his horse to ease up for a while.

The gray gelding seemed reluctant to slow down, so Sol let him tire himself out. It was at that moment that Sol realized he had no schedules to keep and no obligations to meet. There was nobody expecting him at any certain time and he had no bills to pay. He didn't even have a change of clothes, since he'd left everything behind in the room he'd rented at Tilly's Boardinghouse. Sol didn't own much, but he figured that Tilly was bound to find more than enough to square up whatever he owed.

Sol could go anywhere.

It was a freedom that was large enough to excite and overwhelm him at the same time. He'd never seen the world as such a wide-open place before. There had always been tethers of one sort or another holding him back. Most folks were always willing to let him know a man couldn't stray too far, but Sol had never seen the hollowness in those words until he looked out at the horizon stretching in front of him now.

The folks who had told him to stay put and work to scrape together a nice little nest egg were scared. That was all there was to it. They were scared or ignorant or both, because nobody in their right mind would have tried to talk anyone out of what Sol was feeling at that moment.

Why would anyone want to stay in a place like Warren with their faces firmly pressed against a grindstone when there was a whole world out there? The puzzle seemed even more incomprehensible when the man turning that grindstone was someone like Charlie Lowell. Despite the mistakes he'd made along the way, Sol wouldn't have traded his current predicament for all the tea in China. Not even for all the money in the . . .

And then Sol was pulled down from the cloud he'd been riding to be sent face-first to the ground with the rest of the world. He may not have had all the money in the world, but he currently had more than he'd ever thought he could have. He certainly had more than he could spend. In fact, he wondered if he should spend any of it at all.

He'd stolen that money, hadn't he?

Looking back on it that way, Sol felt like he was watching a dream that had come from some lunatic's head. It was close to unthinkable that he could pull a gun on another man and rob him. He'd also tracked down three armed robbers and left one of them dead.

Good Lord, he thought. *What have I done?*

Sol pulled back on his reins and slowed his horse down a bit. His thoughts matched that pace and flowed through him so he had enough time to consider each one. His first decision was to stop thinking about what he'd done. Those things were in the past and there was no taking them back.

Only one man had wound up dead, but that was self-defense.

Sol nodded when he thought about that and said the words out loud just to make them real. "Self-defense," he muttered. "That's right. He was going to shoot me, after all."

With that settled, Sol took a breath and let it out. The biggest matter yet to be settled was where he was headed. He'd ridden this far north, so there was no reason he shouldn't keep going that way. Santa Fe was north. He'd never been there. Sol didn't even know anyone there. He would ride to Santa Fe. It could take him another day or two, but time wasn't exactly a concern.

There were still plenty of things to be decided, but Sol pushed those to the back of his head. When he was hungry, he would scrape up something to eat. When he was tired, he would find a soft spot to stretch out his legs. When he spotted a town that looked inviting, he would stop there.

He was still free.

Despite all the other things rattling around inside him like so many marbles in a jar, Sol was still free.

He continued north, allowing his gelding to go as fast or slow as it wanted to go. Although Sol had done a fair amount of traveling throughout his life, most of it had been out of necessity. He'd needed to leave one town and go to another on account of some job. Once that job dried up, he'd moved again. If someone died, he went to the funeral. If someone in his family was married, he would travel to see them dressed in their finest and enjoy a good meal.

All of it had been placed neatly in front of him, but not anymore. Despite the fact that he could have made it into Santa Fe that evening if he'd snapped his reins a bit more, Sol pulled back on them before he got close enough to see that town. There was a spot that had caught his eye right next to a watering hole, so he made camp there and sat with his back against a log.

He watched the stars come out again and didn't even mind that he wasn't prepared to make any meals or even cover himself in the cold darkness. After making a fire, he stretched out and laid his head on the saddlebags stuffed with money. Feeling like a king, Sol fell asleep while letting his eyes drift between the brilliant little specks above him.

At the first light of dawn, his eyes snapped open and he sat bolt upright. Turning toward the east, Sol rested his chin upon his knees and watched as the sun crept its way up from the spot it had been hiding the previous night. The sky went through its transformation as if an unseen painter couldn't decide whether he preferred purple, red or orange. In the end, pale yellow was the chosen hue and the desert heat soon made its presence known upon Sol's face and shoulders.

He gathered up his few belongings and loaded them onto his horse. Savoring the touch of the sun's rays on his cheek and smelling the morning breeze, Sol didn't sully his mind with thoughts about his future. There were only two things he needed to know: he was hungry and he should be in Santa Fe by noon.

Chapter 10

It was slightly earlier than Sol had anticipated when he rode into Santa Fe. It wasn't quite noon and the sun was blazing down with unrelenting fury. While his gray gelding had been more than willing to gallop most of the way into town, he now dragged his hooves as if his shoes were too heavy to lift. Being the one catching the sun's rays without anything more than the brim of his hat for shade, Sol felt just as sluggish. He kept one arm propped against the saddle horn to hold him up and allowed his head to droop forward.

Santa Fe might have been a beautiful place. It might have been thriving. It might have been a pit favored by the devil himself, but Sol wouldn't have known either way. His throat was parched. His stomach was aching and his skin felt about ready to crack and fall off of him like a muddy crust. As soon as he spotted a place that looked like it would serve food and water, he tied his gelding in front of it and dragged himself inside.

"What can I get for you, mister?" asked a stout Mexican woman with thick black hair tied into a single braid.

"Something to eat and some water. Actually," Sol was quick to add, "lots of water."

"We have plenty of water," she replied with a smile. "There's water for your horse too."

Sol flinched and looked over his shoulder. "What was that?"

"Your horse," she repeated. "It's a fine animal, but you tied him up without watering him."

"Were you watching me?"

She shrugged. "It's a slow day. You can tend to your horse and I'll get your water."

When he came back inside after seeing to his horse, Sol looked over to the nearby tables with disdain. After all the sitting he'd done over the last few days, he wasn't exactly looking forward to doing it again. The chairs in that place were a far cry from a saddle, however, and Sol quickly let out a relieved sigh as he settled into one of them close to the front window. He could see his horse clearly and nodded after he watched a few people pass by the animal without thinking to poke around those saddlebags.

"Here is your water," the Mexican lady said as she set a cup down in front of Sol. Her eyes lingered on him for a bit as she stood beside his table with a pitcher in her hands. Sol drained the water and slapped the empty cup right back down. Refilling the cup, the lady said, "We have more than water if you'd like, but you must pay after this cup."

Suddenly realizing why she'd been looking him over so intently, Sol nodded and dug into his pocket. Before coming into town, he'd taken some of the money from his saddlebags so he wouldn't have to keep digging into them. He held out a generous fistful of cash and showed it to her. "I've got enough to pay for a meal," he declared. "I'd appreciate a steak if you have one."

The lady's eyes widened and she nodded quickly. "Right away, sir. Anything else I can get for you?"

"I'll need a place to stay here in town. Do you have any suggestions?"

"There's a hotel right across the street and down a bit. It's called the Trail's End. They're clean and you can also get a bath."

"Are you trying to tell me something?" Sol asked.

She blushed and looked away. "Not at all. What I meant was—"

"You're right. I can use a bath," Sol told her with a grin. "When I come back here for breakfast, I'll be all cleaned up. Hopefully I'm good enough right now to get that steak."

"Of course. How do you want it cooked?"

"I'll leave that to you, just so long as it doesn't take long."

"Sí, sí."

When she said those last two words, the lady's voice took on a more natural quality that made her seem even prettier. Sol couldn't quite put his finger on it, but he sensed that she'd let her guard down a bit. He wondered if she was nice to all the men who came into that restaurant. He even considered testing the waters to see if she might want to join him some other time for a meal.

Before he could dwell too much on those things, Sol picked up the distinctive scent of steak. Not only that, but the steak was directly in front of him. Sol shook himself out of his thoughts and looked down to see a plate covered with the steak as well as a generous portion of potatoes and a pile of green beans.

"That was quick," he said.

The Mexican lady shrugged and replied, "You looked hungry, so I told the cook to move it along."

"Thanks. I appreciate it."

The woman left and Sol devoured his food. As much as he would have liked to savor every last bite, he was just too hungry to hold himself back. He didn't even realize how hungry he was until he'd taken his first few tastes. After that, it was all he could do to keep from taking a bite out of the plate.

After clearing off the table when he was through, the Mexican woman asked, "Would you like some rhubarb pie?"

"I'll take the biggest piece you're allowed to cut," Sol replied without needing to think about it.

She brought him what could have been considered two pieces and a cup of hot coffee. Sol tore through dessert just as quickly as he had the main course and felt all of his energy returning. Like a ship with a fresh wind in its sails, he got up and strode to where the woman was washing his dishes.

"Here you go," Sol said as he gave her some money. "That should cover it. Keep the rest."

She counted it up quickly and then started to shake her head. "Oh, no. This is too much."

"Go on and keep it. Just make sure you give me another one of those smiles the next time I stop by."

"Sí," she told him in that relaxed manner he'd enjoyed before. "I will."

Sol left the restaurant and looked down the street. Sure enough, just as he'd been told, he saw the Trail's

End Hotel not too far away. Unhitching his horse, Sol led it to the hotel. Rather than tie the horse up again, he kept hold of the reins so he could lead it to a stable he'd spotted just a bit farther down the street. It felt good to stretch his legs and he didn't mind walking off some of his hastily devoured meal.

As Sol took in the sights and sounds of Santa Fe, he felt the same as when he'd stayed up to watch the moon hang up among all the stars or the sun crawl its way through a burning sky. His eyes were more wide-open than they'd ever been and they were soaking up the world in a way he'd rarely been able to before. Sol was so transfixed by what should have been simple things that he didn't notice one particularly important thing.

He was being followed.

Sol didn't realize this until he was leaving the stables with his saddlebags draped over his shoulders. The weight of that money was anything but a burden, although the bags were awkward enough to slow him down. Because of that, Sol got a look at a man with narrow, European features and greasy hair that hung down over his ears and forehead like unruly straw. The man stood across the street, watching the front of the stable. When Sol walked out, he noticed the European man studying him with narrowed, intense eyes.

Meeting the other man's gaze, Sol nodded curtly and kept walking. The European fellow was dressed in ragged clothes and looked as if he hadn't had a proper meal in a month. He didn't even flinch when Sol nodded to him. Instead, the man chewed on his bottom lip and kept watching.

Sol's hand went to the gun at his side, just to rest upon the grip. There wasn't a need to draw the weapon just yet, however, since the European man seemed content to keep watching from a distance. Chalking the encounter up to him being a new face in town, Sol walked into the hotel and paid for a room. He climbed a set of stairs, unlocked the room with the key he'd been given and then finally set the saddlebags down.

Even though his back was thanking him for getting those bags onto the floor, Sol wasn't comfortable with leaving them there. In fact, the longer he stared down at the saddlebags, the more he realized how little thought he'd actually put into the simple matter of what he would do with the money.

The first thing that came to mind was to sit down and count it. So far, just knowing that the bags were full was enough to convince Sol that he would be set with funds for a good long while. Then again, he wasn't about to drag around those saddlebags to every place he decided to go. Sol lugged the saddlebags over to the bed and sat down upon the edge of a firm mattress. Compared to all the dust and horse sweat he'd endured throughout his ride, the scent of fresh linens was as welcome of a change as the feel of the mattress against his bruised backside.

Leaning down to unbuckle the closest bag, Sol opened the leather flap and placed his hand inside. Almost immediately, his fingers came to rest upon the bundles of money. Sol stopped and his breath caught within his chest. There was a lot of money in that bag. He didn't even need to know how to count for him to be certain of that much. He was also certain that it was more money than he'd ever had in his life. The icing on the cake was that it was stolen.

That made Sol's next breath snag in his throat right along with the previous one.

Suddenly, the room began to wobble beneath him and the air became too thick to breathe. Sol got up and went to the window, which was framed by delicate, lace curtains. He pulled those curtains aside, opened the window and stuck his face out into the fresh air. It was most definitely hotter than the day before, but that breeze was a welcome change. Sol filled his lungs a couple of times and then glanced down at the street.

The European man was still there.

He wasn't staring up at Sol's window, but he was still wandering along the street.

Sol shook his head and pulled himself back inside his room. For all he knew, the man always wandered up and down that street. There were plenty of fellows with habits like that back in Warren who ran the gamut from drunks and vagrants to miners who were down on their luck and old-timers who simply took their constitutionals at odd hours. Besides, judging by the European man's clothes, he probably didn't have two cents to rub together and the street was the only home he had.

Leaving the window open, Sol walked to his bed and paused just long enough to glance back down at the saddlebags. The thought of counting all that money churned the steak and rhubarb pie that had so recently settled so nicely into his stomach. Rather than upset that glorious balance, Sol quickly snatched a couple more bundles of cash from the open bag and stuffed them into his pockets. The next thing he checked was his gun.

Going through the motions of tapping his holster or simply brushing his hand against the grip of his pistol had become as reflexive as scratching his nose. The weight of the weapon at his side wasn't so much comforting as it was necessary. It was like the weight of his arm hanging from his shoulder, only Sol would rather have been without an arm than without his gun at this particular moment.

When he stacked his saddlebags under his bed, Sol tried not to think too hard about what he was doing. The fact that he'd gone from scraping by on a miner's wages to stashing bags of money under his bed still sat at the top of his brain and refused to sink in. The roots were taking hold, however, so Sol didn't do anything to pull them up. Once the money was stashed, he left his room and took a walk around Santa Fe.

He was so anxious to get out and about that he forgot to ask the clerk at the Trail's End about a bath. That wasn't a problem for too long, since he spotted a barbershop that also advertised a special price for a haircut, shave and hot bath. Sol stepped into that shop and took the barber up on the offer. It was one of the first times he'd bought so many things without haggling over the price. When he emerged from the barbershop, his face was smooth, his hair was trimmed and he no longer smelled like something that had grown from a horse instead of someone who'd merely sat on top of one for a while.

The sun was still high when Sol continued his walking tour of the town. Everywhere he turned, there were people of all shapes, shades and sizes rushing from one spot to another. Voices filled the air, mixing with the clang of a blacksmith's hammer and the rumble of the occasional wagon wheel. Out of curiosity, Sol glanced over his shoulder every now and then. He couldn't spot out the European man's face, which allowed him to stride with a bit more enthusiasm along the boardwalk. When he reached the door of a tailor's shop, Sol took one more look at the street.

There were so many people going by and not one of them seemed to care whether he was there or not. They all had business of their own to tend to, which was just fine for Sol. Standing there with his hand upon the tailor's door, he let his eyes wander for another second or two before smiling and pulling the door open. His entrance was announced by the tinkle of a small bell nailed into the door frame.

"Hello and good day to you," a thin man with round spectacles chirped. "What brings you here?"

"I could use some clothes," Sol replied.

"Formal or casual?"

"Both, I guess." Holding out his arms as if to mimic one of the wire frames against the wall, Sol added, "This here is all I've got."

"Then you have my condolences, sir. You have most definitely come to the right place. Come on inside and I'll take your measurements."

The tailor looked thinner when he got closer. Even his hair was thin. Black, irregular strands sprouted from the back of his head and were plastered against his scalp in a perfect swirl. His clothes hung on him with just enough room for his arms to move freely. Although his sleeves appeared to be rolled up, Sol could now see that was due to a clever cut of the cuff that kept the sleeves from interfering with the tailor's frenzied movements.

"Step right up here, if you please," the tailor said as he motioned toward a short stool.

Sol did as he was told and went through a series of poses as the tailor measured him from top to bottom. The process was so quick that Sol didn't hop down from the stool once the tailor scooted away to a small desk situated in a corner.

"Is that it?" Sol asked.

"Yes, it is. That is, unless you were planning on growing or shrinking within the next few days."

"Uh, no."

The tailor nodded. "I'll need you to pick out some material and colors, but whatever you choose, I'll need some time to stitch them together."

"I was hoping I could walk out of here with some things. Like I said before, this is all I've got."

"What happened?" the tailor asked with a curious expression. "Did your trunk fall off the back of a stagecoach?"

Sol chuckled at the tailor's easy manner. The truth was that the thin man's explanation was more convincing than the first lie that had sprung to Sol's mind. Also, it served its purpose a whole lot better than the truth. "Yeah," Sol replied. "Something like that."

"Well, how many suits do you need?"

"Suits? Well, I suppose just one fancy one. Maybe another one that's not so fancy. You know, like something dark but that doesn't make me look like I'm going to a funeral?"

Now it was the tailor's turn to chuckle. "Yes, I believe I know what you're talking about. One formal suit and another not so formal."

"What about regular clothes?" Sol asked. "Do you have any of those?"

"Take your pick," the tailor said as he swept his arm toward the racks set up in the back of his shop. "You'll find shirts on the right and pants on the left. Over on that wall there, you'll find jackets, waistcoats and such. I do feel I should mention, though, that my services are the best in town."

Sol nodded and replied, "Good."

"As such . . . they're not without their costs. I do need to purchase whatever material you select. I may have to purchase some other items that I don't have on hand, which is why I normally ask for half of my fee up front."

Sol hadn't visited many tailors in his life, since he'd purchased most of his clothes off a pile in general stores or from the backs of wagons. He did, however, recognize the concern etched onto the tailor's face. Sol did a good job of erasing that concern when he removed some cash from his pocket. "It's all right," he said. "I can pay half now. How much is it?"

The tailor's eyes widened and he smiled graciously. "We can discuss that once we decide on your choice of fabrics. I know of some exquisite silk that just arrived the other day straight from San Francisco. Also, I have some very fine cuff links which I'm certain will complement your suits nicely."

"I don't know about all that, but I could use another bag to carry my new wardrobe in."

"I've got some great ones right over here!" the tailor said excitedly.

Although the tailor was more than happy to give him the grand tour of his store, Sol picked out the color and design of his suits and then made a selection from the more basic sundries hanging from the racks. He paid for the simple clothes, packed them up in a new carpetbag and then put down the deposit required for the suits. By that time, Sol was more than ready to leave the shop.

As Sol opened the door and started to walk outside, the tailor asked, "Where are you staying?"

"Why?"

"So I can send word when your suits are done."

"Oh. At the Trail's End Hotel."

"I know the place," the tailor replied with a smile. "It shouldn't be more than a few days, but I'll be sure to leave a message for you when they're ready."

"All right. Thanks." This time, Sol ducked out of the shop as quickly as possible before the tailor roped him in again. After all was said and done, he'd probably spent more time inside that shop than he'd ever spent talking about clothes in all the years of his life. Once the door shut, Sol raced away like a boy running from the schoolhouse on the first day of summer.

The tailor bustled about his shop, practically dancing between his desk and the piles of fabric, buttons and thread arranged behind a thin folding partition. When he heard the bell at the front door ring again, he hopped out from behind the partition and chirped, "Forget something?"

The tailor trailed off and his smile lost a good deal of its luster when he saw the European man in the rumpled clothes entering the shop. Quickly composing himself and refreshing his smile, the tailor asked, "What can I do for you, sir?"

"I'm a friend of the man that was just in here," the European man grunted. "Know where I can find him?"

Chapter 11

It was a little over a week before Sol received more than a subtle nod from the front desk clerk at the Trail's End Hotel. In that time, Sol had stopped walking the streets of Santa Fe and had been making the rounds at the saloons and poker halls of what most considered to be the less respectable part of town.

At first, Sol wasn't comfortable in the new role he'd taken. Making the change from modest worker to socialite wasn't exactly natural. After a night or two of spending his money just to spend it, Sol settled into more of a routine and became more selective in his pursuits. He'd always enjoyed playing cards, so he put in an appearance at a few different games each day. He brought only a bit of his money and found himself on a lucky streak the likes of which he'd never experienced.

Perhaps it was the money itself. Sol had originally thought the cash might be lucky. After all he'd done to get it, he was lucky to be alive. But he soon realized that it wasn't so much the money as the hand that wasn't afraid to toss it away. The few other times Sol had gambled, he'd been afraid to lose. The occasional game after a hard day of toiling in the silver mine didn't exactly put Sol in the frame of mind where he could risk everything on a hunch. Now that he had money to burn, he could afford to let his instincts have free rein. As it turned out, his instincts were fairly good.

While Sol had hoped to lighten his load a bit by spreading some of Charlie's money around Santa Fe, he wound up keeping more than he lost. Toward the end of that week, Sol guessed he might even be ahead. His winning streak didn't only show through at the card table, either. The more he won, the more handsome he became to the women who chose to spend their nights at the saloons Sol frequented. Although they didn't always state their prices up front, Sol knew working girls when he saw them. He also knew them when he smelled them.

After all that looking and smelling, he figured he might as well do a bit of touching. After all, he figured he'd earned a few indulgences and there was no reason they had to be limited to poker and a few expensive suits. With all of the former, Sol had nearly forgotten about the latter.

The week had gotten by him like an anchor dropping from the end of a coiled rope. The further along it went, the faster it slipped away. When he walked back into the Trail's End, Sol waved to the clerk, but didn't expect much of anything in return. Any other time, he would have been correct in that assumption. This time, however, he was not.

"Mr. Brakefield?"

Sol slowed down and turned around. Once he saw the clerk looking expectantly at him, Sol felt more than a little foolish for feeling so suspicious. Walking up to the desk, he asked, "Yes? What is it?"

"There's a message for you."

Sol's hand drifted toward his gun. "From who?"

"I don't know," the clerk replied as he held out a single folded piece of paper. "I'm not supposed to read them."

Wondering how he hadn't seen that one coming, Sol took the note from the clerk's hand. Before he opened it, he got a sneaking suspicion as to what he might find. Sure enough, that suspicion was proven correct. "One of my suits is ready," he announced.

"Wonderful. I'll see if I can get that into the newspaper."

Sol looked over to the clerk, who had already found something better to do. "I liked you better when you kept quiet."

The clerk shrugged and promptly went about his duties as if Sol had been swept off the face of the earth.

It was approaching the end of the business day, but Sol decided to try his luck with the tailor anyway. The sky was darkening to a pleasant mix of purple and deep blue, which also put a comforting chill into the air. Sol made his way down the boardwalk as if he were already wearing his new silk suit. He walked tall and held his head high. He tipped his hat to an elderly couple crossing the street. He waved to a woman and her little boy on the corner. And he almost said "How do you do" to the European man staring at him from a saloon doorway.

Sol met the European man's gaze and kept walking.

In the last several days, he'd seen plenty of familiar faces in the same spots along several different streets. Santa Fe had its share of folks that were down on their luck and some of them had staked their claim to various alleys or corners. Sol didn't concern himself too much with those folks, just as they didn't seem to think much of him. The European man was different, however. As much as Sol wanted to believe otherwise, there was no denying that man was more than just some territorial vagrant.

As he walked toward the tailor's shop, Sol kept a quick pace and took every opportunity to glance over his shoulder without being too obvious about it. After catching more than one glimpse of the European man behind him, Sol decided subtlety was no longer his biggest concern.

The tailor's shop was in sight when Sol stopped and turned completely around. The European man was still behind him and was even hurrying to catch up with Sol before he made it to the tailor's door.

"Who are you?" Sol demanded as he walked toward the other man and lowered his hand to within an inch or so of his holster. "What do you want?"

"Just want a word with you, fella," the European man replied in a slight Irish accent. "How about you come along with me?"

As the other man reached out to grab Sol's arm, Sol pulled his gun from its holster and took aim. "Don't come another step closer."

"Or what? You kill me like you killed those miners?"

"What miners?"

The European man forced a small grin onto his face, but it didn't stick for long. "Folks are starting to look. You want the law to find you?"

Sol scowled and glanced around at the rest of the street. Sure enough, a good portion of the others walking to and fro in the vicinity of the tailor's shop were watching Sol closely. Women pulled their children away and husbands escorted their wives in the opposite direction. Before Sol could shift his attention back to the European man, he was knocked off the boardwalk and into the narrow walkway between two buildings.

The European man wrestled for control of Sol's gun, but was unable to pull the weapon free. Sol's heart was beating too quickly and his nerves were too frayed for him to be overpowered so easily. Although he kept his fingers locked around his pistol's grip, Sol wasn't able to maintain his footing and soon felt his shoulders slamming against a wall.

Sol struggled to pull his wrist free of the other man's hold. He even felt his wrist coming loose, but Sol was forced to pull it through the European man's long, cracked fingernails. Deep gouges were scraped into Sol's wrists, but he would be free if he could endure the pain. Despite the fact that he might win that struggle, Sol quickly realized he might lose the war.

Someone else had joined the fray, and it wasn't an overly curious bystander. The second man had his gun drawn, but kept it close to his body to keep it out of plain sight. "Having some trouble, Alex?" the second man asked.

Sol tried to fire a shot just to startle the other two, but was diverted when the second man lunged toward him, giving the first a chance to make another grab for Sol's wrist. Although he kicked at both men and swung with his free hand, Sol only managed to make things worse for himself. Both of the other men also stepped up their efforts. Alex grabbed hold of Sol's gun arm with both hands while his partner tenderized Sol's torso with one punch after another.

Tensing his stomach and gritting his teeth, Sol was able to weather the first series of blows. The moment he relaxed enough to pull in another breath, Sol caught a punch in the stomach that forced all the wind from his lungs. The next thing he knew, Sol was no longer able to keep his knees from buckling.

As soon as Sol faltered, Alex pulled the gun from his hand. "That's got him. Check his pockets. This one likes to carry around plenty of money."

Sol was unable to take a full breath at the moment, which meant he was also unable to lift a finger to stop the second man from searching his pockets like a vulture swooping down on a fresh corpse.

"Did you find any money?" Alex asked.

"Just give me a chance, will ya?" the second man replied.

"Who . . . are you?" Sol asked.

Alex grinned. Now that he had his partner with him, his European features took on a livelier sheen. "Who we are don't matter. What matters is that we know who *you* are."

"Yeah," the second man chuckled as he held out the bundle of money he'd found. "You're a gravy train, is what you are!"

"Where's the rest of it?" Alex asked.

Sol shook his head. "I . . . there . . . there isn't

anymore." Before he could get out another word, he felt the numbing impact of a fist slamming against his face. Sol's head knocked against the wall and a warm flow of blood trickled down his face.

"You're lying! I saw you pull a fortune out of them pockets when you paid that tailor. That was only a portion of what you was supposed to pay for them fancy suits, right?"

Blinking away the haze that was creeping into his head, Sol could see the second man leaning forward with his fist cocked back. Although he knew he'd feel plenty of pain in a while, Sol was just numb enough at the moment to keep going through a few more punches. That realization brought a grin to his face.

"You been following . . . me all this . . . time?" Sol wheezed. "And you decided to jump me . . . now? You . . . should've caught me before I went to that . . . last poker game."

The second man punched Sol again and that blow was followed up by one from Alex.

Sol could tell the men were dealing out their worst. Fortunately, their worst wasn't enough to make Sol hurt any more than he already was.

"Where's the rest of that money?" Alex asked. "I know you got more. I know you been winning the last few nights at cards. Where's that money?"

Perhaps Sol had been knocked around worse than he thought and something had come loose. Perhaps he was finding out firsthand what it meant to be punch-drunk. Whatever the reason was, Sol widened his grin and started to laugh. That didn't set well with the other two men at all.

At first, Alex and the second man merely looked at

each other as if they both thought their eyes were deceiving them. When they got another look at Sol's laughing face, they took it upon themselves to knock that smile into oblivion. This time, however, it was Sol who beat them to the punch.

Sol's leg snapped up to catch Alex in the groin. Alex doubled over and let out a hacking wheeze. Since the second man wasn't positioned to catch a foot in the same spot, Sol kicked that one in the knee. The second man grunted and took a halfhearted swing. Sol kicked him in the leg again, forcing the second man to punch the wall instead of his intended target.

Knowing better than to celebrate too early, Sol climbed to his feet. Alex was still groaning and doubled over, so Sol grabbed hold of him to help pull himself up. Once Sol had his legs beneath him, he pulled Alex into the wall and cracked his head against the wooden slats. Sol reached for his gun, but his holster was empty. The second man made the same move, but had the pistol to back it up.

"You're dead!" the second man yelped.

But Sol could see fear in that one's eyes.

Sol reached out to take the gun away from the second man. There was a struggle, but Sol had already taken enough lumps for the second man's punches to feel more like slaps from a baby. The moment Sol's hand closed around the second man's gun, he swung the pistol around to crack it against the man's cheek. There was a solid impact, but the second man was surprised and taken off balance more than anything else. Sol pressed his advantage by shoving the second man into Alex and taking a few steps back.

"You're not just robbers," Sol said.

Alex and the second man bumped against each other before turning to face Sol. Seeing the gun in Sol's hand was enough to take the wind from their sails.

"You can have your money back," Alex said. "We can part ways and that'll be that."

Sol paid no attention to those words. "What do you know about miners that were killed?" he asked.

"It says so on the notice."

As Sol's brow furrowed, the second man stepped in to his friend's defense. "He ain't lying. There's a notice posted about those men you killed."

"What men?"

The second man reached into his pocket, but Sol reflexively aimed his gun directly at him. "I got the notice right here," the second man said. "I brung it to show the law when we handed you in."

Sol thumbed back the gun's hammer and said, "Let's see it, but you'd best be real careful."

Nodding slowly, the second man pulled out a square of paper that was folded into fourths and started to hand it over.

"Show it to me," Sol said.

"All right. Fine. Just settle down," the second man said as he unfolded the paper. When he was finished, he held up the notice so it was facing Sol.

When he saw the crudely drawn portrait of himself beneath the word REWARD written in large block letters, Sol thought he was dreaming. It just didn't seem real to see his face amid such words as "wanted for murder" and "fugitive." Sol snatched the notice from the man's hand and looked it over as best he could without taking his eyes from the other two men. He didn't need to read too far into it to see there was a fifteen-hundred-dollar reward for his capture.

"Where'd you get this?" Sol asked.

"It was posted at the sheriff's office and hereabouts," Alex replied.

"And you were after this money back when I was buying my suits?"

Alex shook his head. "I didn't know about it then. I seen you waving all that cash around. I went back a few times to see if the tailor would let me know where to find you. He wouldn't do it right away, but he sure did once we found that notice and showed it to him."

"I didn't kill any miners," Sol said. "This is a mistake."

"Then tell it to the fella offering up that money."

Sol looked at the bottom of the notice and saw the name Alex had referred to. "Upon capture," the notice read, "contact Charles Lowell in Warren, New Mexico."

When the two men shifted in front of him, Sol snapped his eyes up and tightened his grip on the gun. "Neither of you move."

Both Alex and the second man held their hands up and backed against the wall.

There were more folks moving about, but they passed by the mouth of the alley without thinking to check in the narrow, dirty corridor. The few who did glance down the alley just kept walking when they saw what was going on in there. Sol's stomach clenched with the certainty that he couldn't rely on his privacy lasting much longer.

"Toss your guns," Sol demanded.

Both men nervously glanced back and forth at each other.

"This fight's over as far as we're concerned," Alex said. "No need for—"

"Drop your guns," Sol barked. "Now!"

One man tossed over a pistol, but the other shifted on his feet as if he were about to jump from his skin.

"You already got my gun," the second man said.

"Then start walking," Sol replied. "Better yet, start running."

Neither of the two men had to be told twice. They bolted from the alley as if their backsides had caught fire. After giving them a good head start, Sol collected the rest of the guns, pointed his nose toward the other end of the alley and followed the example set by Alex and his partner.

Sol didn't stop running until he got back to his room.

Chapter 12

Sol did his best to keep from running out of his room like a scalded dog. The saddlebags were slung over his shoulders and they'd never felt heavier. In fact, he never would have imagined what a burden all that money could be. When he got to the front desk, he forced a smile onto his face and set his key down.

"Here's my key," Sol said. "And this should settle up my bill."

"Don't forget about your meals," the clerk replied. "You charged some onto . . ." He swallowed the rest of his words when he saw how much money was piled on the desk. "Actually, this looks like it should be more than enough. I'll get your change."

Sol had been watching the clerk for any trace that he might know about the reward. Apparently, the clerk was more concerned with his job than he was about his customers' entanglements with the law.

"Keep the change," Sol said. "Everything was fine."

The clerk nodded and smiled. Fortunately, Sol's estimate had been close enough to keep him from making the clerk too wealthy. "I appreciate that, sir. Hopefully, you'll come again."

But Sol was already heading for the door and rushing down the boardwalk.

As he made his way to the stable, Sol considered everyone he passed a potential threat. While he might not have recognized anyone on the street, he was certain at least one or two of them recognized him. There could be lawmen about, waiting for their chance to corner him. There could be bounty hunters setting up an ambush. There could even be some more enterprising souls who merely wanted to get their hands on the reward being offered for Sol's head.

Sol got to the stable and hurried past the boy brushing one of the horses. When he pulled open the gate to the stall where his own gray gelding was being kept, Sol tossed down his bags and reached for the saddle propped against the nearby wall.

"You can't go in there, mister!" the stable boy said. "That horse ain't for sale!"

"Don't worry, kid," Sol replied as he dug into his jeans pocket. "This is my horse." He found his ticket and handed it over to the boy.

Once the boy got a look at the ticket, he let out a relieved sigh. "Sorry about that, mister. You want me to help you?"

"No need for that. I'm fixing to leave."

"Oh. I'll get my pa so—"

"Here," Sol interrupted as he shoved some money into the boy's shirt pocket. "Give that to your pa."

The boy let out an amazed gasp as he fished out the money and flipped through the bills. "This is a lot!"

"Here," Sol said as he handed over another wad of money. "This is for you, so don't touch any of your pa's money. You hear?"

Holding two handfuls of money, the kid could do nothing but nod.

"Good. Now, you're getting your own money because I'm playing a game. You like games?"

The kid nodded again.

By this time, Sol was almost done saddling up his gelding. "Some friends of mine may be looking for me and I don't want them to find me. You think you could pretend I wasn't here?"

"You mean like hide-and-seek?"

"That's it exactly," Sol replied as he cinched up one of the final buckles.

"I could tell your friends you went somewhere else! That way, they'll never find you!"

"No. Just pretend like you don't know who I am. In fact, pretend you never even seen my horse. Think you can do that?"

"Yes, sir."

"Perfect." Sol put his saddlebags into place and hung his new carpetbag from the saddle horn. It wasn't a perfect arrangement, but he figured it would do well enough to get him out of Santa Fe. Leading his horse to the front door, Sol cautiously started to peek outside.

"No!" the kid shouted. "Not that way!"

Sol reflexively reached for his holster and almost drew his gun. Fortunately, the boy seemed more affected by the look on Sol's face than the proximity of his hand to his weapon.

"That leads right out to the street," the boy explained meekly. "If your friends are looking for you, they'll spot you easy. You can go out the back way."

Looking to the spot where the boy was pointing,

Sol picked out the shape of a smaller door outlined in light streaming from the outside. He nodded and smiled warmly. "That's a good idea. Thanks."

Not only did the boy cheer up when he saw Sol's grin, but he dashed through the stable to hold open the back door for him. "I'll shut it behind you and then pretend like I never even saw you."

"Perfect."

"I like hide-and-seek."

Sol nodded as he passed the kid by, but wasn't quite able to agree with that sentiment. The stable's back door led out to a small lot that was currently populated by a black Darley Arabian and a few pack mules. Sol led his gray gelding through a gate and onto a winding stretch of rough, narrow road. He quickly got his bearings and headed east, since he was fairly certain that was the quickest way out of town.

The ride to the town's eastern border played havoc with Sol's nerves. By the time he saw open country in front of him, he felt like he'd trudged through miles of enemy terrain with a pack of hounds nipping at his heels. He didn't feel one bit of relief until he snapped the horse's reins and built up some real speed.

As he put Santa Fe behind him, Sol swore he could hear horses at his back. He glanced over his shoulder and got a face full of dirt that had been kicked up by his own horse. Even though he could barely see much of anything at all, he still thought he'd spotted a posse tearing after him like demons that had been loosed from below.

Rather than try to confirm what he thought he'd seen or heard, Sol snapped his reins a few more times and hung on while his horse did all the work. After he'd put some distance between himself and Santa Fe, Sol allowed his horse to ease up a bit. There was no trace of a posse or anyone else behind him. Since the terrain was mostly flat along that stretch, he allowed himself to let out the breath he'd been holding all this time.

As he settled into his saddle, Sol felt like he'd just opened his eyes after a nightmare. He closed his eyes and tried to think of nothing but the wind in his face and the trail spooling out in front of him. It was a tough job under those circumstances, but Sol managed it well enough for his heart to stop kicking like an angry mule trapped in his rib cage. Now that he could think straight, Sol removed the notice that he'd stuffed into his pocket.

He unfolded it and looked the paper over the way he might take in a piece of art hanging on a rich fellow's wall. Sure, Sol could see the lines that made up the picture and could read the words making up the text, but he was too rattled to put them all together. He was, after all, more concerned with staying atop his horse.

After another few breaths, he looked at the notice more carefully. Starting at the top and working his way down, Sol shook his head and wondered just what the blazes had happened to his life.

He was a wanted man.

There was no doubting that much. It was right there in print for anyone to see. Lord only knew how many more had been printed up and tacked to walls or posts for miles in any direction. There had to be plenty of those things plastered all over Warren. Matt had probably seen them by now and Patricia probably told him that she'd always known something like that would happen.

Sol kept reading. Apparently, he was supposed to have killed three men. Either Charlie assumed all three of those robbers were dead, he'd finished the job off himself, or he was just tacking on a few deaths to make Sol look worse. Either way didn't make much difference. As far as anyone knew, Sol had sent all three to their graves. Most of the men who went after that reward money wouldn't even think to ask about the particulars of the killings. So long as Charlie paid up, everyone would be happy all around.

Everyone but Sol, that is.

There wasn't much more to the notice. It was written so it could be read and understood in the time it took to walk past it. Charlie was offering the money and would most certainly pay it. After Sol had put him through the indignity of being shut away in his own closet, Charlie would go an awfully long way to settle that score. Sol had seen that much in Charlie's eyes. Sometimes, when he tried to rest, Sol could still see it.

So, what was left for him to do?

That was the big question that weighed on Sol's mind. What was he to do if he was no longer free?

He still had the money he'd stolen. That bit of knowledge no longer was a comfort to Sol. And, thanks to a lifetime of scraping to get by, he couldn't bring himself to just dump the money and be done with it.

He could keep riding north all the way to Canada or he could turn south and head for Old Mexico.

Neither one of those things set too well with him, either.

Sol was already going north, so he could always go to Denver. It would be a good, long ride, but he had some family up there who would be more than happy to put him up for a few days. When he thought about that, Sol remembered there being some friends of his family who lived even farther north in the Rocky Mountains. One friend in particular sprang to mind. When he thought about that name, Sol felt as if he'd been thinking about it all along and had only recently been reminded of it. That name might very well have been sitting on the tip of his tongue from the moment he drew his gun and aimed it at Charlie. That name was Nester Quarles.

Pulling back on his reins, Sol brought his horse to a stop.

For a moment, he just sat there and looked out into space without seeing much of anything. Several members of his family didn't even speak Nester's name out loud, whether it be for propriety or just plain superstition. Other family members spun tales about Nester Quarles the way others told ghost stories on stormy nights. It was also a name that could turn a lot of heads if it was spoken in the presence of too many lawmen.

As far as the stories went, Nester had buried enough men to populate a village and had stolen enough money to buy a small town. Beyond Sol's family, Nester was suspected of committing any crime that was an offense to God-fearing Christians. Nester was feared by most and worshipped by some. Of course, the type of men who would look up to Nester didn't exactly sing in a choir themselves.

Sol's uncles had once told him that Nester used to ride with some of his cousins. One of Sol's aunts used to say that her half sister used to be courted by Nester whenever he rode through a particular stretch of Kansas. Sol's second cousin never got tired of telling the story about how his brothers once rode on a string of bank robberies with Nester Quarles over the course of six days. At Brakefield family reunions, the incident was referred to as "a dark week for good men."

Sol didn't profess to know what that meant. He barely understood how some of these family members and supposed accomplices of Nester Quarles were even related to him. All that had mattered at the time was that the stories kept making the rounds at all the family gatherings. For a boy flanked on all sides by cousins, aunts, uncles, sewing circles and whittling contests, such tales had always been a blessing.

As the years went on, Nester had become a colorful smudge upon his family lineage. The stories that stuck out the most in Sol's mind anymore were the ones told by a man who lived in Leadville, Colorado. It wasn't a lot to go on, but the man from Leadville had spoken as if he'd seen Nester personally and knew where the outlaw might be hiding.

As it stood, Sol knew he could never return to Warren. For all he knew, there were plenty of towns scattered throughout several counties that he should avoid like the plague. Through this strange mix of bad luck, unfortunate timing and a few poor decisions, Sol was burning his own bridges before he could cross them. The way he saw it, he could either run until he found a quiet spot or he could try to make the best out of a bad situation.

An idea had settled into the back of Sol's mind. It had seemed more like a whim at first, but grew into something more and more solid. Like a bucket of water that hardened into ice, Sol's idea was now something with genuine substance. If done correctly, he could turn this situation into the best opportunity of his life with a dash of payback thrown into the mix. In order to do it correctly, however, he would need the help of a man like Nester Quarles.

Since Sol had no idea where to find his aunt's half sister, his second cousin's brother or any such gnarled branches of his family tree, he decided to make his way to Leadville. It would be a long ride, but he didn't exactly have more pressing matters that required his attention.

Chapter 13

Three weeks later, Leadville, Colorado

There were plenty of quicker ways to get to Leadville. Sol had more than enough cash to purchase a train ticket for himself and his horse. There were stagecoach lines and even several trails that were more accommodating to travelers than the ones Sol used. All of those things required him to be in the open much more than he would have liked, however. For a man with his current troubles with the law, Sol couldn't afford to run in the same circles as more respectable folks.

Within the first few days of his ride north, Sol had spotted the notice with his face on it in four different spots. Fortunately, whoever had drawn the likeness of him for Charlie wasn't a talented artist. Although a few people had seen him in the same vicinity of that notice, only one had paid him any mind before Sol had a chance to tear the notice down.

"Looks like you're famous," a man in his forties had said as he compared the notice to the man standing beside it.

Sol had glanced at the man and then at the notice, while putting on a surprised grin at the sight of that crudely drawn picture. "Guess I am," Sol had replied. "I surrender," he'd said as he held his hands up.

The man, as well as a few others nearby, had chuckled. Sol shrugged and fought every instinct he had to keep from bolting from that spot as if lightning were about to strike there. Rather than stay for the dinner he meant to have, Sol had left that town as soon as he'd ripped his notice from the wall. He slept under the stars that night and ate old jerked venison rather than take his chances in that town again.

As he'd continued to ride, Sol spotted the notices less frequently. Before he'd crossed into Colorado, the notices had all but dried up. Even so, Sol wasn't about to let his guard down. He still had the money stuffed into his saddlebags and he was certain Charlie hadn't written it off.

Sol had learned a hard lesson in Santa Fe. Even after his cuts and bruises had healed, the knowledge he'd gained in that alley would never fade. He kept his head down as much as possible. He kept his money hidden and only displayed small bits of it when it needed to be spent.

Every cross look that was pointed his way was met by a venomous glare that Sol pulled up from the pit of his soul. The nights that he couldn't sleep upon a bed were spent over a fire that sputtered just enough to provide a bit of heat and some light without marking him at a distance. At every opportunity, Sol practiced his draw and fired off a few shots to hone his aim.

When he finally rode into Leadville, Sol felt as if

he'd come a lot farther than the miles that had separated him from there and Santa Fe. The life he'd left behind was a memory that he vaguely recognized and would never visit again. Sol didn't even think about the man he'd once been or the things he'd left behind. There was no sense in it. The dead stayed dead. If there was one certainty in the world, that was it.

Leadville was bigger than Sol had expected. As he rode down Harrison Avenue, he felt a peculiar sort of kinship with the smudged faces he saw and the dirt beneath his horse's hooves. The locals also kept their heads down and only a few bothered to look up at him when he passed them by. Sol didn't have a problem with that. He did, however, have a problem of another sort.

With Leadville being the size it was, the chances of catching Nester's trail were slim at best. Once he added in the fact that Nester was supposed to be either in hiding or dead, those chances grew even slimmer. His only real hope was a man named Daniel Hayes.

Daniel Hayes was one of the men who'd mentioned Leadville at a Brakefield gathering five or six years ago. He could have been a distant cousin, any of a dozen uncles or possibly someone who'd attended the reunion simply to indulge in the beer being served. Hayes had been passing through New Mexico and was a guest of Sol's uncle Kenneth. After supper, over whiskey and cigars, the familiar subject of Nester Quarles had come up. While Hayes hadn't said much, he mentioned something about a new town called Leadville. The rest of what Hayes said blended into the rest of the jumble of stories and rumors that was the familial legend of Nester Quarles.

Having just crossed Third Street, Sol spotted a few saloons clustered in a row and headed for the first one to catch his eye: the Monarch. Whether it had grabbed his attention because of the colorful sign hanging next to its door or the noise coming from within the place, the Monarch was where Sol tied up his gray gelding. He made certain his saddlebags were buckled tightly, but wasn't too concerned about them beyond that. If someone wanted to steal the money, they'd be doing him a favor.

Stopping at the Monarch's entrance, Sol wondered if he might see any more of those notices. For that matter, he wondered if he might be recognized or if he would blend into the crowd. For most men, that wasn't a concern. For Sol, it was the difference between a quiet drink and fighting for his life.

"You gonna move or are you gonna block that door all day?"

Sol was a bit startled by that voice and turned around to find a wrinkled old-timer glaring up at him with bloodshot eyes. Sol stepped aside to let the little old man pass and then followed him into the Monarch.

It wasn't quite late enough for the place to be filled, but the saloon was still doing fairly good business. Most of the tables were occupied. There wasn't much space at the bar. A fellow was even sitting at the piano and rolling up his sleeves. After a bit of finger flexing, the piano player got to work filling the saloon with a lively, if somewhat warbling, melody.

Sol approached the bar and waited to be served.

Before too long, the tall woman serving drinks showed him a smile. She must have outweighed him by at least sixty pounds.

"What can I get for ya?" she asked.

Still thinking back to those family gatherings, Sol asked for a beer.

"Sure thing," she replied. As she turned, the barkeep tossed her thick mane of blond hair over one shoulder and then looked back at Sol as if she knew he'd be watching. While her curves were more than plentiful, the barkeep carried herself well enough to display her ample figure in a way that caught most every man's eye. By the time she stepped back up and placed the beer in front of Sol, he felt as if he'd gotten a show.

"You new in town or just new to this place?" she asked.

Sol took a sip and replied, "Both."

"Looking for a place to stay or maybe a game to sit in on?"

"Maybe later. I was actually hoping to find someone in particular."

"Great," the barkeep said with a wink. "I can meet you in a couple hours."

After all he'd been through in the last month, Sol had nearly forgotten he could blush. Being reminded of that was even more refreshing than the beer. "That . . . uh . . . that sounds . . ."

"Little too much for you right now? Don't worry about it. I've shown plenty of men their limits, but I'll guarantee they all had smiles on their faces when they were through. If you're still interested, I promise I'll be gentle."

"The man I'm looking for is named Daniel Hayes," Sol said.

She watched him for a few seconds as if she hadn't heard what he'd just told her. Before Sol repeated himself, she nodded and said, "I've heard of him. You a friend or debt collector?"

"He's an old friend of my family's. It's been a long time and I don't even know if he'll remember me."

"Well, he comes through here every now and then to play poker, but you'd have better luck looking at Tabor's."

"Tabor's?"

"It's an opera house two doors down from here. They serve liquor in the basement before and after performances, but a few regulars can be found there at odd hours."

"Mr. Hayes drinks there?" Sol asked.

The barkeep nodded. "That's where I'm to send word to him when there's a big game about to be dealt. I don't know if he's there or not right now because I'm a little busy. If you still need some help, I can give you a personal tour of all the little hidey-holes around here."

Suddenly, the barkeep seemed a whole lot prettier than when Sol had first walked into the place. Even so, he kept his response down to a smile and a nod.

"You come on back here after you've washed off some of that trail dust," she told him. "Then maybe you won't be so nervous."

"I might just take you up on that." Holding up his beer, Sol added, "Thanks for pointing me in the right direction."

"Any time."

Sol paid for the beer and left the barkeep a sensible gratuity. He then sipped his beer and took some time to think about what he should do next. Obviously, he wanted to go to this opera house that the barkeep had talked about. But, if Hayes couldn't be found there, Sol would be plumb out of good ideas.

Suddenly Sol felt like he was back in that silver mine and looking at a sparkling bit of ore lodged into the wall directly in front of him. Leaning both elbows against the bar, he waited until the barkeep looked his way before flashing her a friendly smile. She had a few more glasses to fill along the way, but didn't take too long to get back to him.

"Changed your mind already?" she asked. "Can't say as I'm surprised."

"I have another question for you," Sol said as he did his best to match the flirting tone in the voluptuous woman's voice. "There's someone else I'd like to find and I hear he may be in these parts."

"Most of the warm-blooded men in these hills come to see me sooner or later. Which one are you asking about?"

"His name's Nester Quarles. Have you ever heard of him?"

And, like a mouse that had been scooped up by a falcon from a canyon floor, the barkeep's smile disappeared.

She glanced to and fro, while shifting as if she couldn't decide whether she wanted to walk or run away from him. Letting out a short breath, she held her ground and asked, "Why do you want to know about him?"

Although Sol could detect the change that had come

over the woman, he wasn't exactly sure what to do about it. "I was just hoping to find him. That's all."

"That's all? And who the hell are you?"

"I . . . my name is . . ." Sol felt his own words catch in his throat as that crudely drawn likeness of his own face drifted through his mind. He hadn't seen one of those notices for a while, but that didn't mean they weren't about. He surely wasn't going to bet his life on the assumption that nobody in Leadville had seen one.

"I don't care to know your name," she said before Sol got a chance to make one up. "And I don't care to hear your business with . . . with that man. Nobody even knows if he lives around here. Whatever you heard is probably just some damned rumor."

"I'm sorry. I didn't mean to overstep my bounds."

"There ain't no bounds to overstep," the barkeep was quick to reply. "And there's nobody named Quarles around here. If you're the law, you can finish your drink and look somewhere else. If you're . . . some other sort looking to make a name for yourself, you can take your hide out of this place right now."

If Sol had anything in common with the barkeep, it was the discomfort they both obviously felt at drawing anyone else into their discussion. He dropped his voice and leaned forward so he was only an inch or so from climbing over the top of the bar.

"You don't understand," he said. "All I want—"

Sol was cut short when he felt the twin barrels of a shotgun press up under his chin. The barkeep must have already retrieved the weapon because he sure hadn't seen her move to grab it.

"I do understand," she told him in a cool, level tone. "And I don't give a damn what you want. I've had plenty of men come in here, spouting off and waving their guns around because they thought they could get a shot at Nester Quarles. I've heard he may be around, that he was killed and just about everything in between. But if you keep pushing me or if you try to stir up any trouble in here, the only thing you'll hear is this shotgun right before it blasts your head off. Do I make myself clear?"

Sol tried to nod, but the shotgun prevented him from moving more than a fraction of an inch either up or down. That seemed to be enough for the bartender, though.

"Good," she said. "Now leave this place. Don't look back and don't even think about taking me up on any of the offers I made before. If I see you again, you'd best be walking the other way."

Leaning back a bit, Sol tested the waters to see if she would react. Since the barkeep leaned back as well, Sol nodded and straightened his jacket. He glanced to either side and caught a few of the men along the bar trying to keep a straight face. Sol let out the breath he'd been holding and lowered his hands.

"I wouldn't do that," the man beside him whispered.

As Sol heard that, he saw the bartender raise the shotgun a bit more. Only then did Sol realize that his hand had drifted a bit close to his holster. He raised it and backed away from the bar. Knowing that he was still in the woman's sights, Sol turned and walked through the front door as quickly as he could without breaking into a run. Once he was outside, he could hear the rumble of laughter coming from behind him.

"Sorry about that, folks," the bartender bellowed

from her post. "Just trying to keep you all entertained until the real show begins."

There was more laughter, but Sol didn't stay around to see how long it would last. He'd already spotted the opera house and decided it was best to go there when he saw someone rushing out of the Monarch. Recognizing the man as one of the fellows who'd been close enough to hear his exchange with the bartender, Sol set his eyes into a warning glare. "Whatever you got to say, I don't want to hear it, mister," Sol said. "Just because I let that woman talk to me like that don't mean I'll be so generous with you."

The man was Sol's height and had long, stringy hair hanging from beneath a pearl gray hat, and his jaw jutted forward slightly. Lowering his head, the man watched Sol as if he were doing so over a pair of spectacles. "I been in town long enough to know there ain't no shame in letting a woman like Stephie get the drop on you."

"Fine. Thanks."

"Not so fast," the man said as he saw Sol turn to walk away. "My name's Kincaid."

"So what?"

"So I'm a friend of Nester Quarles."

Even though he was looking for Nester himself, Sol wasn't quick to trust another man who claimed to be a known killer's friend. He didn't try to hide that fact as he took another look at the man. Kincaid didn't wear a gun. He wore two of them, holstered in a finely tooled rig that was studded with spare bullets. Despite both guns hanging within his reach, Kincaid had yet to make a move toward them.

"How do you know Nester?" Sol asked.

"I owe the man some money." Narrowing his eyes a bit, Kincaid explained, "Me and Nester played some poker, but never got to settle up. Truth is, I didn't have the money before and Nester ain't exactly the sort who I like to be indebted to. Plus, I got some news he might want to hear." Leaning in a bit as some drunks staggered by, he added, "News about the law catching his scent if you know what I mean. Since we both seem to be looking for the same fellow, I figured we could pool our resources. Where you headed?"

Sol had learned not to trust strangers, but he couldn't exactly take the chance of Nester being caught or killed right now. Besides that, he figured a familiar face might put someone like Quarles or his other friends at ease better than someone showing up from a gathering several years ago. "I was heading for that opera house," Sol said as he pointed to the building a few doors down from the Monarch.

Kincaid looked over there and winced. "Place looks like it might be closed. If your idea doesn't pan out, I've got a few we could try."

"And what do you need me for?"

"If Nester was easy to find, I don't think he'd be breathin'."

Sol had to admit there was nothing wrong with that logic. It also felt comforting to have a backup plan in case the splintered leads he was following happened to fall apart. If he intended on taking up a new trade, Sol figured he would have to get used to taking help whenever he could get it.

Chapter 14

The Tabor Opera House was closed. Seeing as how it was still a bit early in the day for a show, Sol wasn't completely surprised. He was a bit more discouraged when he saw the sign posted on the door declaring when the next show was scheduled.

"Next week?" Sol groaned. "Why have an opera house if you're not going to have performances?"

"Admirer of the stage, are ya?" Kincaid asked.

"Not really. I was just hoping to get in here today."

"Well, there's one way to get in that sometimes works pretty good." Once he saw that Sol's eyes were on him, Kincaid reached out, grabbed the door handle and pulled. The door groaned a bit, but swung open without much fuss.

Sol took a step inside a lobby that was only illuminated by a single lantern and whatever light made it through the windows and doorway. Advertisements from what had to have been the last several shows were tacked to the walls, and before Sol could get a better look at any of those brightly colored displays, he saw a door swing open that couldn't have come much higher than his waist. Once his eyes had gotten used to the dimmer light within the place, Sol could see that the door was actually at the bottom of half a flight of stairs leading down to another room below the main floor.

The man who walked through that lower door came up the stairs and strode across the floor. His suit looked expensive, but was rumpled as if he'd been wearing it for about half a day too long. "The theater is closed," he announced.

"I hear there's a bar in here," Sol replied.

"It's closed, as well."

Kincaid stepped around Sol and moved toward the stairs. Leaning to get a look around the well-dressed fellow, he said, "It don't look closed to me."

The man in the rumpled clothes let out a frustrated sigh. "We do have a bar, but the business hours don't start for a bit. There are some people here, but they have proper business to conduct."

"I'm looking for Daniel Hayes," Sol announced. "If he's here, could you send word that an old friend is here to see him?"

"What old friend?"

"Just go tell him."

Exhaling as if it were a chore in itself, the well-dressed man started to shake his head before another set of footsteps clomped up the stairs leading to the bar in the cellar. When the older gentleman climbed the stairs, it looked more like he was emerging from the floorboards.

"Did I hear my name up here?" the old gentleman asked.

The well-dressed fellow took half a glance over his shoulder. "These men say they know you, Dan. If that's not the case, I can have them removed."

Reaching up from his spot on those stairs, the old man placed his hands upon the floor and gazed out at Sol and Kincaid. Either it was just as dark in the bar or his eyes were a lot sharper than Sol's, because he barely needed to squint as he examined the two men. Gray stubble sprouted from slightly sunken cheeks and a narrow jaw. Although he wasn't as bulky as any of the younger men around him, Dan Hayes looked anything but frail.

"That one there looks familiar," Hayes said as he walked up the rest of the stairs. His eyes were fixed upon Sol and then shifted over to Kincaid. "As for that one . . ."

"You know damn well who I am," Kincaid said as he drew his pistol.

The well-dressed fellow nearly leaped out of his skin. "What's the meaning of this? There'll be no unholstered weapons inside the—" But he was cut short as a gunshot exploded within the confines of the lobby.

Sol had barely seen the gun in Kincaid's hand when that shot went off. Reflexively throwing himself against the closest wall, Sol reached for his own pistol and faced the rest of the room in preparation for a fight. Daniel Hayes was also holding a gun. In fact, the gun in the older man's hand was smoking.

Kincaid dropped to one knee and fired off a round. Hayes ducked and seemed to be swallowed up by the floor as he disappeared from view. That didn't stop Kincaid from firing, however, as he climbed to his feet and rushed toward the top of the stairs leading into the cellar.

"Hey!" Sol said as he reached out to try and grab Kincaid. Only Sol's fingertips managed to get any piece of Kincaid's shirt, but that only lasted for a second before he was shaken loose. "What are you doing?"

Kincaid didn't answer. He didn't even acknowledge Sol's question before firing another shot at the stairs.

The room fell silent. All that remained of the gunshots were the ringing in Sol's ears and the smoke hanging in the air. Seeing that Kincaid wasn't about to be deterred on his way to the bar under the opera house, Sol held on to his gun and peeled himself away from the wall.

"That's enough!" Sol growled.

If Kincaid heard him, he gave no indication. Instead, he inched his way toward the stairs and took a few quick looks at the recessed entry into the bar. When no shots were fired up at him, Kincaid turned toward Sol. "You stay right where you are, or you'll get some of this for yourself," he snarled as he swung his aim toward Sol.

Even though no guns were being aimed at him, the well-dressed man curled up in a corner and wrapped his arms around his head. He whimpered to himself, which put a ghostly murmur into the smoky air.

Sol flinched at the sight of Kincaid's gun turning toward him, but didn't back down. Lowering his pistol, he reluctantly allowed the other man to make his way over to the stairs.

"I'll deal with you in a second," Kincaid said. "Since we both found him, we can split the bounty."

Cursing under his breath, Sol strode toward Kincaid with every intention of stopping him. "I won't let you kill him," he growled. "Do you hear me?"

Kincaid was at the top of the steps now. Responding to the sound of Sol's voice as well as the thump of his approaching footsteps, he pivoted on his heels to look at Sol while also taking aim at him. Kincaid's lips parted to let a couple of words fly and he brought his gun up to sight along the barrel. This time, there was no mistaking the murderous intention in his eyes.

Sol's instinct was to aim and fire before Kincaid could take his shot. He managed to get his finger on his trigger, but wasn't able to pull it before another shot blasted through the otherwise quiet opera house.

Kincaid dropped his hand to slightly higher than waist level and a startled expression worked its way onto his face. He tried to speak, but couldn't. His finger clenched around his trigger, causing his pistol to bark from his hand and send its round into the wall several feet off target. After letting out one more gasp, Kincaid fell sideways down the stairs.

Hesitantly, the well-dressed man who'd been hiding in a nearby corner allowed himself to raise his head and open his eyes. "What happened?" he squeaked. "Is it over?"

Unsure how to answer that question, Sol held his gun in front of him and inched his way toward the top of the stairs. Just as he was about to risk a look down to the cellar, he heard thumping coming from below the floor. There was a short wall topped by a railing to keep folks from toppling into the cellar, so Sol used that for cover before sticking his neck out.

The well-dressed man had regained enough breath to start shuffling toward a set of double doors that must have led into the theater itself.

"Stop," Sol hissed. Although he hadn't meant to snap at the man like he was scolding a dog, Sol also didn't want to announce where he was.

Not only did the well-dressed man obey the stern command, but he also sat and stayed like a good puppy.

Sol listened for another few seconds until he heard grunting and wheezing coming from the bottom of the stairs. Because those didn't sound like they were coming from a younger man, Sol risked a peek over the short wall.

Kincaid lay at the bottom of the stairs with his legs splayed up toward the main floor and his shoulders pointed toward a narrow door marked SPIRITS & SONG. When he saw Kincaid shift his weight, Sol snapped his gun up and sighted along the top of its barrel.

"Anyone . . . ugh . . . up there?" a gasping voice asked.

That voice wasn't Kincaid's.

Still looking over his pistol, Sol asked, "Is that you, Mr. Hayes?"

Kincaid shifted again, but obviously wasn't moving on his own steam. He flopped to one side to reveal the older man lying beneath him. By the looks of it, Hayes might have landed even worse than Kincaid. The older man was wedged sideways under Kincaid with one arm folded beneath him and the other arm tangled up with Kincaid's body. That upper hand was still wrapped around the grip of a pistol.

"Yeah," Hayes grunted. "And I'm in a bit of a . . ."

The door behind Hayes swung inward, allowing the older man to drop onto his back. A slender woman with short black hair yelped in surprise and jumped backward as if a mouse had scrambled over her feet. When she saw the older man on the floor in front of her, she bent down and slipped her hands under Hayes' arms.

"Oh my goodness," the woman said. "Are you shot?"

"Nope," Hayes replied, "but I can't say the same for that one."

Sol got to his feet and lowered his pistol. He was about to walk down the stairs, but stopped when he saw the well-dressed man still huddled obediently in his spot. "It's all right," Sol told the man. "You can get up now."

Although the well-dressed man opened his eyes and looked up, he wasn't quick to jump to his feet. Sol didn't stay around to help him, since it seemed his assistance was needed elsewhere.

Hayes squirmed and fought to pull his legs out from under Kincaid as the slender woman struggled to drag him into the next room. Neither one of them seemed to be having much success.

"Just give me a moment, will you?" Hayes groused.

The woman gritted her teeth and kept pulling. "If you want me to drop you, I'll be more than happy to oblige."

Once Sol made it to the bottom of the stairs, he grabbed Kincaid by the collar, lifted him up and set him down again. Sol let Kincaid flop into a corner at the bottom of the stairwell. He knew the man was dead. Living folks were never that heavy.

"Much obliged, son," Hayes said as he was lifted to his feet by the short-haired woman. "I'd shake your hand, but it seems this little lady don't want to let go of me."

The dark-haired woman rolled her eyes and took her hands off of him. "I swear I don't know why I bothered trying to help. Do you even know who that man is?"

All three of them looked down at Kincaid. Before

Sol could answer the question, Hayes said, "Probably just some fella who wanted to rob the place."

The woman pulled in a quick breath as her eyes immediately snapped over to Sol. "Then is he . . . ?"

Sol shook his head quickly. "No! I came to have a word with Mr. Hayes."

"Do you know this fella?" Hayes asked.

Sol shook his head. Thankfully, he didn't need to lie. "No. I never even laid eyes on him before today."

"Well, the law will straighten this out," the woman said. "I'll just—"

"You'll stay right where you are," Hayes told her. "I won't have a little lady like yourself in harm's way when there may be more armed men about. Besides, we're two able-bodied fellows," he added while slapping Sol's stomach with the back of his hand. "We can fetch the law and tell him what happened here."

"You sure you're all right?" she asked.

"The only thing hurt in that spill was my pride. I'd prefer to set the law straight before you start laughing at me and telling everyone how foolish I looked folded up at the bottom of these stairs."

The woman smiled wearily and straightened the front of her plain brown skirt. "Leaving me with the mess, huh?"

Hayes tipped his hat, winked at her and worked his way slowly up the stairs.

Sol stood in his spot for a moment, waiting for the other shoe to drop. He couldn't see anyone else inside the small room through that door, but he could see the bar and little stage where the spirits and song were supposedly served up. There were a few tables, but most of them were covered by upended chairs. When he turned to see where Hayes had gone, Sol caught sight of a few bullet holes in the woodwork along the stairwell. Since most of those holes were anything but fresh, he had a good idea why these last few shots didn't incite even more panic. As if to refute his last thought, Sol heard a frantic voice coming from upstairs.

"Are you hurt, Mr. Hayes?" the well-dressed man asked. "Who was that man? Where's the other one? I've got to inform the—"

"One step ahead of you," Hayes said from the top of the stairs. "Just stay put and help clean up downstairs. That's a good man."

Sol had to chuckle since he wasn't the only one who ordered that well-dressed fellow around as if he were a bothersome pet.

"You," Hayes barked.

Sol looked up and turned so he could place one foot upon the lowermost step. The old man was up there pointing down at him.

"That's right," Hayes snapped. "You're coming with me."

"I know. That's why I'm here."

"Well, come along, then."

Sol may have been out of sorts. He may even have been a bit rattled. He wasn't, however, about to let himself be shoved around in the same way as the well-dressed man who ran that opera house.

Picking up on the spark in Sol's eyes, Hayes amended himself by adding, "I'd like to have a word with you while we see the law."

Sol nodded and followed the old man through the front door. The moment they were outside, Sol felt an iron grip lock around his elbow. "What are you doing?" Sol asked as he tried unsuccessfully to pull his arm free.

"This way," Hayes snapped. Without waiting for another word from Sol, he pulled the younger man along toward St. Louis Avenue.

Planting his feet, Sol put all of his muscle into his arm and pulled it free from the older man's grasp. Since Hayes had already let him go, Sol wound up making a powerful swing for the sky. "If you intend on taking me to the law," Sol said, "I can't let you do that."

"We're not going to the law."

"What?" Sol asked.

"You heard me, boy." Hayes looked up and down the street. St. Louis Avenue was slightly narrower than the street from which it branched, but still had plenty of activity moving along it. At the moment, however, most of that activity was flowing toward the nearby saloon district.

"Matter of fact," Hayes said in a low voice, "you're damn lucky I don't kill you right here and now."

Having reached the limit of his patience, Sol went for the gun at his side. As his hand brushed against the familiar iron, his eyes caught sight of a smaller gun being held by the older man. Not only had Hayes produced a pistol from somewhere, but he aimed that pistol at Sol's belly.

"What in the hell do you think you're doing?" Sol asked.

Hayes' eyes narrowed and the gun remained steady. "After what just happened back in that opera house, I'd say I was defending myself. Seeing as how I'm the one with the credible witnesses, I'd wager the law would see things my way. That is, if anyone even thought to come to me once they find your body."

"I didn't fire a shot at you, you old fool!"

"Keep your voice down or I'll be forced to end this conversation real quick."

When Sol took another look around, he wasn't encouraged by what he saw. In fact, it was the first time in a while that he was actually disappointed that he wasn't drawing any attention. The occasional local glanced at him and Hayes, but they were on their way to somewhere else. There were no horses or wagons moving along St. Louis Avenue at the moment, and nobody from any of the nearby storefronts seemed interested in butting into Sol's conversation. While Hayes fixed his eyes upon Sol, he also did a real good job of keeping his pistol down low and in close to his body where it couldn't easily be seen.

"Why would I want to kill you?" Sol asked.

"I don't know. Why did that other fella want to kill me?"

"That's a good question. He told me he owed you money."

Hayes let out a sharp laugh. "Is that what he told you? That's rich."

Sol studied the older man's face and asked, "Do you know why that man was after you?"

"Yeah. Probably for the same reason you are. I'm Nester Quarles."

Chapter 15

Nester moved quickly for a man of his age, even though Sol didn't exactly know what Nester's age truly was. The old man was balding and his remaining hair was more the color of salt than pepper. He had some wrinkles on his face, but it was difficult to tell where the wrinkles stopped and where the scars began. The skin on Nester's hands was somewhat loose, but that only narrowed his age down to a range of between fifty to seventy years.

After Nester had introduced himself, the old man had started walking and motioned for Sol to follow. "You're one of the Brakefield kids, ain't you?" he asked.

Sol blinked a few times and replied, "Yes. Yes, I am."

"Which one? Obviously not the one who was taught any manners, or else you would have told me your name already."

"Things have been moving kind of fast, in case you haven't noticed," Sol groused.

"So they have," Nester said as he glanced over to the man walking beside him. "Wouldn't that be your fault? I was just sipping on some expensive whiskey when you and that bounty hunter came stomping along."

"Bounty hunter?"

Tipping his hat politely to a young woman who looked at him like he was her grandpa, Nester said, "That's right."

"How do you know he was a bounty hunter?"

"Because he's been poking his nose around here asking about me. That's why I was sitting in a cellar drinking whiskey during the middle of the day."

Sol shook his head. "So I just happened to come along when there was a bounty hunter after you?"

"Don't feel bad, boy. There's always bounty hunters sniffing around for me. Sometimes," he added with a grin, "they even ask me where to find me. Seems like Daniel Hayes has been known to tell some wild stories when he's had too much whiskey."

"Where are you going?"

"I need to collect a few things before we leave."

"We?" Sol asked. "We're leaving? Both of us?"

"For a man who came looking for me, you don't seem too happy to have found me. I'm starting to think you're downright confused."

"I wanted to have a word with you, not go anywhere. I've come a long way as it is."

"You wanted to talk, so talk. I still need to collect my things because bounty hunters are usually missed when they get killed. Even if that one ain't, he could be recognized by the law when they get a look at his corpse."

"I thought you said you weren't going to the law."

Nester waved his hand dismissively. "The laws always find out when someone gets killed," he grumbled. "Downright ghoulish if you ask me."

"Maybe it wasn't a good idea for me to come here," Sol said.

Pretending as if he hadn't heard that last part, Nester glanced over to Sol and watched him for a few seconds. "You Amelia's boy?"

"Yes."

"I recognized you on account of your chin. All of Amelia's boys had that chin. Which one are you?"

"Solomon."

Nester nodded and waved to someone who'd called out his assumed name from across the street. "If I was the sensitive sort, I would have been hurt you didn't recognize me the moment you laid eyes on me. Course, you were pretty young the last time I seen you."

"It's only been five or six years," Sol reminded him.

That stopped Nester dead in his tracks as he scratched his head. "Couldn't be. You was knee high to a grasshopper and playin' soldier with some other boys."

When Sol heard that, he said, "I used to do that when I was a boy."

"Ain't that what I said the first time?"

"But I saw you talking to my uncle at a family gathering. You were talking about coming to this town when it was just being founded."

After thinking it over for a bit, Nester shrugged and nodded. "I suppose that was the last time I went to one of them things. Yer family's always been friendly enough to put me up and feed me whenever I rode through town. And to think, the first time I met one o' yer kin, it was to rob him blind."

"What?"

"Sure," Nester replied. "I been robbin' since I could lift a pistol. I ain't exactly one to ride around shakin' hands just to meet folks."

"Who did you rob?"

Nester furrowed his brow and slowly shook his head. "There's been so many, I hardly recall. I know it wound up friendlier than I expected, since one of yer cousins was already on the bad side of some lawman. I chased that crooked son of a bitch away and yer cousin was always grateful. At least, I think it was yer cousin. Anyhow, introductions were made and I got to know plenty of yer family. I even went to a whole mess of dinners, parties and whatnot."

"I didn't know we'd ever met," Sol admitted. "I just heard about you from my family."

"Well, I couldn't exactly stroll in usin' my own name. Who in yer family talked about me?"

"Well . . . all of them, pretty much."

Nester chuckled and crossed the street. From there, he turned left onto North Poplar. "So you wait around for a while, think back to the good old days and then decide to head on into Leadville and look for me?"

"There's more to it than that."

Suddenly, Nester stopped and turned around to face Sol directly. "Well, I'm just anxious as hell to hear the rest of yer story, but it'll have to wait."

"Why?"

"You see that wagon over there?"

Sol looked down the street and saw a small cart

that might have been able to carry some tools and a few crates. The cart was tied to a single horse, which looked too tired to hold its head up for very long. "You mean that cart?"

"Yeah. That's my wagon and I can't have it known that ye're coming along with me."

"Why not?"

"Because you know who I am and that makes you the only living soul in this town apart from that horse who knows that much about me. Seein' as how there's plenty more bounty hunters where that other one came from, I'm gonna tell you to get stuffed and ye're gonna walk away."

"But I won't just—"

"I know, I know," Nester grunted quickly. "I got a small spread a few miles west of here, up along a narrow trail leading past an old mine. Meet me there by nightfall."

Sol nodded and let out a tired sigh. "I wish you would've told me that earlier. I left my horse all the way back where we started."

"I wanted you to walk this far with me."

Smiling at what he thought could be some warmth in the old man's voice, Sol said, "I'm happy to oblige."

Patting Sol on the shoulder, Nester explained, "I had to make doubly sure I didn't want to kill you." With that, Nester showed Sol an amicable smirk and walked over to his wagon. "Now get stuffed!" he hollered over his shoulder. "I don't want whatever ye're sellin'!"

Sol watched the old man go and wondered if that could be the man that had inspired so many of his family's legends. Nester Quarles was supposed to be cold as a winter morning and wicked as the day is long. He was supposed to be loyal to his friends and a plague to his enemies. He was supposed to have stolen at least one of everything that could be stolen and fired more bullets than an army.

Sol watched that man wave to anyone who looked his way and climb up into the driver's seat of a little cart as if the effort was almost too much strain upon his back. Sol knew it had been some years since those legends had started, but could Nester Quarles truly be this balding fellow?

And then Sol thought back to what had happened in the opera house. He hadn't seen Hayes pull that trigger, but Kincaid surely hadn't shot himself. The woman with the short hair didn't have a gun as far as Sol could tell, so that left only one man who could have killed Kincaid. And after that, Nester had joked with Sol and done a bit of flirting with the woman.

Yeah, Sol decided. That was Nester Quarles. At least, it was close enough for Sol to turn and run back to the spot where he'd tied his gray gelding so he could follow the directions he'd been given. If he'd had less faith in the man, Sol would have ridden anywhere but up that pass Nester had told him about. Granted, Sol had only spoken to the old man for a few minutes, but that was enough to give him some hope that Nester could provide some of the help he was after.

Sol was still sifting through these thoughts when he turned the corner and set his eyes once more upon the stretch of Harrison Avenue where the Monarch Saloon and Tabor Opera House could be found. The street was bustling with activity and most of it was centered on the opera house. Pulling his hat down low over his face, Sol kept his head down and wound his way through the outer edge of that crowd.

"Anyone know who that man is?" someone asked.

"I heard he was after Nester Quarles!"

Sol slowed his pace so he could hear more. All the while, he prepared himself to make a run for his horse.

"Damn fool," someone grunted.

Sol felt a slap on his shoulder that turned him around to face the opera house. His hand dropped toward his gun, but stopped short of clearing leather.

"You hear about this?" asked a man who was dressed in a dark suit and a string tie.

"No," Sol said quickly, recognizing the man's voice as one of the ones he'd already heard.

The man shook his head and stretched his neck to try and get a better look at the opera house. "Another damn fool came around thinking he'd found Nester Quarles. Can you believe that? Must be the fourth one in as many months."

"Fifth, I think," someone else chimed in.

Sol could see a small woman standing directly in his line of sight. She was short enough that she didn't even try to see through the crowd that might easily have knocked her over. When she saw Sol looking at her, she shook her head and held up two fingers.

"Maybe three," she said just loud enough to be heard.

"However many it is, there's one more to add to the list," the man in the string tie said.

Sol kept moving until he finally emerged from the crowd. Thanks to the commotion, nobody had taken much interest in a single gray gelding no matter how many saddlebags it was carrying. A few quick pats against the saddlebags were enough for Sol to know they were still full. He unbuckled one, took a look inside and then closed it up again when he saw the glimpse of that money. While he was glad the money was there, Sol also wondered how long his good fortune would hold up.

After climbing into his saddle, Sol was high enough to get a better look at the opera house. The well-dressed fellow who'd greeted Sol and Kincaid was now flitting about the front of the opera house like a panicked moth. The dark-haired woman stood on the boardwalk and held the door open so a few men could drag out Kincaid's body. The crowd moved in even closer, so Sol took that opportunity to leave.

Riding through the streets of Leadville, Sol kept his horse moving at a normal walk and kept his head down. He'd come this far and stirred up plenty more fuss than he'd hoped along the way, so he wasn't about to risk being tripped up now. Only after he was out of Leadville did he speed up and start following the directions Nester had given him. Once he was on the proper trail, Sol snapped his reins and let his gray gelding break into a gallop.

The mountain air felt cool against his face and had just enough of a bite to keep him sharp. As he rode, he watched for a trace of the old man's cart. Not only didn't he see the cart, but he couldn't even see a hint that it had come this way. Sol knew he wasn't a master tracker, but he figured he should have caught up to the old man by now. The two possibilities in Sol's mind were that he'd made a wrong turn or had been given the wrong directions. Since he'd already come this far along the trail, he supposed he might as well go a bit farther.

Sol could feel the air thinning out as the trail took him higher and higher into the mountains. Soon, he found the old mine. At least that meant some of the old man's directions had been genuine. Sol pulled back on the reins to give his horse a rest. The gelding wasn't exactly used to the mountain air and his breaths had become increasingly labored.

Sol climbed down from the saddle and led the horse by the reins as he looked for the next trail that was supposed to lead him to Nester's property. Walking closer to that mine, Sol had to smile and shake his head. There wasn't a way he could say for certain it was a silver mine, but he swore he could smell it the way an old dog could sniff out a scarf that had once been worn by its owner.

After looping the reins around a low-hanging branch, Sol took a few more steps toward the mine. He stopped short and glanced up at the sky. It would be a while before nightfall, which meant he had some time before he was expected at Nester's. Approaching the mine carefully, Sol could hear echoes of his days spent chipping away at the stones in New Mexico. The texture of the splintered rock under his callused fingers made Sol feel as if the weight of his pickax was still pulling his other arm down.

According to a couple of small signs posted near the entrance, the mine was closed down. With only a brief acknowledgment of those signs, Sol ducked his head to walk into a rough tunnel that had been blasted into the rock.

There were no tracks for carts laid into the ground.

There were no hooks for lanterns set into the walls. There weren't even any piles of crates or splintered tool handles that had littered every other mine Sol had worked. The men who'd worked in this mine had done so while hunched over and in the dark. Sol knew that because he'd spent plenty of days working in those conditions. Days like that bled into weeks and those weeks became months before he realized that years had finally gone by. Charlie had spent that time with his feet kicked up behind a desk. He'd listened to his workers' gripes, but didn't do anything to alleviate their concerns. When they came in force, hired guns were put onto the payroll to push the miners back into their hole.

Yes, Sol knew dark, filthy caves like that one pretty well. Crouching in that cave like an animal taking shelter from a storm, Sol ran his hand along one wall and nodded slowly to himself. That life was over.

That was why he'd come to Leadville.

That was why he would continue his conversation with Nester Quarles.

Sol would no longer work and die just to make money for someone else. It was his turn to reap the rewards of his own labors, and if someone else had to pay that price for a change, then so be it.

In fact, Sol wasn't going to wait to see what Nester had to say. He would start planning for his own future right then and there. His first move in that direction was to walk back to his horse. After that, it was back into the mine to get a look at some of the more dangerous tunnels.

The sun was well on its way toward the western horizon when the short fellow emerged from the trees.

He waddled toward the mine entrance like a troll coming out of the woods. A battered, wide-brimmed hat was pulled down over his head and was in such bad condition that its thick leather band seemed to be the only thing holding it together. Long whiskers sprouted from his fleshy face, looking more like strands of ink hanging from his chin.

The man held a rifle in his hands, which he brought up to his shoulder as he approached Sol's gray gelding. Reaching out with one hand, he grabbed for the saddlebag and began tugging at the buckle.

"What have we here?" he grumbled.

As he worked to open the bag, the man glanced nervously from the horse to the hole that had been blasted into the nearby rock face. Once the buckle came free, he licked his lips and stuck a trembling hand into the bag.

A shot blazed through the air, sending a piece of lead close enough to the man's hand to cause both him and the gelding to jump. While the short man hopped away from the horse, he fired a wild shot at the cave. Even though he couldn't see anything but inky blackness in the abandoned mine, he fired another round into it just to be certain.

For a moment, there was silence. The echo of those shots rolled into the mountains and was swallowed up by a passing breeze. The short man with the rifle twitched at every rustle he heard and nearly fired at a critter that scampered through some nearby leaves.

Suddenly, a few solid footsteps could be heard. By the time the short man got his rifle pointed in the right direction, Sol was already stepping out of the mine. Without a single word to announce his intentions, Sol aimed his pistol and fired. His bullet caught the short man in the hip.

Rather than return fire, the short man let out a pained grunt and turned to run back toward the trees.

Sol stepped forward and aimed, but didn't pull his trigger. He had an awfully big target, but it was the short man's wide back. A second or two after Sol lowered his pistol, another shot blasted through the air. Sol reflexively slammed his back against the rock face next to the opening as he looked around to see if the short man had a partner. If that was the case, the shooter was one of the worst partners a man could have.

The short man took another step, dropped to his knees and flopped forward. He was still sputtering into the dirt when another man dressed in buckskins sauntered out of the same group of trees from which the short man had emerged.

Sighting along the top of his pistol, Sol kept his back to the rock. Even after he got a better look at the third man's weathered face, Sol kept his gun in hand and ready to be fired. He was looking at the same old man he'd met at the opera house, but Sol still felt like he was in the presence of someone else. This old man had the same face and same wiry frame, but carried himself with easy confidence and looked down at the twitching body as if he were admiring a bubbling stream.

This old man's eyes were cold and his hands were steadier than the rocks at Sol's back. This was the Nester Quarles that Sol had been expecting.

"Don't think he'll be robbing you or anyone else again," Nester said as he stepped up to the short man's body and nudged him with the toe of his boot. "Neither will the other two I found in them trees."

"What the hell are you doing sneaking up on me like that?" Sol asked.

Nester chuckled and holstered the pistol he'd used to send the short man to his grave. "I thought you might've gotten lost."

"I wasn't supposed to be there until nightfall."

"Yeah, but you still got a ways to go. You waited around here so long that it would've probably taken you until well past dark before you got to my house."

Looking up at the sky as if to point out the warm glow of early evening, Sol asked, "And how did you know I wasn't still on my way?"

"Because I can keep watch on most of the trail leading up to my spot. That's why I chose it. Now come on. I know plenty of shortcuts and we might just be able to make it back before it gets too dark."

Sol looked down at the body on the ground between them, but Nester had already seemed to have forgotten about it. In fact, Nester was grinning.

"You know him?" the old man asked.

Sol walked over to the squat corpse and patted the dead man's shirt pockets. There was nothing to be found, but Sol struck pay dirt when he reached into the inner pocket of the dead man's jacket. He was fairly certain he knew what the folded paper was, but unfolded it just to be certain. Sure enough, it was the reward notice with Sol's likeness drawn on it.

"Either of those other men go by the name of Alex?" Sol asked.

"Hell if I know," the old man replied as he turned and walked away. "I didn't bother shakin' hands."

Sol folded up the notice and put it in his pocket. He considered describing Alex's European features to Nester or asking to get a look at the other two men's faces, but kept his mouth shut instead. It was clear what those men were after. Knowing more than that simply wouldn't have done Sol any good.

Chapter 16

No matter what else could be said about Nester Quarles, Sol couldn't claim the man was a liar. While it might not have been a long stretch between that mine and Nester's property, the trail connecting the two wound through some rocky ground and had plenty of sharp drop-offs. Even if he had been moving along at a slow pace on his own, Sol thought he would have gotten lost a few times. As it was, he had a difficult enough time just trying to keep up with his guide.

Nester rode the narrow pass as if he were strolling through a field of daisies. When he wasn't gazing up at the scenery, he was glancing over his shoulder to check on Sol. He didn't say much apart from the occasional "Watch that bit there" or "Mind that cliff." By the time the trail straightened out, the sun was well below the horizon and only a faint smear of orange colored the sky.

Of course, despite the fact that the trail was straight, Sol had to hang on for dear life as his gray gelding struggled to maintain its footing against what felt like a near-vertical climb.

"What's his name?" Nester called back.

Sol's knuckles were white as they wrapped around the reins and the saddle horn. He was well past the point of keeping up the appearance that he wasn't worried about falling to his death. By this point, he was more concerned with preventing himself or his horse from skidding down the side of a mountain.

"Wh . . . what?" Sol gasped.

Nester was already at the top of the pass and looking down at him. "Your horse," he replied. "He's been doing real good. Seems like a fighter. What's his name?"

"Oh. Smoky. His name's Smoky."

"I never heard you call him by name. Never even heard you talk to him."

"I don't write him letters, either. Is that a problem?"

Nester chuckled and slipped his fingers beneath his hat so he could scratch his head. "I guess it's fine, since he's doing his part well enough, but you should talk to your horse. It'll make him more of a partner than just some pack animal."

After a bit more struggling, Sol felt the ground level out. He was feeling dizzy and wobbling a bit in the saddle, but that was only because he realized that he'd been holding his breath over the last couple of yards. Sol exhaled and wiped the sweat from his brow. "I suppose he had been doing a good job," he admitted. "I guess it just seemed sort of . . . well . . . odd to talk to him."

Nester nodded and turned his own horse away from him. It was the same chestnut brown Morgan that had pulled Nester's cart, but seemed much livelier now that it was on its own and not attached to anything with wheels. As he led the way down a gravel trail, Nester reached out to scratch his horse's ear. "Everyone needs a friend," he said.

Nester's house wasn't much to look at. It was less of a spread and more of a lonely shack on top of a rocky hill surrounded by trees. While Sol had never spent a lot of time in the mountains, he never thought he had much of a fear of heights. That all changed when he turned to look back in the direction from which he'd arrived.

Suddenly, Sol felt as if he'd been picked up and tossed a thousand feet into the air. His stomach clenched at the sight of all those treetops scattered beneath him. The trail Smoky had negotiated looked more like a line that dropped straight down a jagged, rocky slope. If it were brighter at the moment, Sol might have been able to see Leadville from that vantage.

"Nice, ain't it?" Nester asked. "It didn't cost much of anything, neither." When he didn't hear a reply, the old man looked over and asked, "What's the matter, Solomon? You afraid you might start to skid? You feeling light-headed?" Nester grinned and slapped Sol on the back. "Don't worry. You'll get your legs beneath you by the time you walk to the house."

Feeling that slap on his back immediately put visions into Sol's mind of all the various ways he could topple down that mountain. Gritting his teeth, he declared, "It's Sol."

"What?"

"You heard me."

Nester stopped and turned to look back at the

younger man. There was more than enough fire in the old man's eyes to make Sol glad it was only half a stare.

Trying not to squirm too much under that gaze, Sol added, "Only my mother and a few aunts called me Solomon. My grandmother did too."

As he turned to face the house again, Nester said, "I recall your grandma. She was real nice."

The house was crooked, but it was difficult to tell if that was due to uneven ground, tough conditions or bad craftsmanship. There was a brick chimney holding up one end of the house, which was straighter than anything else in sight. In fact, it seemed as if that chimney was keeping the rest of the place from falling over.

"You were a mason, weren't you?" Sol asked.

Climbing down from his saddle, Nester replied, "Yeah, way back when I was a pup."

"Did you build this house?"

"Nah, but I did put that chimney together. I just happened to find this house."

"Isn't this your property?" Sol asked.

"Sure . . . when I took possession of it, I found this house. You wanna come inside or are you content to stay out here until you catch yer breath?"

Sol climbed down from his saddle and led Smoky to the same tree where Nester had tied his own horse. The Morgan scraped a few times at the ground, but soon lowered its head before a cold breeze whipped through like a set of nails through Sol's flesh. Pulling his jacket in tight around him, Sol stepped into Nester's house.

The inside of the house wasn't any more impressive

than the outside. It consisted of one room and, as one might have guessed, the fireplace was the centerpiece. Apart from a cot, some cooking implements and a few stools, there wasn't much else to see.

"So," Nester said as he walked over to the fireplace and started stacking a few logs, "are you gonna tell me who that fella was that tried to ambush you?"

Sol winced, but didn't know what to say to that. A few months ago, the very notion that someone could be gunning for him would have been ridiculous. Now it was a fact of life.

In the silence that had followed his question, Nester nodded and kept building the fire. "I see. You ain't used to tellin' folks yer sins. Not much of a church type, are ya?"

"No, but I suppose that man could have been coming after me. That's mostly the reason why I wanted to try and find you."

"So you could pass some of those enemies on to me? Thank you kindly."

Sol chuckled.

"Why did you come here, Sol? After what you cost me today, I think I have a right to know that much."

"What I cost you?"

The fire sparked and smoke started to curl up from the pile of wood. Shifting to look at Sol, Nester growled, "I had a nice little life goin' here. Ain't nobody knew who I was and the occasional gunman that came sniffing around was thrown off my trail easily enough once they saw an old man 'stead of an outlaw with fire in his eyes."

"So nobody's found you?" Sol asked.

"Well, there were a few that were more persistent than the others," Nester admitted. "They seemed to have gotten lost in these mountains and were never heard from again."

Those words came out of Nester's mouth like breath that had been frozen into steam. Whoever those persistent fellows had been, it was Sol's guess they were now joined by the three men who'd meant to attack Sol at the abandoned mine.

"You know how long it took for me to build this up?" Nester asked. "You know how long it took for me to get situated in a town where I could sit and rest for a while in one place?"

Sol didn't know what to say, so he kept quiet.

"Answer me, boy!"

Nester's voice boomed like a cannon within the confines of that house. Sol twitched at the sound of it and reflexively placed his hand over his gun. That reflex did not go unnoticed.

"You gonna draw on me, boy?" Nester snapped as he stared directly into Sol's soul. "You come all this way to swap lead with me, then you'd best be faster than you look! An' if ye're tryin' to scare me, ye're gonna have to do a whole lot more'n that."

For a second, Sol didn't even realize he'd made a move toward his gun. He had to look down to see how close his hand was to his holster. Once he saw that, he held his hands up where they could be seen. "I . . . didn't mean anything like that."

Nester squinted and eased up a bit. He barely moved more than a few muscles, but the air within the house suddenly became much easier to breathe.

Finally, Nester reached around behind him for a stool and then plopped down onto it. "What the hell you got yerself into?"

"I . . . well . . . I'm wanted for a murder I didn't do."

That was one of the few times Sol had given voice to that thought. Part of him was ashamed to say the words and the other part didn't want to believe they were true.

Despite all of that, Nester only chuckled. "A murder you didn't do, huh? I've been there. Plenty of times, actually."

"I'm serious, Nester."

"I'll bet you are."

"I killed one man, but that was all," Sol admitted.

"Now it comes out. Why don't you tell me the story from the beginning?"

Sol shifted on his feet and then pulled up a stool that only had three good legs beneath it. The fourth leg required some balance and a bit of guesswork to keep from collapsing. It did Sol some good to have a diversion as he spooled out what had happened, starting from the point when he'd agreed to chase down the men who'd robbed Charlie.

Nester listened with a minimum of interruptions. Mostly he just nodded and rubbed his chin thoughtfully. Every now and then, he would laugh at a part he found amusing. Even though Sol didn't find any of it amusing, he did find it ironic that he was now the one telling stories to Nester Quarles.

"You want to know yer first mistake?" Nester asked when Sol reached the end of his account.

"What?" Sol asked.

"You trusted a rich man. Ain't nobody can trust a rich man."

"That's all you can say?"

Nester shrugged. "Ye're takin' the word of some bounty hunter that ye're wanted? That rich fella probably just put a price on yer head and spread the word a bit."

"Well," Sol said as he dug into another pocket, "he's spread the word a lot more than just a bit." With that, Sol handed over the folded notice. "The man who ambushed me earlier today was carrying that."

Taking the paper from Sol's hand, Nester unfolded it and looked it over. He then let out a low whistle and nodded approvingly. "Fifteen hundred, huh? Not a bad start. Once this blows over, you can frame that and impress a few ladies."

"I'm not about to wait for this to blow over. I don't want to hide and I don't want to ride somewhere else with my tail between my legs in the hopes that nobody will look at me too many times or figure out who I am." Sol glanced about the simple room and then to the man sitting across from him. "No offense meant."

While Nester might have looked angered for a moment, it didn't last long. There was a shade of a grin on his face as he said, "You did a good job of running, since ye're a good ways from New Mexico. You came here lookin' for Daniel Hayes who was supposed to point you to Nester Quarles, right?"

"That was the last I heard," Sol replied.

"And after all your recent escapades," Nester said as he held up the notice, "you must want to see if I can do something to help you out of yer current dilemma."

"I want you to help me in a robbery."

"A robbery?" Nester sneered. "Little Solomon Brakefield picks up a gun and suddenly thinks he's a bad man? Is that it?"

Sol didn't speak up to defend himself, but he also didn't speak up to deny what Nester was saying.

Reading that silence perfectly, Nester scowled and nodded as he shifted his attention to the fire. He picked up a poker and used it to nudge the logs into place so they could burn more evenly without smothering the fire he'd put together. Every time he used the poker, he was careful not to scrape it against the bricks of the fireplace unless it absolutely couldn't be helped.

"You must'a heard some real good stories about me, boy," Nester said. "I suppose that's partly my fault since I told plenty of tall tales whenever I would visit yer pa and uncles. I didn't think any of them stories were told to the young'uns."

"Everybody in my family heard those stories," Sol replied.

"Yeah, I suppose that ain't too big of a surprise. Did you also hear about all the time I spent in jail?"

"Some."

"What about the men I killed?" Nester asked as he carefully pushed one log into a gap between two others that had partially crumpled into ash. "Did you just think I did them murders for fun? Did you think I liked it?"

"No. I would never think that."

"Well, maybe you should'a thought about that."

"I had to kill a man and it wasn't for fun. It was because I didn't have any other choice."

"That ain't what I mean," Nester said in a voice that could barely be heard above the crackle of the fire. "I meant that maybe you should have thought that I might've enjoyed what I done. Leastways, that I wasn't ashamed of it."

Sol didn't know what to say to that, so he said nothing.

"The men I killed . . ." Nester said. "Some of 'em tried to kill me, some of 'em got in my way. Some of 'em were just in the wrong place at the wrong time. What about that short fella back at that mine?"

For a moment, Sol could only think back to the silver mine in New Mexico. Then he recalled the mine that he'd been to earlier that night. "What about him?" he asked.

"Why were you about to give him another free shot at you?"

"I scared him away," Sol said in his own defense. "I shot at him and I believe I hit him."

"But you didn't put him down. You were about to let him run away."

"Sure. He was running away, so I was going to let him—"

"You were going to let him put some ground between you, screw up some more courage and then take another shot at you," Nester snapped. "Y'see, kid, I been goin' down this road for a while and I've had plenty of pups with fire in their eyes come to me so they can prove one thing or another. Usually, they do all their proving without saying a word. They plead their own case by just doin' what they do." Seeing that Sol was about to speak up for himself, Nester silenced him with a quickly raised hand. "You fired a shot at a man who had a gun and meant to use it. Once you scared that man off, you were set to watch him go."

"And how do you know what I meant to do?" Sol asked defiantly.

"I got eyes, don't I? Was I wrong?"

Sol wanted to tell Nester he was dead wrong. He kept quiet because he was fairly certain that lying about it wasn't going to do him one bit of good.

"Fact is," Nester continued, "it don't matter if that man was after you or if he was after me. You might've known who he was or I might've known. It just don't matter. All that does matter is that he stepped up against you and needed to be put down. You want to be a bad man? That's a rule you got to live by no matter what else is goin' on around you."

"So you can uphold your reputation?" Sol asked.

Nester shook his head. "So you can stay alive. You think I'm up here hiding? You'd be right. I called down too much hell and needed to seek some shelter from the storm. After the storm passed, maybe I got a bit set in my ways and enjoyed my afternoon drinks in that cellar."

"Seems like you've got a nice place here," Sol said. "Plenty of folks in town seemed to like you."

Letting out a short, grunting laugh, Nester said, "I chose to live in Leadville because it's up in the mountains and just short of lawless. I live in this shack because I can see someone comin' for me long before they get here. I drink in that cellar because there's only one way in and one way out. All them folks who wave and tip their hats to me don't know who the hell I am and if they found out, I'd have to shoot 'em."

Sol waited for Nester to start laughing at the joke he'd made. When Nester didn't laugh, Sol realized the old man hadn't been joking.

"Whatever you do," Nester said, "just ride out the storm. You leave behind a wife or any family in New Mex?"

Sol shook his head. "No."

"Good. Then you can start over somewhere else. Anywhere else. The world is your oyster, kid."

"That's why I came to find you," Sol quickly said. "Because I'm tired of scraping by and doing a job just so I can beg for my pay like a vagrant with his hand out. Most everyone else I know is in the same spot. They all tell me that's just the way things are and that I should do what I need to do in order to get by. Well, I don't want to get by. I want to get ahead and if I have to do that by breaking someone else's laws, then that's the way I want it."

"Someone else's laws, huh? You some sort of traitor to yer country?" Nester asked.

"No. I'm sick of begging. Only when I stopped begging and started taking what I earned did I even start to get ahead."

"Ahead?" Nester scoffed. "You came runnin' to me trying to convince me you got the sand to be a bad man. If that's what you call ahead, then I'd hate to see the piss-poor existence you had before."

Sol nodded and chewed on his tongue as if he were punishing it for saying the wrong words or not saying the right ones.

"You seen a bit of how I live," Nester continued.

"And this ain't even a bad day. Because of what happened at that opera house, this town is done for me."

"What? Why?"

"When men came lookin' before, they didn't find anything. Now that bounty hunter friend of yers wound up dead and for all I know, that fella at the mine today could'a been one of his partners."

"He was after me," Sol said. "Did one of those other two have pale skin and a European face?"

"Maybe."

"I think those other two you killed were the ones who attacked me in Santa Fe. I let them go too. They could have followed me here."

"No offense or nothin', but fifteen hundred dollars ain't exactly a mother lode to bounty hunters. It'd take a lot more'n that to bring three of 'em all the way up here from Santa Fe."

Rather than say anything more, Sol got up and walked outside. When he came back, he was carrying his set of saddlebags. Sol set them down and said, "It could be that fellow from the mine today knew about that."

Nester looked up at him without shifting from his stool. He grudgingly reached for the bag and pulled it open. When he got a look at what was inside, he leaned down as if to make absolutely certain his eyes weren't deceiving him. "I'll be damned. Is that the money you stole from your boss in New Mexico?"

Sol nodded.

"Haven't you been careful enough to keep this hid?" Nester asked.

"When I first took off running, I didn't exactly know

how to keep it hidden or where to hide it. I . . . I just didn't think it through."

"Hell, I would'a thought it'd be common horse sense to hide this."

"Maybe for you," Sol said as he sat back down in front of the fire. "That's why I came here. I already got started along this road, but I need to be shown how to keep riding it. A man just doesn't roll out of bed knowing how to be a robber, just like he doesn't know how to be a blacksmith without being shown."

"You want to be my apprentice. That what ye're sayin'?"

"Yes. That's what I'm saying."

Nester shifted his eyes away from Sol so he could watch the fire crackle. He still had the poker in hand and used it to absently prod at the logs. Grinding the poker into some glowing embers, he said, "I suppose I've heard crazier things."

"How did you become the man you are?" Sol asked.

"By making a lot of mistakes and listening to the wrong people."

Sol shook his head. "I remember you talking to my father and uncles when you would visit. You might have called yourself by another name, but it was you, wasn't it?"

Keeping his eyes locked on to the fire, Nester muttered, "Yeah, it was me. You were just a wild-eyed cuss back then."

"You talked about your life and the things you've done with pride and don't tell me otherwise."

"I was drunk."

"Then why haven't you set up shop somewhere to make an honest living?" Sol asked. "How do you pay for those drinks or this place?"

"That ain't yer concern."

Sol nodded and smiled. "Exactly. If your life was so terrible, you would've given it up by now. Either that, or you'd be dead or in jail somewhere, but you're not. You're alive and well, living in Colorado. I know plenty of men who are doing a whole lot worse. Why else would some folks look up to you as a hero?"

"They're misguided, that's why," Nester grunted. Eventually, his eyes drifted back to the saddlebag full of money on the floor beside him. "How much is in there?"

"I haven't counted it yet."

"Any reason why you wouldn't just put that money in a bank somewhere far away from anyone who would'a heard of you or this Charlie fella?"

"Because I don't want to keep my head down and hide for the rest of my life." Although he'd said those words proudly, Sol quickly winced and looked away from Nester. "Not that I mean you're hiding . . . or that you should—"

"Eh, I know what ye're sayin'," Nester interrupted before Sol had much time to squirm. "I came here to cool my heels for a bit, not curl up and die. Fact is, I got a real good idea of what ye're sayin' and you ain't the first to come around askin' me to take them under my wing."

"So you have helped other men learn to be outlaws?"

Nester chuckled and shook his head. "Hell no, I

haven't. That just sounds ridiculous when you say it like that. I ain't about to open a school or some such nonsense. My only concern here is that I do know yer father and uncles . . . or I used to. They still aboveground?"

"My father died a few years ago and one of my uncles passed on before that. The rest of the family is doing well enough, though."

"I don't suppose any of them, wherever they may be, would like it if I corrupted you the way ye're askin'."

"I've already killed a man. I've already robbed another and I'm already on the run from the law with a price on my head. I've survived this far because of some quick thinking and a whole lot of luck, but I know those things won't hold up forever."

Nester nodded slowly as if he were listening to an entirely separate conversation. Even though Sol couldn't quite hear the same things the old man was hearing, he could tell as soon as Nester came to some sort of agreement with those other voices. The old man turned to look at him again.

"You mucked up my situation here, but good, boy," Nester snarled. "I can't risk going back into town on account of the law might want to have a word with me. Whether that short fella at the mine down the road was after you, me or them saddlebags, it's a safe bet there'll be more coming after them. What was the name of that bounty hunter friend of yers?"

"Kincaid," Sol replied. "And he wasn't my friend."

"If Kincaid got this close to me, anyone else he might be workin' with will be lookin' to make someone answer for his death. That means he'll be comin' after me, as well. None of this bodes well for either of us."

"I agree," Sol replied.

"You don't need to agree or disagree to that. It just is what it is."

Although Sol nodded, he kept his mouth shut.

Letting out a sigh, Nester said, "I'll be movin' on from here before sunup. I got some old friends I can check in on and a few stops to make so's I can set myself up in a new situation. Since you had a hand in messing this one up, you'll come along with me to help set things right."

Sol smiled and nodded. "You won't regret this."

"You're damn right I won't. You make a move against me or show yerself to be untrustworthy and I'll kill you."

"No need for that," Sol replied. "I didn't come all this way just to let you down."

But Nester wasn't accepting those words. In fact, he glared at Sol as if he only heard chatter coming from a yelping animal. When he spoke again, it was in a low, even tone that didn't leave any room for bluster. "You best hear what I tell you, boy. You step out of line and I will kill you. There won't be nothin' you can do about it and there won't be any getting around it. You will be dead, you hear? Dead."

"I understand," Sol replied.

Nester shook his head and shifted his attention back to the fire. "Maybe I shouldn't do this. None of yer kin would appreciate it one bit."

"If they knew about how rich we could both wind up, they'd understand."

"What the hell are you talkin' about?" Nester asked.

"You know the money in that bag?"

Nester nodded.

"There's plenty more where that came from."

"Where?" Nester grunted.

"Albuquerque."

The old man studied Sol as a grin slowly appeared upon his face. "You got some sorta plan you ain't spoken of yet?"

Sol shrugged and replied, "I needed to make sure you were the man for the job and that I could trust you."

"I can vouch for the first, but the second's up to you," Nester said. "How much money are we talkin' about?"

"I've seen ten thousand get sent back to the Jessup Mining Company at one time. Sometimes, there's a few shipments a week. If those bosses are stealing a percentage of that money, they've got to be storing it somewhere. Since it's basically stolen money, my guess is it's not just in a bank."

Nester chuckled and shook his head. "You'd be surprised, boy. Most money in banks is dirtier than dirt."

"Then maybe we can just get our hands on one shipment," Sol said. "That should be enough to set us both up for a while. And if this is being sent in from Warren, there's got to be more coming in from other small mines scattered here and there."

"You say this is a big company?" Nester asked.

Sol nodded. "Big enough."

"Could be a lot of mines."

"Could be."

Nester's eyes narrowed as he glanced sideways over to Sol. "This could be a big job. Could be messy too. You really think you can see it through?"

"Not by myself. The two of us could have a good chance. Besides, if we get there and it looks impossible, we can always forget about it."

Shaking his head, Nester said, "You can't just decide to come and go from this. You do it or you don't. I can't afford to just let you traipse in, tip my hand to the killers gunning for me and traipse out again."

"I started this and I intend to see it through," Sol vowed.

"That's good, because there ain't no backing out now."

Chapter 17

True to his word, Nester was up the next morning before the sun had had a chance to touch the sky. The air had acquired a set of cold teeth, which sank especially deep in the early hour. Some folks called it "bracing," or some other such nonsense, but Sol had always found it to be as bracing as getting clubbed with a frozen length of iron.

Sol hardly remembered waking up. He was shaken from his sleep, booted from the pile of blankets Nester had provided and then told to get the horses ready. Before Sol could peel his eyelids all the way apart, he was on Smoky's back and heading down the mountain. His eyes snapped open real quickly when he found himself half a step away from toppling down the side of that mountain. Smoky had taken a step onto some loose gravel and started to skid, which caused Sol to grip his reins as if his life depended on it.

"I told you to follow me close," Nester growled over his shoulder. "You wanna take lessons from me, then here's a good one. Watch yer own damn self, because nobody can do that for ya."

"I like that advice."

"Good. Now steer away from that patch o' dirt before yer horse breaks its neck."

Sol leaned forward, spotted the dirt and pulled his reins to the left. Smoky reacted fairly well, but still managed to scrape one hoof through the edge of that dirt. The gray gelding slipped a bit and then recovered. Sol didn't care to think about what would have happened if the horse had slipped any worse.

Although Nester shifted a bit, he was merely adjusting his own motions to accommodate his own horse's gait. As he flicked his reins, Nester made a clicking sound with his tongue.

"Where are we going?"

"Jesus, Mary and Joseph, you sure do like the sound o' yer own voice."

"I was just—"

"I know and we're going where I said we was going," Nester cut in. "You want to ride right down the same way you came up? If there's anyone else coming after us apart from those two we found yesterday, they'll just love it if we come straight to them along the very trail they're probably watching."

"But there might not be anyone watching," Sol pointed out.

Nester chuckled and replied, "You gotta always think someone's watching you. That way, you'll be ready for the occasional spot where ye're right."

Nodding, Sol leaned back and focused upon Smoky's movements and the curve of the trail directly in front of him. For the rest of the ride down the mountain, Sol matched Nester's pace and rode only in the spots where Nester had ridden. He kept his mouth shut until the ground leveled out and the mountain was behind him. It seemed that was the best way to stay on Nester's good side.

It took a bit longer than Sol had expected, but they eventually made their way to a wider stretch of trail that led out to some open terrain. Sol's ears were still cramped enough to let him know he was a ways up, but at least there wasn't a drop-off directly beside him.

Now that he was on even ground, Sol took a moment to look up at the sky. "I don't suppose you brought some food," he said.

"You rode all the way up from New Mex without carrying any food?"

"I wasn't exactly planning on bolting out of here so quickly."

"I got another lesson for ya."

But this time, it was Sol who interrupted. "Let me guess. Always be ready for anything."

"Now ye're learnin'!"

"Great," Sol muttered to himself. "There's a gem I couldn't have gotten on my own."

Nester led Sol along a trail that eventually curved to the north. Even though Sol could see where the trail cut through a low mountain pass, he wasn't being led in that direction. Instead, Nester took him to a wide patch of grass. By the time they were close enough to the grass for Nester to dismount, Sol could see a small creek trickling along the edge of the grass. Nester led his horse to the creek, dropped the reins and motioned for Sol to do the same.

After Sol had climbed down from his saddle and stretched his legs a bit, he saw Nester turn and face him. The old man's hand hovered less than an inch over his holstered pistol.

"All right, boy," Nester said. "I want you to hand over that saddlebag full o' money."

"Pardon me?"

"You heard me well enough. Hand it over or I'll come and take it."

Sol narrowed his eyes to study Nester. It was difficult to tell whether the old man was serious or giving him another test. Either way, Sol only came up with one way to answer Nester's challenge. "No," he said defiantly. "I won't hand it over."

Nodding slowly, Nester adjusted his stance so he could square his shoulders to Sol. "All right, then. We do this the hard way."

For a few moments, Nester stared at Sol as if he were reading the small print upon his soul. Every so often, Nester would shift his gaze just a bit and look deeper. Finally, he snapped his hand down and up again to aim his pistol and thumb the hammer back.

Sol hadn't even seen the old man's gun clear leather.

"Ye're dead," Nester stated. "But you got some promise."

Letting out the breath that had caught in his throat, Sol only realized at that moment that he'd gotten to his own weapon. This pistol was still pointed toward the ground and his finger was hooked around the outside of the trigger guard, but Sol had indeed managed to draw without needing to waste more than half a thought on the process.

Chuckling, Sol let out a deep breath. "I thought you meant to take that money from me."

"I do."

Sol blinked, but didn't know if he should stop smiling or not. "You can have a share of the money, if that'll make up for how I messed up your situation in Leadville."

Nester shook his head. "Take out what's in that saddlebag and we'll split it between us. Whatever we can't carry stays here. An' you can wipe that mean look offa yer face while ye're at it. We won't get anywhere if we're too busy lookin' after that much cash."

As much sense as that made, Sol still didn't like the sound of it. Dropping that set of saddlebags was like dropping his gun and waiting for the hammer to fall. It hit the ground with a heavy thump. Nester descended upon it, pulled the bag open and started sifting through it.

"There's a lot here," the old man said.

"I know."

"Here," Nester said as he started tossing bundles of cash to Sol. "Stuff this into yer pockets and tell me when you ain't got any more room."

Sol caught several bundles and tucked them into his pockets. Just as he'd promised, Nester kept tossing them until Sol ran out of free space. After that, Nester packed some money away for himself. It took considerably less time for the nimble-fingered old man to finish his task. When he was finished, there was still about half of one pouch remaining.

"We should bury the rest right here an' we'll come back for it later," Nester announced.

"No," Sol replied. Seeing the warning glare in Nester's eyes, he added, "We don't know if we'll even make it back here. We might not even be able to come back this way after we're through in Albuquerque."

Nester's eyes snapped back and forth between Sol and the saddlebags. "You really think there's all that money to be had, boy?"

Sol nodded without hesitation. "I heard as much from Charlie himself."

"He could'a been lyin'."

"He wasn't lying. He was too scared to be lying."

After studying the saddlebags some more, Nester finally shrugged. "I gotta admit I like yer instinct. I expect you'll want to haul that money around?"

"I've brought it this far," Sol said cautiously.

"Fine. Keep it hidden and if anything happens to it, I expect you to hand over a portion of yer own cut to make up for the portion I lost."

"That's fair."

"Damn right it is. Now let's have a look at what sort of lead ye're slingin'."

As Nester walked forward, he reached out to take Sol's gun from him the way he might take it away from a child that was about to hurt himself. The old man's gun was back in its place at his side and, once again, Sol hadn't seen the pistol move.

"It's all right, boy," Nester said. "If I meant to shoot, I would'a done it."

Reluctantly, Sol released his grip on the gun so Nester could take it away. "You'll have to work on yer draw," Nester said as he examined the pistol. "An old Cavalry model, huh? By the look of it, an 1873 model."

Sol nodded. "Yeah. I think it is."

"I just said it was. You'll have to get something better. These are good when they're new, but I had one stick on me after being exposed to the elements."

"I've taken good care of it," Sol said in his own defense.

"You been cleanin' it after every time it was fired? Making sure all the moving parts is dry?"

"Mostly."

"Yeah? Well, yer finger didn't even make it through the trigger guard," Nester replied. "What you got to say about that?"

Sol grinned and shrugged. "I suppose you've got me there."

"Take a shot at that tree," Nester said as he pointed to a nearby specimen. "Clip a few of them branches."

Pulling in a breath, Sol fixed his eyes upon a target and grabbed his gun from its holster. Once again, his finger snagged upon the guard.

"Don't try for speed," Nester scolded. "I wanna see accuracy."

Sol nodded and rested his finger upon the trigger. From there, he raised his arm and fired. Several branches shook as the bullet tore through them, but the proper one didn't fall. Keeping his head up, Sol took another few shots.

"Never mind," Nester grunted.

"I can do better. Just let me get set."

But the old man waved at him as if he were erasing Sol's last few words from a chalkboard. Stepping in Sol's line of fire without the slightest hesitation, he said, "None of that matters. You ain't out here to shoot targets and you won't never get the chance to set yer feet."

Sol nodded and reloaded his pistol. "I can practice my draw."

"Any man can practice till he gets quick, but you

won't get much of anywhere if'n you can't draw yer gun without getting tripped up on the guard. Besides, that ol' thing's too heavy. You need a better one."

"Do you have another gun?" Sol asked.

"Nope. Don't need one."

"Then where do you suppose I'll find one?"

Nester grinned and replied, "Sometimes the easiest answers are the best ones."

Chapter 18

The trading post was just over five miles south of the little creek where Sol had shot down those unfortunate branches. It was the largest of a small cluster of buildings huddled on either side of the road like a patch of mulberry bushes that had sprung up through nothing but pure chance and a stiff wind. Apart from the trading post, there was a small shelter for horses and a pair of outhouses. Sol thought the last building at the end could have been a post office, but there was no sign in the window and no other way for him to be sure.

Nester wasn't too interested in the other buildings anyway. After riding up to the trading post, he dismounted and snapped his reins around a post. "There's a case of guns to the right after you walk in. Pick out something smaller than what you got now and newer, as well. And don't forget a new holster and some ammunition."

Feeling like he was being sent on an errand by one of his grandparents, Sol nodded at Nester's demands and sauntered into the store. As he walked past the tables stacked high with blankets, shirts, socks and other sundries, Sol mused at how normal it felt to be there. He needed some things, so he went to the store. Even after his tracking down an infamous legend like Nester Quarles, some things remained the same. It did him a whole lot of good to know that.

"Looking for anything special?" a spindly man with glasses asked.

Sol looked over to the man who'd spoken and found the narrow-boned fellow straightening a rack of fringed coats along the wall. "Yes. I need a gun."

"Right this way." As he walked to a counter situated to the right of where Sol had walked in, the spindly fellow brushed his hands against the apron he wore and flexed his fingers. "Looking to do some hunting?"

Before the salesman could reach for one of the rifles hanging from a rack behind the counter, Sol replied, "Not as such. I need a pistol."

"I've got a fine selection." The salesman stuck a few fingers into his shirt pocket and glanced at the opposite end of the store. He saw Nester over there speaking to a woman who looked to be the same age and build as the salesman. There was also a kid of no more than ten or eleven years darting back and forth between Nester and the woman. Finally, the salesman took his eyes away from Nester and smiled. "Any particular model you're looking for?" he asked as he removed a small key from his pocket.

Sol was looking down through the glass top of the case. As his eyes wandered among the shiny firearms, he thought about how much money was in his pockets. Judging by the look of some of those guns, he might just have to step outside and get some more so nobody would see all the bundles he needed to flip through. Sol decided that would be just fine. He was investing in his future, after all.

"What's that one?" Sol asked as he pointed to a finely polished gun resting upon a velvet cushion.

The salesman grinned like a snake that had unhinged its jaw to welcome a stray mouse. "Ahh, that's a great choice," he said as he unlocked the case and reached inside. "Thirty-eight-caliber Colt. Nickel-plated. You ever fire one of these beauties?"

"No, I . . ." Shifting his attention from the salesman to the other end of the trading post, Sol took notice of a few burly men who'd stepped into the place. Those men seemed to have taken a shine to Nester and were walking straight over to him. Sol then looked at Nester and got an easy nod in return. Since Nester wasn't too concerned about those men, Sol continued what he'd been doing.

"I've never fired one," Sol said. "Mind if I get a feel for it?"

The salesman already had the gun out of the case and was giving it a few last-minute polishes using another piece of velvet. "Help yourself," he said as he draped the gun over one arm and handed it over. "There's a few targets out back, if you'd prefer."

Sol held the gun in his hand and let it sit there like a deadweight that had been tied to his wrist. "I don't like it."

"Well, how about this one?" the salesman asked as he started to reach for another one in the case.

Before the salesman could lift the second gun, Sol stopped him. "Not that one, either," he said, since that second gun looked to be about the same size as the one he already had. "I need something lighter. Something I can work on."

"Work on? You mean you want to modify it?"

Sol nodded, but was distracted by more activity coming from the other end of the trading post. It seemed that Nester was drawing a crowd. The old man faced them all and was saying something to one of the men who'd recently walked in. Before Sol could see much of anything else, he caught the glint of polished metal in the corner of his eye. Sol turned toward the salesman to find him holding out another pistol.

"Why don't you try this one?" the salesman asked. "It's a .44 Smith and Wesson. Carved grips. Fires like a dream and I hear it can be modified easily enough. Of course, you'll have to take care of that on your own. I'm hardly a gunsmith."

"Hey," Nester shouted from the front of the trading post. "You find anything yet?"

"Yeah. I might have."

"Good. Wrap it up and take it home."

The longer Sol held on to that Smith & Wesson, the more he liked it. Rather than being a weight in his hand, it felt more like an extension of his arm. When he thumbed back the hammer, it sounded like a soft, metallic kiss. It shouldn't take much for him to remove that trigger guard. After that, he'd be ready for business.

"How much?" Sol asked.

The salesman rubbed his hands together and glanced at a list that was tacked to the back of the case. "Will you need ammunition as well?"

"Yes, please."

"Hey!" Nester shouted. "You find what you need?"

Sol nodded. "I think I found just the one. It might need a little work, though."

The salesman nodded and looked over toward Nester as well. "I can recommend some good men who can work on this pistol."

Ignoring the salesman, Nester asked, "What about a holster?"

Placing his own gun on the counter, Sol picked up the .44 and asked, "You mind if I see how this one fits?"

The salesman didn't look too happy about it, but he consented with a nod.

Sol dropped the gun into his holster and could feel there was some extra space in there. The leather was comfortably worn, but all Sol had to do was take a step or two as he paced in front of the display case and he could feel the new gun jostling about against his hip. When he went to take the gun out, the pistol snagged upon the leather.

"Why not?" Sol decided. "If I'm buying a good gun, I should get a good holster for it."

"Most definitely," the salesman replied. Even though Sol only paused to think about how much money he would be spending, the salesman filled the silence with a quick "If you buy the gun and some ammunition to go along with it, I can take a quarter of the price off the holster."

"Make it half price and you've got a deal," Sol said.

After glancing down at his list of prices tacked to the back of the case, the salesman grinned and nodded. "You run a hard bargain, sir, but I will agree to that."

"Excellent. I'll take the pistol, the holster and a few boxes of ammunition."

Without wasting another moment, the salesman turned and collected all of the items with a flurry of reaching arms and clawing fingers.

"You find yer gun or not?" Nester hollered.

"I sure did."

"You get the bullets too?"

"Yes, sir," Sol replied as if he were placating a nagging parent.

The old man waved once and said, "Fine and dandy!" He then turned toward the people that had been gathered in his section of the trading post and raised his voice so he could be heard clearly throughout the entire place. "It's been fun and all, but we've got appointments to keep. If you'd all be so kind as to toss your valuables into one of them sacks over there."

The salesman froze and looked up at Sol. When Sol looked back at him with a similar amount of confusion etched into his face, he turned and leaned to get a better look at Nester and the rest of the people in the building.

Nester waved his gun at all of the folks in front of him, but kept it centered mostly upon the men who'd walked in most recently. When one of the younger fellows decided to make his move, the old man spotted it and answered by pulling his trigger. The younger fellow staggered back and knocked his shin against one of the display tables. He made a halfhearted attempt to draw his gun and then fell over.

"Anyone else want to try their luck?" Nester snarled.

Nobody accepted the offer.

Sol felt as if he stood there motionless for a good half hour. It was actually closer to a few seconds.

"Why don't you get a rifle for me while ye're over there?" Nester shouted. "And be quick about it."

Slowly shifting his eyes away from Nester, Sol spotted his gun lying on top of the display case. When he looked up, he noticed the salesman had spotted the very same thing. The salesman twitched, and Sol lunged for his pistol. There was no way for Sol to know if the salesman had been trying to grab the gun or if he was about to scratch his nose. The only thing Sol knew for certain was that he got to the gun first.

"You heard him," Sol said as he fumbled to get his finger beneath the trigger guard. "Get me one of those shotguns . . . and . . . and a box of shells."

The salesman stood up and held both hands up high. "Y-you don't have to do this. Please . . . I . . ."

"Shut up," Sol said as he extended his arm and shoved the gun closer to the salesman's face. "Just do what I told you."

Contending with hands that wouldn't stop shaking, the salesman took the closest shotgun from the rack. "Is . . . this the one you wanted?"

"Yes. That one's fine."

"The shells are behind me in a crate. Can I . . . ?"

Sol nodded and waved the pistol at him. "Just do it fast."

The salesman lowered himself so unsteadily that Sol swore he could actually hear the man's knees knocking. Some of the shotgun shells clattered against the floor and rolled along the base of the display case as the salesman fumbled to scoop them up.

"Keep quiet," Nester snarled. "You hear me? Keep quiet!"

"I think you killed him," a woman sobbed.

"He ain't dead," Nester replied as he took a few steps toward the spot where the younger man had dropped.

Sol leaned to get a look at what Nester was doing. The old man sauntered across one aisle and over to another. As he moved, Nester scattered another pair of men who looked like they should have been big enough to toss Nester through the front window. Rather than try anything so bold, those men scampered away on all fours before Nester could get too close.

Leaning down a bit, Nester asked, "You dead, boy?"

The grunts that followed weren't exactly clear, but they had plenty of steam behind them.

"See?" Nester said as he swung around and corralled the remaining customers and workers into one group. "He just stepped out of line, is all. Hopefully the rest of you learned yer lessons. What about you, Sol? You get that shotgun yet?"

"Just about."

The rattling behind the counter had stopped. Sol took another look at the salesman and found him fumbling while trying to get a bullet into the cylinder of one of the display pieces. As soon as he saw he'd been spotted, the salesman shoved the bullet in as best he could.

"Don't," Sol said as he pointed his gun at the salesman.

Either the salesman had gotten a big dose of courage or he was too scared to hear, because he didn't take Sol's advice. Instead, he held the pistol in trembling hands and gritted his teeth as he tightened his finger around the trigger. Fortunately for Sol, the salesman had grabbed a single-action revolver and was so nervous he hadn't cocked the hammer back.

The joy of still being alive flooded through Sol in a rush. And, in another rush, it was replaced by blinding anger directed at the man who'd taken it upon himself to try and end his life. It wasn't charity or good sense that had kept Sol alive. Instead, the salesman was just too stupid to get the job done.

"Gimme that gun," Sol growled as he reached out to snatch the pistol from the salesman's hand. "What's the matter with you? I wasn't gonna shoot. I told you not to try anything!"

"Sorry," the salesman whined. "Sorry!"

"Where's the damn guns I wanted?"

Fumbling to gather up the shotgun and pistol Sol had chosen, he groaned, "Right here! They're right here, just please don't shoot me."

"Shut your mouth, you sniveling little rat."

"All right. I will. Just, please don't kill me."

The more the salesman begged, the more Sol wanted to fire. He didn't even know where the desire came from. What puzzled him even more was the way his own anger grew as the salesman kept groveling and whimpering. If Sol had come across an animal behaving like that, he would have shot it just to put it out of its misery.

"Here," the salesman muttered. "It's all here. Please!"

"The money too," Sol growled.

"What?"

"Oh, now you wake up?" Sol asked. "That man over there has already shot someone, I'm pointing a gun at you and you don't grow a spine until someone threatens your money?"

The fire in the salesman's eyes flared up in a way someone might expect from a mother protecting her young. As it turned out, the salesman was protecting eighty-four dollars and sixty-two cents. As he dumped the money into the sack that also contained the guns and other items, the salesman balled up his fists and took another run at Sol.

Since scooping the money from the till had been such a gut-wrenching affair for the salesman, Sol had been expecting some sort of final display before letting it go. He just hadn't expected the display to be so pathetic.

The salesman's first punch landed and bounced off of Sol's shoulder without enough force to put a dent in his jacket. Judging by the vicious snarl on the salesman's lips, however, one might have thought he'd just single-handedly won a war.

"Get away from me," Sol barked as he backhanded the salesman to the floor. "Just sit there and stay put."

A second ago, the salesman was making a stand. Now he was back to crying. "Yes, sir, I'm so sorry."

It was all Sol could do to keep from pulling his trigger. He wanted to at least wound the salesman out of principle for being such a sniveling, impotent little coward. Since money was all the other man seemed to care about, taking that from him made Sol feel a little better.

Nester nodded proudly as he backed toward the front door. He held his gun in hand and smiled when he saw Sol rush toward him carrying the sack full of money and guns.

"You folks have been real good," Nester announced. "With a few exceptions, of course. Now, we'll be on our way. You folks be sure to sit tight and don't stick yer heads out of this store or . . ." Nester pulled his trigger and sent a round through a rack of dishes against the wall. The gunshot and shattering that followed was enough to make everyone in that trading post press themselves flat against the floor and clench their eyes shut.

"After you, Sol," Nester said as he stepped away from the door.

Sol winced at the sound of his own name being announced so prominently, but figured that was the least of his problems. Every step he took through the front door felt like there was a grizzly running after him and he was forced to walk for his life when he so desperately wanted to run. But he knew better than to run. He didn't know how he knew.

He just did.

Once he was outside, Sol pulled in a shallow breath of the sweetest air he'd ever tasted. The only thing that smelled sweeter was the scent of horses as he climbed into his saddle and took hold of Smoky's reins.

Nester strolled outside with a smile on his face and a spring in his step. For a moment, he looked like he might even take a bow. Instead, he fired another shot into the trading post.

"What in the—"

Waving off Sol's exclamation, Nester said, "Just breaking some more plates and making sure they stay put. Let's get moving." After hopping into his saddle quicker than any man his age had a right to be, Nester snapped his reins and emptied the rest of his bullets into the upper portion of the trading post. The victorious yelp he let out was plenty loud enough to be heard over all that shooting.

Sol took hold of his own reins and cinched the upper portion of the burlap sack around his saddle horn. He saw some movement in the trading post and couldn't tell if it was someone walking to the window or just light reflecting off of broken glass. Just to be safe, he fired a couple of rounds into the wall. The rest of his bullets blazed up to the heavens.

"That's the spirit, boy!" Nester shouted.

Suddenly, Sol opened his mouth and let out a war cry that would have made any Indian brave proud. Smoky started to rear, but then responded to the snap of his reins and broke into a run.

Both men raced away from the trading post amid the thunder of hooves and battle cries. The blood was pumping so quickly through Sol's veins that he could barely see straight.

Nester led the way through a small field and then across a river. Rather than circle around to meet up with the trail they'd agreed upon earlier, Nester steered his horse back to the river.

"Keep yer horse's feet wet for as long as you can manage," Nester said cheerily. "A mile would be good. That way, there ain't no tracks for the law to follow."

"We need to ride in the river for a mile?"

"Only if you can. You shouldn't have to go nearly

that far, on account of most lawmen bein' a good mix of lazy and easily discouraged."

Sol chuckled and shook his head. "How much did you get, Nester?" he asked.

"Hell, I don't know. Some food and a canteen." Digging into his pockets, the old man produced a bundle of porcelain napkin rings. "I don't even know what these are! Hot *damn*, it is good to be out and about again!"

Chapter 19

"You did good back there, kid," Nester said. "You did real good."

Sol and the old man were sitting with their backs against a tree and their legs stretched out in front of them. The burlap sack that Sol had filled was next to him and another smaller sack was next to Nester. Upon closer examination, Sol realized that Nester's collection hadn't been put into a sack at all.

"Is that a pillowcase?" Sol asked.

Picking up the cotton cover, Nester looked it over. His eyes seemed particularly drawn to the floral pattern stitched around the edge. "I suppose it is," the old man replied. "There wasn't much of a selection." Upending the pillowcase, Nester dumped its contents onto the ground and shook it just to be certain everything was accounted for. There were several sticks of candy and dried strips of jerky, some pouches of coffee and tobacco, sugar cubes, soap, a file and another set of napkin rings.

Sol dumped out his burlap sack and found the shotgun, the pistol and a generous mix of ammunition that covered both guns as well as a few that neither man possessed. Apart from that, there was also a holster and gun belt, a pencil and the money. Sol let his hands drift through the money as he recalled the look on the salesman's face when he'd been forced to give it up. Soon, Sol's thoughts were interrupted when he felt Nester's hand push his aside.

"We split everything," Nester grunted as he helped himself to a more than generous portion of the cash. "That's the way it always goes, no matter who ye're ridin' with. If someone tries to tell you to keep only what you stole, you tell them you'll only fire at the assholes that're firing at you on the next job. That'll change their tune real quick."

Sol nodded and let the old man help himself.

As Nester took his money and stuffed it into his pockets, he reached for the remainder of the cash sitting on the ground. Sol glanced down at the cash, but didn't make a move to stop Nester from going in for seconds. Nester closed his fingers around a handful of that money, clenched those fingers into a fist and then cracked that fist against the side of Sol's head.

"Hey!" Sol snapped. "What in the . . . ?"

"Wake up, boy! Ye're dealin' with thieves now. Don't never forget that. The other men you ride with may save yer skin and you may save theirs, but ye're all a bunch'a thieves. Someone's always gonna try to steal from you when ye're splittin' up the take. You don't let nobody step on you then, just like you don't ever let nobody step on you ever! You hear me?"

"Yeah."

Nester's fist cracked against Sol's head in the exact spot it had landed before. "You weren't paying attention! I can tell. Now do you hear me?"

This time, Sol forced himself to look Nester in the eyes and make his voice sound a whole lot calmer than he felt. "Yes," he replied. "I hear you."

The old man nodded and kept his fist up where they both could see it. "Good. You never, ever just sit by and watch someone take what's yers. I don't give a damn if it's money or a button you found on the ground that caught yer eye. You start letting folks take from you and they'll keep on taking. What's worse is that they'll think ye're weak. And if you sit back and let someone take from you, you are weak."

Sol nodded. "All right. Can we just count up this money and dismiss school for the day?"

Nester scowled and asked, "You all right? You did real good back at that store. You should be proud."

"You should've told me you were going to rob the place."

"I wasn't all the way sure until we got there. Besides, you should always be thinkin' of the next place ye're gonna hit. I found some of my biggest hauls just 'cause my eyes were open at the right time."

"And that man you shot," Sol muttered. "Did you just decide about that when the chance presented itself?"

Nester kept his eyes on Sol for a few seconds. His face went through a couple of different changes, but Sol couldn't tell what the old man was thinking. Finally, Nester grinned and asked, "You feel sorry for that fella?"

"No."

"Good. Don't. He thought he could walk over me without even drawing his gun. Can you believe that?

He came at me with some ax handle he'd picked up from a bucket or somewheres else they were out for sale. The second I let that happen, I might as well start wearing a dress."

"Did you have to shoot him to prove your point?"

"Yeah," Nester replied without hesitation. "I did. You gettin' soft on me, boy? Or maybe you was always soft."

When Sol jumped to his feet, he didn't even know what he was planning on doing. When he grabbed Nester's collar and hoisted the old man off the ground, Sol didn't know how he was going to get out of this situation without losing a whole lot of blood.

Adjusting his legs so he could support himself, Nester allowed his body to hang from the ends of Sol's fists like a scarecrow dangling from a pair of hooks. His easy smile was still intact and his eyes were still relaxed and slightly amused, which was exactly how they'd been before Sol had reacted.

And then, ever so slightly, Nester's eyes changed. It looked as if a small fire had been lit inside each eye, and they grew brighter the longer they were allowed to burn.

"That's more like it," Nester said. "At least you got a bit of sand in you."

"I got plenty of sand. Just because I don't go around shooting anyone I can doesn't mean otherwise."

Nester's smile widened. "You want to be an outlaw, then you gotta be ready to use that gun of yours. That shopkeeper's got the law on his side. You want to take yer money, you ain't about to be paid like that shopkeeper. I thought you was tired of lining up with yer hand out."

"I was," Sol said. His eyes hardened before he added, "I am."

"Then you'd best be ready to take yer money my way. An' since folks ain't about to pay you on account of yer good looks, you gotta be ready to take it from them." Cocking his head to one side, Nester asked, "You sure you want this kind of life, boy?"

"You know one thing I noticed?" Sol asked. "You call me boy when you're looking at me like I'm something less than what's on the bottom of your boot."

"You got real good eyes, boy."

Sol shoved Nester away from him in the hopes of knocking the old man against a tree. Instead, Nester got his feet set and steadied himself before staggering back more than a foot. Somehow, the old man managed to keep his eyes on Sol and his chin up the entire time.

"You didn't know what was comin' back there, but you made it through just fine," Nester said. "Not only that, but you came out with a profit. Tell you the truth, I was just hopin' you'd make it outside without gettin' shot."

"And what if I did get shot?" Sol asked.

"Then both of us would be through with this little adventure of yers. What'd you think?" Nester asked. "That this would be one ride after another and free money bein' tossed yer way? That haul you got from yer old employer was a fluke. You were in the right spot at the right time, but a man can't live his life hopin' for another fluke. Things just don't happen that way.

"Ye're just learnin', is all," Nester added as he stepped forward to drape an arm around Sol's shoulders. "Since there ain't no school for what I do, you gotta learn the same way any other outlaw learns how to conduct himself. You watch someone who's kept himself alive for more than a few days on the run and you get some good partners to keep you alive until ye're ready to run on yer own."

As he listened to the old man, Sol felt the burning in his gullet die down. He even smirked as he said, "I've sure learned not to trust my partners when they say they just want to look around inside a store."

Nester chuckled and said, "There you go! That's exactly right. And the best way to make sure you know about the job you take next is to be the one that's doin' the planning."

When he looked over to see the eager smile on Nester's face, Sol didn't know quite what to make of it. One thing he knew for certain was that he didn't like being the one who was literally under the old man's wing at that particular moment. The last man to put his arm around Sol like that had been his father. With a sideways step and a twist of his upper body, Sol pulled away from Nester and took a few steps before turning back around to face him.

"Can we do anything to modify this gun?" Sol asked as he walked over to pick up the Smith & Wesson.

Reaching into his pile of mismatched stolen items, Nester replied, "That's what I stole this file for. Hand over that pistol."

Sol held on to the pistol and turned it so it caught the light in different ways. "Will this be ready by the time we reach Albuquerque?"

Wearing a rattlesnake's grin, Nester asked, "You'll

get yer chance for payback against that mining company. Just promise me one thing, Solomon. Don't set revenge in yer mind above everything else. Vengeful men don't make good partners."

Sol shook his head. "Whatever revenge I wanted, I got by taking Charlie's money away from him. Seems like that's all anyone truly cares about anyway."

"Ye're in a spot to take away a whole lot more'n that and you know it. Just the fact that ye're thinking about riding back with that price on yer head tells me that you'd like another shot at those boss men. Maybe you'd like to finish what you started?"

"No," Sol replied. "It's not like that. Charlie was holding back a whole lot of money. There's no reason why he should just get away with that."

"You remember what I said to you about thieves bein' thieves and stealin' from everyone including each other?" Nester asked.

"Yes."

"Businessmen ain't nothin' but thieves in fancier clothes. The worst things you can do when facing a thief is to turn yer back on 'im or underestimate 'im. You go riding into Albuquerque all filled with righteous fire and you'll get sloppy. This may be a big job and it may be a job you got some other stake in, but it's just a job. Keep yer head on yer shoulders and be smart or you'll make a mistake that'll cost yer life. Maybe both our lives. You got that?"

Sol nodded. "Yeah."

Nester snapped his hand out as if he meant to crack Sol against the head again. This time, Sol ducked to one side and raised a hand to defend himself. The old man smirked and nodded approvingly. "You got that?"

"Yes. I do."

"All right, then. Now hand over that gun so I can start in on these modifications."

Sol handed over the gun and sat down again.

Reclaiming his spot against a tree, Nester got to work filing away the .44's trigger guard as if he were whittling on a lazy summer evening. "We should hit a federal bank or maybe raid an armory. You'd be amazed how much money we could get selling stolen guns. You'd also meet a whole new class of businessmen that way."

Sol shook his head and then broke into a laugh. "You're either kidding, very confident in me or crazy," he said. "I can't decide which."

"How about most of one and a bit of the other two?"

"Fair enough."

Chapter 20

Sol was glad he'd found that Smith & Wesson for two reasons. First of all, it fit in his hand a whole lot better than the old gun he'd been carrying around before. Each time they stopped to water the horses or work the kinks from their necks, Sol and Nester went through a few rounds of target practice. While Sol could see an improvement in his own skill, the old man improved a whole lot quicker. It seemed the tales of Nester's ability with a firearm weren't too far from the truth.

The second reason why Sol appreciated that .44 was the modifications it needed. Filing off the trigger guard, filing down the sights and tinkering with the weapon in any other number of ways was enough to keep Nester occupied during most of the ride into New Mexico. Even after they'd crossed back into Sol's familiar stomping grounds, Nester was content to point out a few old trails they could use to move about unnoticed and reminisce about his younger years rather than look for more stores to rob or federal armories to raid.

Sol actually grew to enjoy those stories, since a lot

of them involved his own family members in one way or another. For one thing, Sol learned that one of his uncles used to ride with Nester on a string of train robberies. Those robberies were all carried out in Missouri, where there was no shortage of other more prominent robbers to take the blame for Nester's deeds. Thinking back to how many laws he'd broken in someone else's name put a fond smile upon Nester's face.

Also, one or two cousins had sought him out in much the same way that Sol had come looking for him in Leadville. Apparently, one of those cousins was nearly killed in a stagecoach robbery and another wasn't even able to contend with the icy glares of Nester's old gang before he ran back home.

"They was all just foolin' about," Nester recalled. "You know, making like they was gonna tan his hide or use him for target practice. I never seen a boy run so fast as that cousin of yers when he tore away from that camp. Come to think of it, I don't even think he got to his horse. I believe he ran all the way from Wichita to Dodge City." After letting out a slow whistle, he added, "That boy must've spread some sort of word, because I didn't never see another eager young Brakefield come callin' until you showed up on my doorstep."

"Thanks for making me sound like a lost puppy," Sol groaned. "I appreciate that."

"I don't know about the puppy part, but I think you may be lost."

"What gave you that idea?"

"This mining company, for starters," Nester replied. "I been riding along following you without saying much of anything one way or another. Still, you haven't told me much of anything we'd need to know about this mining company of yers."

"I told you where it is."

"Sure. Albuquerque. You gotta know somethin' more than that!"

Sol nodded and looked out to the horizon where the first traces of Albuquerque could be seen. The flat, sandy terrain was plenty more familiar to Sol than the mountains of Colorado. Throughout the entire ride, he'd breathed different air as he'd gone from one elevation to another. This was the first day that he wasn't feeling some sort of effect from the change of climate. Sol felt even better now that he could see Albuquerque in the distance like some sort of hazy, angular mirage.

"Jessup Mining Company. That's the name of the company that Charlie works for. I saw that name printed upon the bundles that were sent out and I know those bundles were sent to Albuquerque in New Mexico. Is that enough for you, old man?"

It hadn't taken Sol long to know just how to say those last two words so they'd grate upon Nester's nerves. He bared his teeth slightly and asked, "You know where to find this mining company? It ain't like this is some one-horse town we're about to ride into."

Sol closed his eyes and put some effort into trying to recall more details from the front of those bundles he'd handed over to be delivered. Smoky carried him diligently onward in a strong, easy stride as Sol clenched his eyes shut so he could concentrate. When he opened them, Sol was shaking his head. "I can think of a street name or number, but I don't know if it's right."

"Since you don't know whether it's a name or number, I'd bet on it not bein' right." This time, Nester was the one to let out a sigh as he gazed at the distant city. "You sure about the name, boy?"

"Yes."

"Then that should be enough. Do me a favor, though, and let me be the one to go out askin' about the place."

"Why?" Sol asked with a scowl.

Nester turned to look at Sol in silence. It was a look that Sol had gotten to know fairly well in the amount of time he'd spent with the outlaw.

"I don't care if this is another one of your tests or not," Sol said. "Tell me why and don't make me guess."

"I'm startin' to think I knocked you on the head a bit too hard. Did you forget about that notice? You seemed awfully proud of it when you showed it to me before. Fifteen hundred dollars may not be a lot to a mining company, but I'd bet they've seen that notice and will have committed that likeness of you to memory."

As much as Sol would have liked to argue, he simply couldn't. "All right, then," he said. "What do you suggest?"

"I'll be the one to scout out this Jessup Company," the old man replied. "While I'm doing that, you can scout out the rest of the town."

"You mean scout out Albuquerque?"

"That's just what I mean."

"The whole town?" Sol asked.

"Are you going deaf? Yes!"

"What would I be looking for, exactly?"

Nester held up one hand so he could mark each of his points with a finger and then tic them off one by one. "First of all, we need a place to sleep. It's gotta have a good view of the street, be well hidden and easy to get out of if the need arises. Second, we need a place to put the horses and that's gotta have all those same things as the hotel. Third, we need to know where the law is and how good they are at making their rounds. Fourth, we need—"

"Stop," Sol interrupted. "My head hurts."

Grinning over at the younger man with his hands still marking the points he'd been making, Nester asked, "This all ain't as easy as you thought it'd be, huh?"

Sol shook his head. "Sometimes, I think you're just putting me through these paces to keep me out of your way."

"And why would I do that?"

"I don't know," Sol replied. "Perhaps you'd like to move in, clean out that mining company and then ride off while I'm scouting for the right stable when the law comes looking for me."

Nester chuckled and replied, "I see you've been listening to me, after all. That's a good way to think, but I ain't tryin' to steer you away from anything."

"Then how come all the robbers I've ever heard about ride in like a thunderstorm, shoot a place up and then ride away? And before you tell me they scouted all those places out, I'll cut you off right now by saying I don't believe that nonsense."

"How many outlaws have you ever ridden with?" Nester asked.

"One."

"So how do you know all of this ye're sayin' right now?"

"I've read plenty of newspapers and heard plenty of folks talk." Before he could be interrupted, Sol added, "And lots of them were talking from first-hand experience."

"Okay. Take all of them stories and mix 'em up with everything else you heard about every other outlaw who kicked up enough dust to get noticed. How'd most of them end up?"

Wincing a bit, Sol said, "Some were killed. Some were put in jail or hung. But some got away, like you."

"Most were put in jail, killed or hung," Nester corrected. "You know why that is?"

Slowly, Sol lowered his head and let out all the steam he'd built up in one long breath. "Because they didn't scout their jobs ahead of time?"

Nester smiled victoriously. "You got that right. I lived in Leadville as a fine, upstanding citizen and that's because I took a good long time making sure everything was—"

"I heard you, the first time you told that story. I'm sorry I mucked things up for you there. For the love of all that's holy, please just stop rubbing it in," Sol begged. "I'll go and find the hotel, stable and even a place for supper. How's that? Good enough?" With that, Sol snapped his reins and got moving a bit quicker toward town.

"Wait," Nester said.

Sol pulled back on the leather straps until Smoky was down to a slow walk.

Riding up to him, Nester kept right on going. Turning to look over his shoulder, he said, "I'm going in first. If your face is plastered all over the walls, I don't want you bringing down all the fire and brimstone in that city."

"So what do you want me to do?"

"Wait out here for a bit and then ride in using the same road I take. If ye're the scourge of Albuquerque, I'll ride right back out to warn you. If not, you can go about yer scouting. We'll meet up over by that fence out yonder."

Sol glanced in the direction Nester had pointed and saw the broken fence. When he looked back to the old man, Nester was far enough away that he had to shout to be heard. "And what if you can't find me to warn me?"

"Then I guess we won't meet up. Coming here was yer idea, remember?" Nester snapped his reins and raced toward the spot where trail became street and open country became a town. He waved over his shoulder and then leaned forward over his horse's neck.

When Sol caught himself waving to Nester's back, he felt like the biggest fool in New Mexico. "Yeah, I remember," he grumbled.

The place Sol settled on for a room was a long, short building that looked and smelled as if it had originally been made for horses. Ironically enough, the stable he found nearby was a lot cleaner and newer than the place where Sol rented rooms for himself and

Nester. The hotel had no name and was only marked by a faded old sign that said HOTEL in pale green letters. The beds were both uncomfortable and one room smelled slightly worse than the other. Sol knew this for a fact because he'd started off in the worse-smelling of the two and then moved his things to the second. If Nester wanted to force the scouting duties upon someone else, he should be ready for the consequences.

Rather than concern himself with what Nester was doing, Sol decided to take his lessons to heart and continue scouting. He kept his hat pulled down as far as possible in the event there were more of those notices about and kept his eyes pointed forward. Fortunately, nobody who passed Sol on the street seemed too concerned with looking at him anyway.

In the space of a few hours, Sol not only found several different ways to go from the hotel to the stable and then out of town, but he also spotted a few clean-looking restaurants and a cantina that had a two-man band playing loudly enough to be heard from the street. Sol kept walking until he found what looked to be a business district. The buildings were a bit taller and better maintained. There were more shingles hanging from doorways, and the boardwalks felt sturdier beneath his boots.

Glancing up, Sol could see the sun had a little ways to go before it started dipping below the horizon. That meant he had a bit of time before he would need to meet Nester. Since a promising shingle hung not too far in front of him, Sol decided to spend his bit of extra time as best he could. And if he beat Nester to the punch, so be it.

The sign that had caught Sol's eye was for a local surveyor's office. A smaller shingle hanging from the sign advertised assayer's services, which were also available at that same location. Sol walked up to the front door and knocked. When he knocked a second time, he noticed the third sign hanging behind the glass of the front window. That one told him the place was closed.

"Can I help you?" a stout man in his forties asked. He wore a rumpled brown suit and used a walking stick. Judging by the chips and cracks on that stick, it wasn't carried for decorative purposes.

"Do you know when this office will be open again?" Sol asked.

Without looking at the window or any other part of the office, the man replied, "Eight o'clock tomorrow morning. That is, unless you have an appointment."

"I don't have an appointment."

"Would you like to make one?" Noticing the heightened scrutiny that response brought about, the man in the rumpled suit shifted his walking stick to his left hand and extended his right to Sol. "My name's Dennis Farley. I own this establishment."

Catching himself before he spoke a name that might be that of a locally wanted man, Sol cleared his throat and said, "So . . . nice to meet you. I just got into town, so I apologize if I'm a bit out of sorts."

Despite looking a bit confused by Sol's stammering, Dennis maintained his polite air. "You could always come back tomorrow after you've had a chance to rest."

"Actually, I think I'll do that. I have some other business to take care of while I'm in town. Do you know where I might be able to find the offices for the Jessup Mining Company?"

Dennis' eyes widened a bit at the mention of what was obviously a competitor. "If you would like to come in and talk business now, I'd be more than happy to reopen for a bit."

"Oh, well, that business is separate from the business I meant to talk to you about. Since you're on your way out, I could handle one and then come back tomorrow to talk to you about the other."

Sol knew his line of manure wasn't very convincing. Dennis must have been either a trusting soul or he really wanted to go home, because he gave up on digging his keys from his pocket and shifted his walking stick back to his right hand. "The Jessup offices are, I believe, four or five streets that way," he said while using his walking stick to point. "Make a left when you see the Chinese tailor and keep walking. You won't be able to miss it. The Jessup offices take up all three floors of a fairly large building."

"I appreciate your help and I'll catch up with you tomorrow," Sol said.

It seemed the earnest first half of Sol's statement wasn't marred by the lie that was tacked onto the end, because Dennis accepted them both without question. "Nice meeting you and I'll be sure to clear an appointment for you in the morning. What was your name again?"

But Sol had already left. He heard the question, but had made it far enough away for him to keep from making up a name on the spot. Since another question didn't follow, Sol knew he'd escaped Dennis well enough. After that, it was a simple matter of following the instructions he'd been given.

Chapter 21

At times, when he'd had a moment to think about such things after working in the silver mine or sitting in his room back in Warren, Sol had thought about how much fun it would be to just pick up and ride away to some new place. Now that he'd made that jump, Sol couldn't help but wonder why he hadn't made it sooner. Then again, he'd jumped in a different direction than he would have expected back in those tired moments after work.

Rather than walk the unfamiliar streets and soak up the unfamiliar sights and sounds, Sol kept his head down and his eyes in motion. He didn't savor the things he hadn't seen before. Instead, he watched for anyone who looked at him for too long or groups of men who kept pace with him for any longer than they should have.

Plenty of men he saw were armed. That was nothing new.

Plenty of folks glanced his way. That was nothing new, either.

The way Sol looked back at all those folks was new.

It felt like a new suit of clothes that he'd been forced to wear. It itched in spots and fit perfectly in others. It also made him act differently, the way a formal suit made a man act differently than when he was wearing his favorite pair of jeans and an old shirt.

Like it or not, Sol wore his new suit and couldn't just take it off at the end of the day. It wasn't a second skin. It was his only skin.

The Jessup Mining Company could be seen as soon as Sol rounded the next corner. There was no way for him to miss the large building that stood out from all the others huddled around it. Unlike many of its stucco-coated neighbors, the Jessup building looked as if it had been plucked from New York City and dropped down onto the New Mexico street. It didn't fit in with the rest and obviously wasn't about to try and change any time soon.

Sol approached the building, but stopped when he was across the street from it. Now that he was there, he didn't know quite what to do. His hand brushed against his new pistol, but the only target he had was the large building itself. As attractive as the notion of shooting holes in some of those windows might have been, Sol knew better than to draw his gun and start firing like some kid with his nose out of joint.

When he spotted the figure on the corner across from him, Sol thought he might have just been given the target he'd been looking for. The figure kept still until he knew he'd been spotted. Then the figure turned toward Sol and began stalking straight toward him. Sol's first impulse was to look around and make certain he wasn't being set up for an ambush. The last thing he needed was to ruin this plan by announcing his presence at the wrong time. When Sol looked back to the figure, however, he couldn't find him.

Sol twitched to look at something moving toward him from a slightly different angle, but it was already too late. The other man was upon him and shoving Sol against a building.

Night hadn't quite fallen yet, but the sun was at such a drastic angle that half the town was in shadow and the other half was bathed in light. That bright light sliced in just right so the shadows seemed even blacker. When Sol landed in one of those shadows, he thought he'd knocked his head against the wall hard enough to temporarily blind him.

"What in the blazes are you doing here?" the other man snarled.

Sol blinked and asked, "Nester? Is that you?"

"Yeah, it's me. I'm supposed to be scouting this place out, remember? What's yer excuse for bein' here?"

Trying to knock the old man's hand away from him, Sol merely cracked his wrist against what felt like an iron post. Only after he made sure Sol knew he hadn't forced him to let go, Nester relaxed his grip.

"Come on," Nester said as he shoved Sol away from the Jessup building and walked beside him. "Let's get away from this spot before someone catches sight of you."

After they'd rounded a corner and put the Jessup building well behind them, Nester growled, "Start explainin' yerself."

"I finished what I was supposed to do, so I came over here to get a look at this place. After coming all this way, I couldn't bear to just circle around this spot rather than—"

"Rather than dive in like a danged fool?" Nester cut in.

Sol shrugged, but didn't have much else to say.

"Eh, no harm done, I suppose," Nester muttered. "Besides, it's good you got the look you were after, because we ain't staying around here much longer."

"Why?"

"Because you ruffled a lot more feathers than I gave ya credit for, that's why," Nester replied with a smirk. Glancing up and down the street, he lowered his voice to a rasping whisper as he lowered his head so nobody could even see his lips moving. "The shipment's already here, but they're movin' it to some other spot."

"How do you know that?" Sol asked.

"I skulked around long enough to catch sight of a bunch of well-dressed fellas marching to a lot out back. There's a wagon and a real nice stagecoach bein' prepared, but I'd say they won't be leaving until the morning."

Sol looked at the old man suspiciously. "How do you know who's traveling, where they're going and why?"

Scowling back at the younger man, Nester snapped, "Here I thought you'd be happy to hear about this. With them on the move, it'll be a whole lot easier to hit them."

"I'll be happy once I know it's accurate."

"There's that instinct of yers," Nester said. "I heard most of this after I got into the building. All I needed to do was follow the sounds of voices. It wasn't hard, on account of the place was mostly empty at this time of night and the man who did most of the talking was real loud about it. Seems like you ain't much of a favorite son around here. That price on yer head was upped to twenty-five hundred."

Sol blinked and took a moment for that last part to sink in. "What?"

Nester nodded like a father watching his boy win a footrace. "Only a little ways out and you already got a decent price for yer scalp. Do you know how long it took for me ta be worth that much? Of course, that was a few years ago and rewards weren't quite as high as they are now."

"So if there's more money being offered for me, that means there'll be more bounty hunters after me?"

Nester kept nodding. "That's what bounty hunters do. Then again, it also depends on how many of them notices were posted. Could be that nobody worth mentioning has seen them yet. We could always make sure they get seen, though."

"Why would we do that?"

"So you get more men gunnin' for ya," Nester replied as if he were explaining the simplest thing in the world. "The more men you got gunnin' for ya, the more folks are out there spreadin' the word about what a tough hombre you are. That sort of word of mouth's invaluable."

"And what happens when they find me?" Sol asked.

"Then you deal with 'em, of course. That's how this whole thing works. The more of a reputation you build, the easier the jobs get. Soon, folks'd rather hand over what you want than fight you. An ounce of fear's worth a gallon of spilt blood. That lesson's worth more'n you know, boy."

Feeling as if his head were filled with a dozen swarming bees, Sol forced himself to look through the confusion and steer himself back onto his original path. "All I care about right now is this shipment you're talking about. Are you sure you heard enough to know all the details?"

"I heard plenty," Nester replied. "The rest I got from a real good source."

"What source is that?"

Now the old men grinned and showed a set of small teeth that ground against each other. His slender face could barely contain the excitement that was so obviously churning in him. "You want to know how I know? Why don't you come along with me and see fer yerself?"

"Can't you just tell me?" Sol asked.

Nester shook his head. "Nah. I think you're gonna want to see this for yerself."

Sol didn't like the grin on Nester's face any more than he liked the tone in the old man's voice. What burned Sol even more was the knowledge that he would have to play the old man's game for now if there was any hope of getting the answers he wanted. Finally, Sol said, "All right, then. Show me."

Nester led the way to a small shack that Sol guessed was an outhouse. Upon closer examination, the shack was slightly bigger than an outhouse and too small to be a home. Any more of Sol's guesses as to why the shack had been built were forgotten when he got a look at what was inside.

The man in the shack looked to be in his forties and might have been wearing fancy clothes at the start of the evening. Those clothes were ripped and dirty now, however. He was also gagged, blindfolded and hog-tied. When he heard the door open, the man squirmed and flopped in his corner as he struggled to get himself upright.

Although he tried to talk, the man's words were reduced to a muffled flow of grunts and groans thanks to the knotted bandana that was stuffed into his mouth.

Sol couldn't take his eyes off of the man. The fact that he was even seeing a captive in that state was enough to root him to his spot. He wasn't shaken out of his trance until he heard Nester's voice.

"He thinks I left another fella in here with him," the old man whispered. He then stepped forward so he could pull the bandana away from the captive's mouth.

"Is that still you?" the captive asked. "Is there someone else here? I demand to know what's going on! My employers will not tolerate this!"

"Hush up now," Nester said in a tranquil voice that seemed genuinely peculiar in comparison to that of the captive. "Remember what I told you before."

The captive's mouth hung open, but he kept any more words from escaping it. Instead, he nodded vigorously.

"Good," Nester said. "Now tell me once more about that shipment."

"I didn't tell you anything. I won't . . ."

When Nester raised his hand, he was holding his pistol in front of the captive's face. Although the blindfolded man couldn't see the gun, he could certainly hear the metallic click of the hammer being thumbed back.

"It doesn't matter if you know or not," the captive quickly explained. "You won't be able to get to it."

"Tell me anyways," Nester prodded. "What's being shipped?"

"It's . . ." The captive's throat pinched shut, which obviously required every bit of the man's will. His efforts were quickly broken down when Nester placed the barrel of his gun against his forehead. "It's a shipment of funds coming from some of our mining interests," the captive spat.

"How much?" Nester asked.

"I don't know for certain. It's several shipments that were held up since there have been some concerns with moving it safely. It would normally come here and stay here, but there's been problems. There was a robbery of an earlier shipment, so we're taking extra precautions."

Nester glanced over to Sol and gave him a knowing grin. "Where's the shipment going?" Nester asked.

"I don't know the name of the town, but it's about two days' ride from here."

"Which way?"

"East," the captive sputtered as though he was on the verge of tears. "Two days' ride east of here. Can I go now?"

"I don't know," Nester replied. "We'll see if my associate and I can come to an agreement once you've told us everything."

"That's all there is. I swear it!"

"Why's it being shipped anywhere?" Sol asked. "Aren't there banks here?"

The sound of another man's voice made the captive jump and tremble. When he spoke, he sounded several steps closer to blubbering. "This money is kept separate from the rest."

"Why?" Sol snapped. "Because it's skimmed off the top before you send it on down the line?"

"Yes," the captive sobbed. "Mr. Oberlee wants to make sure his share isn't at risk if there's going to be another robbery. Please just let me go now. That's all I know!"

Kicking the shack's door shut, Nester pulled the bandana back up around the man's face and stuffed it into his mouth. The captive squirmed and thrashed as if he were fighting for his life.

Sol could barely stand to watch.

Nester stepped outside and motioned for Sol to follow. "Anything else you want to ask? I'd say he'll answer damn near anything right now."

"No," Sol said. "Just let him go."

Judging by the look on Nester's face, someone might have thought he'd just been asked to cut off one of his own hands. "Let him go? Why would we do something like that?"

"What else are we supposed to do with him?"

Nester cocked his head to one side and didn't say a word. He didn't need to say anything, since his intentions were written clearly enough across his face.

"No," Sol said to the unspoken verdict. "I won't be a party to an execution."

Apparently, Sol had spoken a bit louder than he'd hoped. From inside the shack, the muffled voice lamented through the bandana in a series of shuddering moans.

Chuckling under his breath, Nester said, "I think

you just hurt the man a lot more than I was plannin' on."

"You weren't going to kill him?"

Squinting so he could study every line in Sol's face, Nester replied, "Not unless you think it'd be best."

Sol pulled in a breath and shook his head. "Maybe we should find out what sort of precautions he was talking about. Other than that, I'd say he's told us plenty and we should let him go. That is . . . if you think he was telling us the truth."

Nester chuckled. "If that fella could lie well enough to fool us in the state he's in, he'd be working at a poker table instead'a at some crooked mining outfit. You go in and get what you need. I'll stay outside to make sure you don't get interrupted."

"All right. I think I can manage." Before Sol could walk back into the shack, he felt Nester's iron grip close around his forearm.

"Don't you let him go," Nester said in an icy tone. "You do that and we might as well ride right out of here and forget about that shipment."

Sol nodded and took a few deep breaths. He let them out like steam being pushed through a piston and then stomped into the shack. If he was asked about it later, he might not have been able to recall exactly what he'd said to that man who was bound and gagged. All Sol cared about was that the job didn't take long. When he stepped outside again, Sol was glad to feel the cool air upon his face.

"Well?" Nester asked.

"There's going to be some hired guns riding along with the shipment," Sol reported. "There's also going to be a few riflemen hanging back a ways to scout for an ambush and pick off anyone who tries to attack the shipment head-on."

Nester's eyebrows lifted and he let out a low whistle. "Sharpshooters, huh? I didn't hear that when I questioned him before."

"Let him go," Sol said.

Shaking his head, Nester replied, "Can't do that. He'll scamper off and warn the others."

"He's already missing. Maybe you should have thought about that before you kidnapped him."

"He may be missing," Nester said, "but he won't be missed. He was sent away while all them others got the wagons prepared. His job's to get a message to a courier and that's been done."

"What did the message say?" Sol asked. When he got a casual shrug, Sol didn't hesitate to press the matter. "You must have talked about that before I got here. What did it say?"

Nester smirked. "Just that everything was fine on this end. That means the shipment must be ready to roll. Hopefully whatever men they hired in that other town won't have itchy trigger fingers."

"I thought that town was supposed to be two days' ride from here."

"Sure," Nester replied. "It'd take that long for a team of wagons. A single rider on a good horse could cut that down a hell of a lot. Fact is, I heard of some messengers who could bolt outta one place and get where they're goin' in—"

Cutting the old man off with a few frustrated waves, Sol said, "I'll take your word for it. I just don't want that man killed, is all."

"Why?" Nester asked. "You squeamish?"

"No. I'm already wanted for one murder and I'd rather not have another one tacked on for no good reason."

Before too long, Nester nodded and gave half a shrug. "Fine, I suppose. My knots should hold long enough for us to get outta here. I can get him situated so he won't be a bother to anyone till we're long gone."

"But . . . you said . . ."

"I said I didn't wanna let him go," Nester replied. "You need to listen to yer elders."

"Good. The matter's settled. I'm getting something to drink." With that, Sol turned his back to Nester and walked away.

But Sol didn't put that shack too far behind him. Instead, he doubled back after several paces and found a nice, dark spot from which he could watch Nester slink back into the dirty old building. For a few hard moments, Sol couldn't hear anything. Then the door opened and Nester walked outside. The old man turned to look into the shack and snarled something at the captive that Sol couldn't hear.

Nester eyed the captive the way a cat watched a mouse moments before it tore the rodent's head off. The old man's hand remained upon the grip of his pistol, but his pistol remained in its holster. As the wind howled and dust was kicked up from the ground, everything was set into motion. Even the shack swayed and groaned beneath the push of the breeze.

Nester, however, didn't move.

Sol held his breath and waited for the old man to put the captive down with one shot. He was ready to draw his gun and chase Nester away, but Sol wasn't even certain he could do so and follow it up with anything worthwhile. If he drew too slowly, it wouldn't count for anything. If he made too much noise, he could catch one of Nester's bullets for himself. If he fired and missed, he would end up the same way. No matter what, all of those outcomes ended with that captive dead on the ground and Sol unable to do much of anything. It might be too late for Sol, but it was sure too late for that pathetic man in the shack.

And so Sol waited.

Nester finished what he had to say, shut the door, wedged some rocks under it to keep it in place and then walked away from the shack. After that, he glanced over to Sol and winked.

"Testin' me now, huh?" Nester asked. "Keep them instincts, boy."

Chapter 22

Sol couldn't get any sleep. Despite the fact that he felt almost too tired to stand upright, his thoughts were racing around at a dizzying pace and his muscles were too drained to keep up. The first hints of dawn had crept into the sky by the time Sol drifted off. Shortly after he was finally asleep, he was awakened by a couple of sharp shakes. The effect was more than a little disconcerting.

"Get yer clothes on and get ready to ride," Nester growled. "Them wagons have already rolled out of that lot behind the Jessup building."

Swinging his legs over the side of his bed, Sol ran his fingers through his hair and focused his eyes. He didn't know how Nester had gotten into his room and surely didn't know how the old man had managed to sneak up on him.

"This is gonna be one hell of a day, boy," Nester declared. "I can feel it in my bones." Judging by the smirk upon Nester's face, nobody would have guessed that he didn't like the earlier hours of the day. The old man drew his pistol, spun it around his finger and then dropped it into its holster. After that, he left the room and whistled all the way down the hall.

Sol gathered up his remaining belongings, pulled on his clothes and set about the necessary tasks. Fees for the hotel and stable were squared away and the horses were saddled by the time Nester showed his face again. After climbing onto his horse's back, Nester snapped his reins and led the way out of town.

The desert air hung like a sandy curtain draped over Albuquerque. Within an hour after leaving, Sol and Nester spotted the wagons that had been behind the Jessup building, so they steered away from the trail and circled around to put plenty of space between them and the shipment. After signaling for them to fall back even more, Nester pointed toward a rocky slope that would give them a vantage from higher ground. The two of them made it to the slope, ditched their horses halfway along the rocky surface and crawled to the top upon their bellies.

It wasn't a steep rise, but was good enough to keep the horses hidden while Sol and Nester gazed out upon the caravan. Sol wished he had a spyglass, but Nester seemed to be doing just fine with the eyes God had given him.

The caravan was a slow-moving beast that crawled as though each horse was a limb scraping at the sandy ground to gain another inch. Two wagons made up the body of this beast and they rolled along noisily enough to be heard with just a bit of concentration on Sol's behalf. He could only assume there were two men on each of the wagons, but there could easily have been more. Riding alongside the wagons, spaced fairly evenly to the left and right, were three riders on each side. Six men on horseback accompanied the wagons: One man on either side rode a few yards ahead of the wagons. Another two rode a few yards behind and the remaining two drifted in between. Every now and then, a stray beam from the sun would glint off of bared gunmetal, but Sol figured it would be safest to guess that all the men in that group were armed.

"See them over there?" Nester asked as he pointed away from the caravan and to the southeast.

Sol squinted and shook his head. "No."

"Don't spend so much time gawkin' at what's easiest to see. That'll still be there when you want to look again. Try gettin' a glance at what's off to the sides. That's where the real goodies are."

Rather than rebuke the old man's advice, Sol took it. He shifted his eyes away from the rolling caravan and gazed off in the direction that Nester was pointing. It took a bit of scowling and squinting, but Sol eventually caught a glimpse of another horseman at least a hundred yards or so away.

"How in blazes did you see that?" Sol asked.

Nester chuckled without taking his eyes from the sight. "I know what to look for, is all. I count two other riders keeping clear of the rest. How about you?"

"I only see one. Wait a second. There might be another one even farther ahead."

"That's my two."

Sol would have loved to catch sight of another rider keeping pace with the caravan, just to get one over on the old man. Then again, the notion of there being even more guns out there only served to tighten the knot in Sol's gut. Once he'd drifted to both ends of that scale, Sol settled somewhere in between and took an earnest look at what was in front of him. "Just those two," he finally admitted. "That's all I see."

"Good. That makes things easier."

"Easier? There's eight men on horses and at least two or three on each of those wagons!"

Nester slapped his hand against Sol's mouth and then shoved him toward the ground. Sliding down so his own shoulders were scraping rock and dirt, the old man snarled, "Keep yer voice down. You wanna give us away?"

Sol lowered his voice, but didn't take any of the edge from it. "None of those men can hear us. And how the hell do you consider this easy? We should turn back."

"This is the life, boy. You wanna be a bad man, you gotta be ready to ride in and take what you want. You think the only thing keepin' men like us from bein' rich is the letter of the law? Most men carry guns to shoot two things: snakes and us. The difference in fights like this comes in who's more prepared to shoot back. Right now, that'd be us."

"How do you figure?"

"Because we see them and they don't see us. That's just about all it takes."

"Just about?" Sol asked.

Nester drew his gun and held it up to his cheek as if he were about to kiss it. The weapon was dented and worn away in spots, which made it look as if it had been brought into this world at about the same time as its owner. With a flick of his fingers, Nester checked the rounds inside the cylinder. He closed it with a snap of his wrist and rolled onto his belly so he could get another look at the caravan. "I'd say the only way for us to get close to them wagons would be for you to take out that rear guard first. That should buy me enough time to ride in and drop a few of them guards. After that, you can ride in behind and catch a few of them boys by surprise."

"I've got a better idea," Sol said. "I'll go in first."

"And what?" Nester snapped. "Show that famous face o' yours to a bunch'a men who plastered them notices all over creation? What the hell you got in that head of yers? It's gotta be mush or some sort of stew because it sure as hell ain't brains."

"Riding at them now would be like trying to charge a fort that's already barricaded and ready for an attack," Sol said. "Especially this early when they're all sharp and ready to shoot at something. I'll sneak in to get a closer look at what's in there."

"Why you?"

Sol didn't hesitate one bit before replying, "Because I'm not the one itching for a fight. I'm also the one who helped put a few of Charlie's shipments together back in Warren. All that money won't just be sitting in those wagons. It'll be locked up in a safe or a lockbox or . . . I don't know. It'll be locked up, that's for sure. I've worked in enough mines and whatever's shipped out of there is always locked up. They use decoys or any number of tricks and I might be able to see through whatever tricks these men are using."

Nester scowled at Sol for a few seconds and then took a few quick glances at the wagons. Just when it seemed his eyes couldn't be angry enough, the storm behind them lifted and he shrugged. "All right. Fine.

You wanna go in and try to get in close to get yer revenge? You best do it real careful. If you take a wrong step and ruin this, ye're on yer own. I ain't about to risk my neck comin' in to rescue you."

Sol nodded. "That's fine. This isn't about revenge. I've already told you that."

"So glad you agree."

"And tonight, when they're in camp," Sol added, "I'll sneak in and have a word with one of them bosses."

Nester snapped his head back and looked Sol over as if he were inspecting the younger man for the first time. "Just crawl right into their camp, huh? You could barely handle robbin' a trading post and now you think you can handle this?"

"It's why I'm here."

"Damn, boy. You might have a bit of sand in ya, after all. Still some mush between yer ears," Nester added, "but plenty of sand."

True to his word, Nester rode along for the rest of that day without firing a shot at the caravan or even riding too close to it. The old man focused so much attention on those wagons and the horses surrounding them that he barely seemed to blink. The only other words he spoke during daylight hours were the occasional grunt to signal for a stop and another grunt when it was safe to ride again.

It didn't take long for Sol to pick up on what Nester was doing and what caused him to do it. By midday, Sol could spot the scouts that rode ahead and behind the wagons. Sometimes, Sol would only see a wisp of dust kicked up by those distant horses, and other times, he could spot when one of those scouts slipped up and skylined himself by cresting a rise or dwelling for too long upon a tempting piece of high ground. When that happened, both outlaws got behind cover and stayed there until the scouts moved on. If there wasn't available cover, Sol and Nester would drop from their saddles and pull the horses down along with them so all four of them could lie on the ground with their bellies against the dirt. It didn't take long before the horses were more accustomed to this drill than Sol himself.

Throughout all of this following, watching and hiding, Sol never stopped thinking about what he intended on doing. It was obvious that Nester was the better choice to sneak among those wagons when they would eventually come to a stop. Still, Sol meant to follow through on his declared course of action. As he'd already told Nester, it was why he'd come this far.

If the rest of that mining company would get their comeuppance for all the cheating and stealing they'd done, Sol was going to be there when it happened. He'd been there to put Charlie in his place, so it was only fitting that Sol finish the job.

It wasn't revenge. Sol had told himself that over and over again.

Nester didn't speak out against Sol's plan the entire day. It wasn't until nightfall that the old man even broached the subject. The wagons had come to a stop alongside a wide stream that wasn't much deeper than a puddle. The horses were being unhitched from the wagons and the scouts had taken up positions about sixty yards to the north and south of the camp.

Having left their own horses several paces back,

Nester and Sol crawled in from the east to watch as men guarding the shipment prepared for supper and a pair of dandies stepped out of the wagons to stretch their legs.

"You still intendin' on sneakin' into that camp?" Nester asked.

Sol nodded, despite the doubts that circled his mind. "Yeah."

"Then wait until after they eat. I don't know what they brought for food, but folks tend to let their eyes wander while they're fixin' their meals and while they're eatin' 'em. Afterwards, they tend to talk, smoke or give their eyes a rest. That should be a good time to get closer." Glancing at the sky, he added, "It'll be darker by then too."

"What will you be doing while I'm away?" Closing his eyes and steeling himself, Sol added, "Should I even try to look for you if things go bad?"

Reaching out to slap Sol on the back, Nester said, "I'll be doin' my part to see to it it don't go bad. That's what partners do."

"What about all that suspicion talk?"

"Oh, that still holds true. Partners can still be suspicious of each other, but that don't mean we want to see them get killed. If them suspicions turn out to be true, it's best that you put the traitor down yerself. That way, it keeps the gang from looking weak."

Sol watched the old man for a few seconds, but quickly saw the flicker of a smile on his face. "So we're a gang now, huh?"

"Not hardly, but nobody else needs to know that. Do you recall any stories about me robbin' a Cavalry payroll bound for a fort in Sioux country?"

"Yes," Sol replied as he jumped onto the new path the conversation had taken. "Wasn't that the one where you and your partners hit two stagecoaches at once and fought your way through a dozen guards?"

"More or less. There was only one partner and the rest was all talk."

"So you didn't rob that payroll?" Sol asked.

Nester chuckled and was quick to say, "Oh, we robbed the hell out of that payroll. It was just me and one other partner. By the time we got to them coaches, the soldiers had heard so many stories about Nester Quarles and his gang of marauding hell-raisers that they thought it best to hide a portion of the money and hand over the rest just to see if we would take it and leave."

"So you robbed two stagecoaches using only two men?" Sol asked.

"Nah. We kicked up a lot of dust and took the piece of that payroll they were willing to hand over. The point is, we walked away with some easy money and didn't have to fire a shot because we worked hard to be feared and never showed one sign of weakness. If'n you get into that camp and spy enough for us to hit them wagons at just the right spot, you'll make us look like a force to be reckoned with and that's somethin' we can bank for later. So go do what you gotta do. Just keep yer eyes open and watch yerself."

Sol nodded and pulled in a deep breath. Although it felt good to taste the night air as it filled his lungs, it didn't do much to dispel the nervousness that had filled him up like mold in a dank cellar.

As if sensing Sol's hesitancy, Nester pointed toward the camp and said, "It ain't so hard. Just look for the darkest spots and crawl in through 'em. There are bound to be a boss or two in one of them big tents next to those wagons. They'll know about any tricks or lockboxes and such."

Sure enough, there had been two tents pitched between the wagons. Two more were scattered closer to the fire, but those were more like sheets propped up by a pair of sticks. "You think I'll be able to sneak past the gunmen?" Sol asked.

"If ye're light on yer feet, maybe. I wasn't never too good at that sort of thing myself, but I knew a fella we used to call Weasel who could—"

Sol cut the story short with a quickly raised hand. "Maybe you can tell that story later."

"Sure," Nester grunted with a nod of his head. "If you get seen by a guard, stab him or cut his throat. You don't want to make noise by firing a gun unless you got no other choice."

Even with that bit of advice tucked away inside his head, Sol didn't feel much better about his chances. Then again, after allowing himself to skid this far down the slope, there wasn't much else to do than keep rolling and pray that he didn't break too many bones before hitting the bottom.

Chapter 23

No matter how many stories Sol had heard about the infamous Nester Quarles, he still found himself amazed that the old man could hit the nail on the head so perfectly. Not only was he able to get close to the camp using some of Nester's advice, but he was able to get even closer because the men in the caravan were lazing about after finishing their supper. The acrid hint of cigar smoke hung in the air along with the lazy banter among the men.

Every so often, Sol would swear that he'd been spotted. He could feel eyes on his back like spiders crawling beneath his shirt. He froze and held his breath, but nothing happened. There were no alarmed shouts or shots fired, so Sol kept moving. When he got close enough to touch one of the wagons, Sol could scarcely believe it. When he heard footsteps approaching that wagon, Sol was certain his game was about to be brought to an end.

Reacting out of nothing but instinct, Sol dropped flat against the ground and rolled beneath the closest wagon. When he came to a stop, he swore he could see Patricia's frightened face staring back at him in the darkness. In the blink of an eye, Sol was taken back to that night in Warren when he'd heard those shots fired and he'd thought someone was trying to rob Charlie. Now he was the robber sneaking around in the night and he was the one skulking about in the shadows.

Since he wasn't quite certain how to swallow that notion, Sol pushed it from his mind and concentrated on the task at hand.

Whoever had been approaching the wagon kept walking. Sol could see the man's boots pass by a few paces and then pause just long enough for Sol to think he might have been spotted. He heard a wet cough, which was followed by a juicy wad of spit that landed within inches of Sol's face. Although Sol managed to keep from getting wet, he still got dirt kicked into his face as the other man walked away from the wagon.

Sol didn't have any time to count his blessings. Another pair of men appeared and walked toward him. One set of feet was wrapped in old boots and the other was clad in more expensive, albeit dusty, shoes.

"Fine meal, Cam. Fine meal," one of the men declared in a smooth, even tone.

The second man chuckled, but was obviously trying not to laugh too hard. "There's only so much a man can do with beans and jerky, Mr. Oberlee. Hopefully it didn't stick in your craw too much."

Now that they were talking, Sol didn't have any trouble guessing which voice belonged to which set of feet.

"On the contrary! It was splendid. Of course, the whiskey didn't hurt."

Both men laughed as one of them pulled on the wagon's door.

Sol's fingers clenched at the ground as thoughts of the wagon moving slowly away to leave him in the open churned through his head. Even though the wheels surrounding him didn't move, both men were still close enough to hear if Sol let out so much as a hiccup. In fact, they were facing the wagon as if contemplating on hunkering down to get a look underneath.

"Locked up tight?" the more refined of the two voices asked.

After a bit more rattling from the wagon, the other man replied, "Looks that way, Mr. Oberlee. You should probably be heading to your tent for the night."

"You think any robbers will attack me in the four steps it'll take me to get there?"

After a brief pause, the gruffer of the two replied, "I suppose not. Just shout if you catch sight of anything peculiar."

"I'll be sure to do that, Cam. Have a good night."

"I'm on first watch, so my good night won't start for a bit. Thanks all the same, though."

Sol forced himself to look at the ground rather than at the feet directly in front of him. He'd been staring at those ankles so intently that he thought the men attached to them might just feel it. After the time it would have taken to tip a few hats, the boots turned away from the dusty shoes and walked away. The shoes turned around, but stayed put. Sol almost knocked his head against the bottom of the wagon when he saw something drop down directly to the right of his spot.

Thankfully, it wasn't a gun barrel or set of eyes

being pointed at him. It was a match that had been dropped directly beside the wagon. Judging by the smoke still curling from the matchstick's charred tip, it was recently struck and promptly blown out.

In a matter of seconds, Sol could smell more cigar smoke. If Mr. Oberlee meant to have one last cigar before retiring for the night, Sol figured he could accommodate him.

The rifleman sat with his legs stretched out in front of him and his back against a rock. It wasn't the most comfortable spot he could have picked, but it did allow him to watch over the camp from a good height and at a safe distance. From where he was sitting, the rifleman could see both wagons, the campfire and all the tents without having to move his eyes. His rifle was propped against the rock beside him and his horse was tied to a branch a few paces behind the rock.

A place for everything and everything in its place.

While he wasn't close enough to smell the cooking fires or the cigars that had followed the meal, the rifleman could watch as the men in the camp had their little social and prepared for a comfortable night's sleep. Surely, the dandies traveling surrounded by all those guards would have considered the accommodations barbaric, but it beat the stuffing out of eating some scraps of jerky and washing them down with water. Running his tongue along the top of his mouth, the rifleman swore he could still taste the bit of rust that had formed at the bottom of his canteen.

Not wanting to make the noise of spitting the sourness from his mouth, the rifleman swallowed it and reached for another swig of rusty water. His eyes never strayed from the camp. He'd been paid to watch it, so that's what he intended on doing.

When he got his canteen in hand, he brought it to his lips and tilted it back. Just then he spotted some movement that seemed out of place. What caused his hackles to rise was the fact that the movement came from beneath one of the wagons.

The rifleman took his sip of water and narrowed his eyes as if he could filter out the shadows from the little bit of starlight. He still couldn't see much more than some movement on the fringe of the camp, so he reached out with his other hand for the spyglass lying on the ground next to him. While letting the water trickle from the canteen into his mouth, he put the spyglass to his eye and settled his view upon the wagon.

"What the hell?" he muttered.

Despite what he'd just seen, the rifleman wasn't about to dump his last canteen. He set it down so it would remain upright and then used both hands to steady the spyglass. Sure enough, it wasn't just some critter scampering out from beneath that wagon. It was a man. Now that man was sliding along the back-side of the wagon and making his way toward the largest tent.

The rifleman didn't hear anything that didn't belong in the night. There was a bit of wind and some dust or fallen leaves brushing against the rock, but nothing whatsoever that would have alerted him before the leathery hand clamped around his mouth from some-where behind his spot.

He tried to reach for his rifle, but the weapon was gone. The rifleman's fingertips scraped against rock as he was pulled backward over the same boulder he'd been leaning against. Before he could do anything about it, his legs were flailing toward the sky and his back was being dragged against the top of the rock.

For a few seconds, the rifleman was upside down. Once gravity had its way with him, the rifleman slid toward the ground and landed awkwardly upon his neck and shoulders. His next breath became wedged in his lungs as the lower half of his body folded down to crush what was normally the upper half.

Reflexively, the rifleman swatted at the hand that still pressed tightly against his mouth. His hands knocked against forearms that felt more like thin iron bars. The hand that kept the rifleman quiet now pushed down hard enough to press the back of the rifleman's head into the dirt.

Still flailing and fighting, the rifleman felt one of his boots connect with something solid. He knew it wasn't rock, because whatever he'd hit gave way for a second and then came right back at him. In the next moment, the rifleman could see only a gnarled old face scowling down at him like a kid inspecting a trapped spider through greedy fingers.

" 'Fraid that wasn't good enough," Nester said as he raised his free hand up close to his ear. "This just ain't yer lucky night."

Rather than stare too long at Nester's leering face, the rifleman caught the glint of metal in Nester's hand. The knife clutched in the old man's hand had a short, curved blade that had a wickedness in its very shape. Using all the strength he could muster, the rifleman twisted to one side before he was slit open by that blade. He pulled his head and torso in the same direction, straining to clear a path for the incoming blade. He pulled his legs that way as well, hoping against hope to catch Nester with any sort of kick.

Gritting his teeth, the rifleman felt the rush of air next to his face as Nester's fist dropped. The blade drove into the dirt like a stake and didn't stop moving until the knife's guard thumped against the earth. Rather than waste a single moment, the rifleman kept twisting at the waist until his shins caught Nester in the ribs.

The old man grunted and rolled with the impact. He moved swiftly for someone of his years, but never let go of his knife. Instead, Nester pivoted around the embedded knife until he'd put some distance between himself and another kick. As soon as he saw the rifleman get himself upended, Nester gathered his own legs beneath him and locked eyes with his opponent.

Squatting with his back to the rock, the rifleman glanced around for his weapon and couldn't find it. His hand then went to the pistol at his side and immediately wrapped around the carved wooden grip. Before he could get the pistol from its holster, the rifleman saw Nester move again. This time, the old man lunged forward. Nester's right arm snapped out, pulling the knife from the ground and delivering it straight into the rifleman's midsection.

For a moment, the rifleman couldn't breathe. Then, like some sort of miracle, he was able to pull in a gulp of air. The action didn't even hurt much. That was when he realized the old man hadn't been able to flip the knife around and had only managed to deliver a blow using the blunt end of the knife's handle. Although he wasn't gutted just yet, the rifleman had been hit hard enough to force the wind from his lungs. When he saw the old man flip the knife around so its blade was pointed at him, the rifleman leaped away from the incoming swing and refilled his lungs before landing on his side. Nester's blade slashed through empty air, hissing loudly enough to be heard over the sound of the rifleman's landing.

"I don't know who the hell you are," the rifleman wheezed, "but you just made the last mistake of your life."

Nester grinned and tossed the knife back and forth between his two hands. "Oh, we'll just have'ta see about that."

Sol chose a quiet moment to crawl out from under the wagon. He regretted his decision the second he realized that it was so quiet that he could hear every one of his own breaths echoing in his ears. Hopefully, the rest of the camp wasn't able to hear him so well. Since it was too late to take back what noise he'd made, Sol was a bit more careful as he kept going.

The few gunmen he could see were in their spots around the camp's perimeter. Since they were expecting trouble to be coming at them from the outside, not one of those hired guns was paying much attention to what was going on within the camp itself. Figuring he'd know soon enough if he'd been discovered, Sol continued working his way toward the largest tent.

A dim flicker glowed from within that tent to cast a man's hazy outline upon the canvas. The outline of that figure looked like a charcoal drawing that had somehow come to life. It made its way from one end of the tent to another before finally growing big enough to blot out one entire half of the tent. After a quick exhale, the man inside blew out the flickering light and the shadows reclaimed their territory around the dying campfire.

Sol briefly entertained the notion of getting out while he was ahead and crawling away from the camp. That thought flew from his mind as soon as Sol reminded himself of why he was there. Matt had been shot, but Charlie didn't care about that. All he or any of these bosses cared about was their money and making certain it was escorted safely so it could be stashed away.

Sol was glad he'd stolen Charlie's shipment. The longer he thought about what had brought him to where he was now, the more Sol wanted to push the situation further. Whether he was doing the right thing or not, he was taking a stand. Things might not have gone the way he would have liked, but he couldn't change them now. He was in his spot and playing his role, so he might as well see it through. At the very least, he'd let these greedy bosses know what it was like to be trampled.

Sol nodded as he squared all of that away within his head. All of his senses had become clearer. He could taste the air and feel the grit against his skin. His ears picked up every crunch of nearby boots against the ground and every tired clearing of a throat. The guards were still content to watch for threats coming from outside the camp, so Sol approached the big tent.

From what he could hear, the men inside that tent were settling in for the night. Sol could tell there was someone brushing against the canvas from the inside.

Having been pitched in a rush, the tent wasn't tied down as securely as it could have been. As such, the bottom edge fluttered loosely against the ground. Sol made his way to a spot midway between two stakes and tested the lowest edge of the canvas.

As he'd hoped, there was just enough room for Sol to get a look inside. He pulled the bottom up a few inches and saw the legs of a folded cot and the sagging canvas where a figure was suspended just above the dirt. There was no light within the tent and one man's snores were already drifting through the air. Sol pulled the tent up a bit more and squeezed beneath it until he was inside.

At his first opportunity, Sol propped himself up on all fours. In the middle of the tent, there was a post to support the canvas ceiling. Hanging from the post, there was a shaving mirror and a small, unlit lantern. Two cots took up most of the space within the tent, each of which held a man wrapped up in a bundle of blankets. Next to each cot was a stool. The stool closest to Sol was topped by a set of neatly folded clothes and a small pistol that was so well cared for, it sparkled in what little light made it into the tent. Sol could also see something else in the darkness: a pair of frightened eyes staring at him.

The man was lying upon the closest cot and he was too frightened to move. For a moment, Sol was also frozen. Both men regained their senses at the same time and both of them made a lunge for the pistol resting upon the stool.

Since he'd been the one that was creeping in the dark, Sol wasn't caught quite as off guard as the man in the cot. Therefore, Sol was able to snap his hand out and grab the pistol while the man in the cot flailed for the weapon in a blind panic. As soon as Sol got a hold of the shiny weapon, he jumped to his feet.

The man in the cot looked up and opened his mouth to say something, but was cut short when Sol pointed the shiny pistol at him.

"What's all the . . . ?"

The man in the second cot was just stirring and had gotten those words out when he saw Sol standing in the middle of the tent with the gun in his hand.

Before he had a chance to think twice about it, Sol drew his own pistol and aimed it at the tent's other resident. Now he held a gun in each hand and had both of the men in check. Since the first man was closest to leaving his cot, Sol moved in that direction and glared at him.

"Just sit still," Sol whispered.

"Take it easy now, mister," the second man said in a voice that was a bit too loud for Sol's liking. "Whoever you are, I'm sure we can—"

"Be quiet," Sol hissed.

Although he was quiet, the man in the first cot was still moving. He made a clumsy grab for the shiny pistol in Sol's hand, leaping from beneath his blanket in the process. Seeing the sudden burst of motion, Sol lashed out to crack the gun against the man's temple.

There was a dull thump followed by the snap of wood as the shiny gun's owner fell onto the side of his cot with enough force to crack one of the legs holding it up. That man let out a groan and rolled onto his back, letting one of his arms dangle over the side.

Sol blinked in confusion as he took a look at how

the brief scuffle had ended. Still holding a gun in each hand, Sol turned to face the man in the second cot. That fellow's eyes were wide as saucers as he held out both hands in a vain attempt to keep Sol away.

Backing up a step so he was out of both men's reach, Sol kept his eyes bouncing back and forth between the other two until he was certain the first man was down for the count. The moment he saw the second man open his mouth, Sol aimed both guns at him and thumbed back the hammers. Those metallic clicks seemed louder than a pair of cooking pots bouncing against a tin floor.

"Everything all right in there?" asked a voice from outside the tent.

Sol felt a mix of panic and fear stab through his chest. Doing his best to hide those things, Sol fixed his eyes upon the second man and wished he could put on the same murderous glare that Nester had shown him so many times over the last several days. If he couldn't manage that, Sol knew he might just have to shoot his way out of that tent.

Whether the man in the second cot saw a glare or desperate intent in Sol's eyes, he nodded and waved his hands in quick surrender.

"Mr. Oberlee?" the man outside asked.

Sol glanced quickly to the man in the first cot and saw him still lying with one arm hanging off the edge. If that fellow hadn't moved a muscle yet, Sol figured he would be out for a while longer. He turned his attention back to the second man and stared at him hard enough to burn holes through stone.

"No need to worry," the second man announced in a steady, if somewhat forced, voice.

"I thought I heard something in there."

Smiling as if the man outside could see him, Oberlee replied, "Yes, well, Henry just slipped out of his cot."

"That's all?"

Nodding at Sol, Oberlee replied, "That's all."

"I can get you another cot, sir. Just give me a moment."

Sol gritted his teeth, which was enough to get his point across. Oberlee sat up and dropped back into his cot a moment later. "I think there was a possum in here," he said. "Or maybe a rabbit."

"Fine. I'll see if I can flush it out."

"No!" Oberlee snapped. "It's gone. Henry tripped. That's all there is to it. I just want to get back to sleep!"

Either the guards were accustomed to being snapped at like that or the man outside wasn't very anxious to tuck a couple of rich men under their covers. Either way, the man outside didn't make an effort to come into the tent. After a bit of a pause, he replied, "All right, then. Have a good night." Those words were followed by the crunch of boots against dirt.

Taking another page from Nester's book, Sol inched forward while trying to maintain his glare. The mixture of that glare and the guns in Sol's hands kept Oberlee squirming and cowering like a beaten dog waiting to be swatted on the nose.

Once he was close enough to Oberlee, Sol pressed the barrel of his gun beneath the man's chin. "Good job," he whispered. "Now we can have a little chat."

Chapter 24

The rifleman's knuckles cracked against Nester's jaw and sent the old man staggering backward. Shaking his aching hand, the rifleman smiled to show a set of teeth that had been bloodied only a few seconds before. Before he could give voice to the taunt he'd been thinking, the rifleman felt a sting in his eyes as a handful of dirt was thrown into his face.

Nester let his mouth hang open so the air could cool the pain that flooded through his head. That last punch wasn't the first that had landed and all of those blows had turned Nester's already grizzled face into a mess. Even so, he wasn't about to let the younger man get over on him.

Ducking beneath a hooking punch, Nester stepped forward to deliver a punch of his own that landed in the rifleman's gut and doubled the younger man over. Nester straightened up, raised his left arm over his head and dropped it straight down so his elbow slammed against the rifleman's neck.

The rifleman didn't so much as glance toward the camp as he put some distance between himself and Nester. He swallowed his pride and scurried around the rock he'd been using as a backrest before the fight began. It wasn't until he'd scampered all the way around that the rifleman finally found the very thing he'd been looking for. The Sharps rifle lay upon the ground against the back side of the rock, covered in shadow so well that the rifleman might not have seen it unless he was so close to the ground.

Snatching up the Sharps, the rifleman rolled onto his back in preparation for Nester's next attack. He was ready to fire the moment he got a target in his sights, but that target never arrived. Content to alert the camp if he couldn't shoot Nester right away, the rifleman took aim at the sky over the wagons.

Suddenly, sharpened steel cut through the air and opened a bloody gash in the rifleman's forearm. Letting out a snarled curse, he tried to pull his trigger, but instead found his finger trapped within the guard. Nester had come around the rock and now had a hold of the rifle in one hand. The old man twisted the rifle around even more as he lashed out with the knife in his other hand.

The rifleman tried to let go of the Sharps so he could get away from the incoming blade, but his finger was still caught under the trigger guard. Turning away from Nester, he felt the knife cut into him again. This time, the blade raked along the back of his shoulder.

Nester's face was twisted with rage. He snarled like an animal as he viciously tried to pull the Sharps away from its owner. After he heard the wet snap of a finger bone cracking in half, Nester was able to wrest the Sharps out of the younger man's grasp.

The rifleman started to yelp in pain, but Nester pressed the side of the rifle against the back of the man's head and shoved his face into the dirt. That way, when the younger man did yell out, the only sound he made was a muffled groan that could barely be heard over the rush of the wind.

"Stay down," Nester growled.

The rifleman squirmed and kicked while trying to turn onto his back.

Somehow, Nester managed to keep the younger man down as he shoved the rifleman's face even harder against the dirt. "Stay down, damn you. I'll tie yer hands together and be on my way."

Not only did the rifleman keep struggling, but he also managed to land a few glancing blows with his wild swings and thrashing legs.

Nester brought the rifle up an inch or so and then slammed it down again. When that impact didn't slow the younger man down, Nester pressed his knife hand against the rifle as well and pushed all of his weight down upon the back of the man's head.

Breathing through gritted teeth, Nester smacked the handle of his knife against the younger man's head to keep him from turning his face away from the dirt. The old man took a quick look up and around to find no real movement in the camp and nobody coming toward the rifleman's perch. By the time Nester looked down again, the rifleman was only fighting with half the force he'd had before. It became easier and easier for Nester to keep him down now that the younger man was losing his steam.

"There you go," Nester whispered. "Sleep tight, now."

When the rifleman's body went limp, Nester pushed on the back of his head just to be certain. The rifleman didn't budge. Nester eased up on the Sharps, but was ready to lunge forward if the need should arise. The rifleman still didn't budge. Pulling the Sharps up, Nester watched the rifleman for a few more seconds and then glanced toward the camp.

Everything was still fairly quiet in the distance, but Nester wasn't the sort to put too much faith in a run of good luck. He nodded, took a deep breath and then checked the Sharps to see how many bullets were left in the rifle.

The rifleman twisted around like a creature that had just come back from the dead. He grabbed hold of Nester's shirt and delivered a sharp, straight punch to the old man's face. Nester's head snapped back, but he was too shocked to feel any pain from the blow. He was also just a bit too slow to keep the rifleman from reclaiming his Sharps.

The rifle slipped from Nester's fingers and the younger man crawled away with it. Gasping for air, the rifleman placed his hand around the grip and was just about to touch the trigger when he felt a powerful blow to his ribs.

Nester kicked the younger man and planted his foot to settle in above his prey. From there, Nester wrapped a fist around a portion of the younger man's shirt and slammed the rifleman's shoulder against the ground. Nester's other hand dropped straight down to bury the blade of his knife into the rifleman's chest.

There was no mistaking it this time. Nester didn't have to wait and see if the younger man would stop moving and he didn't issue any commands. Instead, Nester glared directly into the rifleman's eyes and pushed the blade in all the way to the hilt.

It took a moment for the pain to set in, but the rifleman started to feel it before long. When a groan worked its way up from the back of his throat, it was silenced by a callused, leathery hand placed directly over his mouth.

Nester's face had become colder than the desert night. He barely even concerned himself with the rifleman any longer. Instead, Nester took in his surroundings with the sharp, calculating eyes of a true predator.

The camp was still quiet.

No shots had been fired.

Nobody was coming to check on the man that had just been killed.

When he looked back to the young man's face, Nester paid no attention to the smell of death that drifted through the air. He gave the knife one last stab just to see if there would be any reaction in the rifleman.

There was none.

The younger man was gone.

Nester pulled the blade free and used the rifleman's shirt to clean it off. The shirt was loose and came free easily, since the rifleman had worn it more as a jacket over his other clothes. Now that the outer shirt was pulled aside, Nester could see something much more interesting worn by the younger man: a badge.

Nester bent down to pull the badge away from the dead man's shirt. After studying the tin star, Nester let two words drift through the night.

"Aww, hell."

Sol moved one of the two stools inside the tent to a spot where he could sit and keep an eye on both of the other men. Henry was still stretched out on his cot and Oberlee was sitting with his legs hanging over the side of his own cot. Since Oberlee was only wearing a baggy nightshirt without any place to hide a weapon, Sol didn't see the harm in letting the man sit up like an adult.

"Your name's Oberlee?" Sol asked.

"Yes." When he saw the warning glare in Sol's eyes, Oberlee lowered his voice to a whisper. "It is," he said quietly. "Morgan Oberlee."

"And you work for the Jessup Mining Company."

Oberlee nodded.

"You know a man named Charlie Lowell?" Sol asked.

Furrowing his brow, Oberlee concentrated until the effort seemed to give him a cramp behind the eyes. "It sounds familiar. Does he work at one of our interests in New Mexico?"

This time, Sol nodded. "A silver mine in Warren."

Oberlee's eyes widened a bit as if he might forget himself and speak loudly enough to alert some of the nearby gunmen. Just then, Sol realized there wasn't a lot he could do to keep Oberlee quiet other than stuffing a gag in his mouth. Since that would defeat the purpose of his visit, Sol put some more fire into his eyes and pressed the pistol a bit more against Oberlee's neck.

"I do remember that name," Oberlee said in a whisper that was so quiet, Sol could barely hear it. "He manages the mine in Warren. Been doing so for quite a while."

"Do you know who I am?"

Letting out a slow breath, Oberlee nodded again.

Pale resignation settled upon his face and he closed his eyes as though he was standing at the wrong end of a firing squad. "You're the one who robbed that shipment."

"Yes."

"You also killed those men. I assure you, there's no reason to kill me."

"What men?" Sol asked. "The only man I shot was one of the men who was supposed to be robbing Charlie. If there was supposed to be more than that, Charlie just cooked up some story to make me look bad."

"Right," Oberlee sighed. "I'm sure it was all a big misunderstanding."

"Believe what you want, but you should believe your own eyes first. I didn't kill you and I didn't kill that other one over there, even though neither of those tasks would have been too difficult."

Oberlee glanced over at Henry and found him still crumpled in his cot. The other man might not have been in the best condition, but he was most definitely breathing. Dead men didn't pant and twitch in their sleep like they were dreaming about chasing rabbits. Looking back at Sol, he asked, "What do you want from me?"

"Charlie did a whole lot of talking when I had him at gunpoint. He told me all about the way your company shaves off a cut of the profits while the miners are allowed to starve or are shot when they complain about how they're treated."

"Really?" Oberlee said. "That's terrible."

"But you already knew about all that, didn't you? I can see it in your eyes."

Oberlee shook his head. "No. I swear." Since his

voice had started to get louder, he dropped it back to a whisper and fixed pleading eyes upon Sol. "If Charlie was cheating me, I can look into it. I can have him investigated. We have accountants who can go over the ledgers and see what he's been doing. If he's mistreated his workers, I can investigate that too. Just give me a chance."

Sol shook his head as things began to come into focus. "You want to clear things up? Then start by telling me where this money is going. Aren't there perfectly good banks in Albuquerque?"

"What money?"

Fighting to keep his voice down, Sol growled, "The money that was shaved off of the official profits. Don't sit there telling me you don't know about any of this."

"I don't. I swear. This shipment may be a little light to make up for some of what was stolen, but—"

"But nothing," Sol cut in. "You're going to tell me what's in those wagons and how I can get inside them."

"Fine, fine. If there's a problem with Charlie Lowell, I can try to rectify it. If there's any wrongdoing, the proper men should be the ones to pay for it. If you kill me or my associate, it won't solve anything."

"Or I could take you and those wagons out of here so you can show me what's in that shipment," Sol said as he felt the anger inside him grow into an inferno. "I'll need to take those wagons out where I can look through them properly."

Chuckling nervously, Oberlee said, "I don't know how you can do that. The guards won't allow it."

"They will if you come along with me."

"And what should I tell them?"

Keeping his gun pointed at Oberlee, Sol walked over to the stool where Henry's clothes were neatly folded and stacked. "Just tell them that you and your partner want to double-check the money. I'm sure that's not anything too unusual."

Oberlee shrugged, but Sol wasn't too interested in what the man had to say about it. Sol pulled on Henry's coat, put on his hat and kept his gun aimed at Oberlee. When he was done, Sol felt downright proud of himself for being able to do two things at once.

"All right," Sol said as he stuffed his gun hand into Henry's coat pocket and pushed it through until the pistol ripped the seams so the gun's barrel poked out from beneath the coat. "I'll have this on you the whole time. You make one wrong move and I'll shoot."

"What do you want me to do?"

"Once we drive those wagons away from here, you'll open the lockboxes or safes or whatever is in there and we'll see how your story holds up."

"If there is money in the lockboxes, that doesn't prove anything."

"It proves you're in on this dirty dealing and that you're a liar and a cheat," Sol snapped. "It'll also make things real difficult for you to explain to the rest of the company when they realize how short you are in another shipment."

Oberlee twitched when he heard that, so Sol knew he'd hit a tender spot.

"You're coming with me to those wagons and if you don't get those lockboxes open or if you raise any sort of alarm . . ."

Oberlee nodded in resignation. "I know," he sighed. "You'll shoot."

"Very good. Play your cards right and we'll all walk away from this."

When Sol waved him toward the door using his partially concealed gun, Oberlee headed for the tent's flap and pulled it open. He took a step outside without making a sound and turned to walk in the direction of the wagons.

Henry's hat didn't fit too well, but its brim covered most of Sol's face. As he walked out of the tent with his chin held low, Sol felt proud of himself. Not only would this robbery happen without a single shot being fired, but he'd drag a snake even bigger than Charlie out of its hole. That sunny outlook lasted right until Sol took another step outside of the tent.

Oberlee was standing a few paces to Sol's left. The businessman had turned around to face Sol and was grinning from ear to ear. "Just so you know," he said, "my partner's name isn't Henry and the walls of that tent are a lot thinner than you must think." Shaking his head, Oberlee added, "You're really not too good at this, are you?"

Flanking Oberlee on all sides were men who all had their guns drawn and their sights set upon Sol. One or two of them had shotguns. Another carried a hunting rifle. Two were even wearing badges, but none of those men caught Sol's eye more than the one who stood at the edge of the group. The last time Sol had seen that man, they'd been shooting at each other over another batch of money around a campfire outside of Warren. That time, however, Sol had been in a slightly better spot.

"You?" Garver grunted. "What in the hell are you doing here?"

"You know this man?" Oberlee asked.

Garver nodded. "He's one of the fellas who robbed that money from me and the kid a while back. He's the one who shot Bill."

"One of the fellas who robbed you?" Sol chuckled. "I was the only one and I wounded you to boot. How long did it take you to crawl back to town after that?"

Garver's lips curled into an angry snarl and he lunged toward Sol. Before Garver could get too close, a shot cracked through the air and something hissed through the gap between Garver's and Sol's heads. Sol tripped over his own feet while shuffling back into the tent. Garver jumped and reflexively fired a shot that missed Sol by a matter of inches. After that, all hell was unleashed as other men in the group fired into the darkness or into the tent to answer the shot that had gotten the ball rolling.

Even before his backside hit the dirt, Sol could feel hot lead ripping through the air all around him. Some of the shots clawed at his arms and shoulders, but most of them passed over his head. Fortunately, the tent flap had been loose enough to cover all but his feet once he'd fallen backward. As he blinked to clear his head the best he could, Sol could see holes being torn through the canvas in the spot where he'd been standing less than a second ago.

Outside, Oberlee turned to the man beside him and slapped him directly on the spot where the badge was pinned to his chest. "Arrest that man! Shoot him! String him up! Do something to earn what I pay you!"

Chapter 25

Henry was still in his cot. Whatever that man's real name was, Sol didn't need to think of him as anything but Henry. Cursing himself under his breath, Sol wondered how he could be so arrogant as to think he could waltz into this camp and waltz back out again without starting any ruckus. Rather than waste any more time thinking it over, Sol made sure his guns were loaded and then scooted toward the back of the tent.

"You're going to kill me, aren't you?" Henry asked.

Ignoring the man completely, Sol dove for the loose section of the tent under which he'd crawled earlier. It took a bit of squirming, but Sol made it out in short order. His mind churned on everything that had gone wrong. But the whole night wasn't a loss. If Garver was there taking orders from Oberlee, that meant that whatever was happening with the money shipments was linked all the way to that level of the Jessup Mining Company. Since Oberlee had at least one lawman working for him, that meant he was more dangerous than some thieving boss. Either that, or Oberlee was a concerned businessman trying to protect his money from a bunch of robbers.

"Good Lord," Sol groaned as more shots were fired and a few men started making their way inside the tent. "What was I thinking?"

Everything rushed through Sol's mind so quickly that he felt as if he might just get thrown off the face of the earth and into empty air. Forcing himself to get moving again, Sol tripped and twisted to one side to keep from landing on his face.

He hit the ground on his left arm, which sent an explosion of pain through his entire body. Although it wasn't a graceful landing, he didn't think it should have hurt so badly. When he looked down, he saw his arm was bleeding in several spots. Only then did Sol remember being grazed by a few bullets from the first bunch that had ripped through the tent.

Whether it was the sight of his own blood or the pain that flowed from those wounds, Sol was snapped out of his haze quicker than if he'd been doused with cold water. He bolted away from the tent and made it a bit farther than he'd hoped, but wasn't about to celebrate just yet.

The hailstorm of lead continued, but most of it erupted from the front of the biggest tent. Every so often, a shot was fired from somewhere in the distance that sounded more like whip cracks than gunshots. Even stranger was the fact that those shots seemed to come from a slightly different angle each time.

Hearing voices to his right, Sol looked in that direction and saw a group of men slowly approaching him. They were about ten paces away and immediately backed up when they spotted Sol. Gritting his teeth through the pain of his small wounds, Sol prepared to defend himself. All he needed to do, however, was wave his gun toward that group of men to send them scurrying away as quickly as their legs would carry them. Not only were those men unarmed, but they were barely dressed. They covered their heads with their hands and rushed toward the smaller tents situated next to the wagons.

If only the rest could be sent away so easily.

When Sol saw Garver and two of the other gunmen running around the large tent, he immediately took aim with both guns. Before he could think twice about it, he pulled his triggers and sent a barrage of lead through the air. Sol didn't even know if he hit anything. All he could see was the smoke from his pistols and all he could feel were the guns bucking against his palms.

Men scattered in every direction. A few of the gunmen dove for the ground, but Garver dropped straight down and kept his eyes on Sol.

"You got lucky once," Garver shouted. "It ain't about to happen again!"

Sol stopped firing and suddenly wished he knew how many bullets he'd spent. He looked to see where the other gunmen were and caught one of them sitting up to sight along the top of his pistol. Just then, another one of those distant shots cracked through the air and delivered a piece of lead into the gunman's back. As that gunman fell over, Sol turned and made a run for the edge of the camp.

"Where are my drivers?" Oberlee shouted. "Get over here and get these wagons moving!"

Those petrified, half-dressed men whom Sol had

sent running before now emerged from behind the wagons. They traded some words with Oberlee, who shoved them toward the horses and barked at them to get the teams hitched into their harnesses. If Oberlee had had a whip in his hand, he would have undoubtedly used it to make the frightened drivers work faster.

As he ran away from the camp, Sol felt like he was trapped inside a bad dream. Even though his legs were moving, he wasn't completely sure if he was covering any ground. And if he was, he didn't quite know where he was headed. Every part of him hurt to some degree or another. No matter how unlikely it seemed that he would make it out of that camp alive, Sol wasn't about to stop trying. He'd already gotten himself in too deep to try and rest now.

Suddenly, a pair of men ran around the edge of the camp to circle toward Sol from the right. Sol's boots skidded upon the rocks in his haste to change directions, but he managed to do so as a shotgun blast erupted from behind him. A shot from the distance hissed past Sol's head and continued over his shoulder, but Sol didn't turn around to see where that bullet landed.

Behind Sol, one of the men hollered. Another shotgun was fired, but Sol had already been forced to circle around the camp. Oberlee, the man with the badge and one other had made their way to the wagons. A few more men who looked as if they'd only just been pulled out of their bedrolls were scrambling around to hitch the horses to the wagons. One of those men, wearing a wide-brimmed hat and a pair of long underwear, raced to climb into the lead wagon's driver's seat. Even before he'd gotten the reins in his hands, another man carrying a shotgun and wearing a nightshirt climbed into the seat beside him.

"Get these wagons out of here!" Oberlee shouted. "Right now, before any more of those robbers come swarming down on us!"

With a good number of men from the camp gathered around the wagons, Sol turned to run in the opposite direction. He made it less than two steps before charging directly into Garver's fist.

The punch had come as such a surprise that Sol barely even felt it. Instead, he was knocked straight back and nearly off his feet. Garver took one step forward and delivered a punishing kick to Sol's ribs.

"That's for shooting me back when you stole Charlie's money," Garver grunted. He brought up his gun, thumbed back the hammer and said, "This is for shooting Bill."

Sol lay flat on his back so he could lift both hands and fire with both guns. One of them only let out a single round before it was empty. The other spat three shots in fairly quick succession before it fell silent. Even after he knew he was out of ammunition, Sol kept pulling his triggers.

Pulling himself to his feet, Sol held the guns in front of him as if they were something more than iron weights. Even though he carried fresh bullets in his gun belt, he was too rattled to reload. Sol couldn't look away from the sight of Garver flopping on the ground like a fish that had been plucked from the stream.

Garver's shirt was a bloody mess. He locked eyes with Sol as he forced out a painful cough. The rage in his glare slowly faded until it was replaced by sorrowful confusion. Then, like so many before him, Garver was gone.

The rumble of wagon wheels brought Sol back to the world of the living in a hurry. By the sound of it, Oberlee's men had gotten both teams hitched to their wagons and were in the process of putting the camp behind them. The shots had died down a bit, since most of the activity was now centered on the wagons.

Sol was no longer worried about the money in that shipment. All he wanted was to stay alive. Sol kept that singular purpose in mind as he looked for the darkest, quietest spot that could be used as an avenue of escape.

"Stop that man!" someone shouted.

Forcing himself to keep moving despite all the pain from his various nicks and bruises, Sol hurried past the small tents on the farthest edge of the camp. A few shots were fired at him and the ones that didn't punch into the dirt whipped past him like swarming bees.

Behind Sol, the wagons were gathering speed. Those wheels rolled and the drivers whipped their teams to go faster.

Men were shouting, but most of those voices faded at the same rate as the rumble of the wagons.

Another shot was fired at Sol's back. This one was close enough to sound more like a hungry animal barking in his ear.

"One more step and you're dead!"

When Sol heard those words, he truly felt like an outlaw. It wasn't the thrill he'd imagined when he was a child listening to all those stories about Nester Quarles. It was a simple choice that drifted through his mind: He could keep running, or he could turn and see if he could hurt those men bad enough for him to escape. Since his guns were dry, he knew he'd be forced to test his luck with the blade hanging from his belt.

Sol had never imagined that the thought of spilling another man's blood would come to him so easily. At the moment he tried to figure which man he should take out first, he might as well have been deciding if he wanted honey or syrup on his biscuits.

Closing his eyes and bowing his head in shame, Sol planted his feet and raised his hands.

"Now drop them guns!" the man behind him ordered.

Sol opened his fists and let the empty pistols hit the dirt.

There were heavy steps behind him as rough hands grabbed Sol's wrists and pulled his arms down behind his back.

"That hurt?" the man growled into Sol's ear. "I should break your arms and every other bone in your body for what you done. Three men are dead." After tying Sol's wrists together with a length of rope, the man spun Sol around so he could look directly into his eyes.

As Sol had guessed, the man who'd tied his wrists together was the one with the badge. Only a lawman would shout so much when a bullet to the back would have gotten the job done twice as fast.

Another man hunkered down a few paces back. He

had a bit more panic in his eyes when he looked up and, as far as Sol could tell, he wasn't wearing a badge. "There's another one over here, Cam."

The man with the badge turned toward the other one and dragged Sol along with him. "Another body?"

"Yeah. It's Garver."

Cam winced, but seemed somewhat relieved. "What about Wayne or Andy?"

"They haven't come into the camp yet. Maybe it was them that was firing the rifles earlier."

"Are you stupid?" Cam snapped. "Why would one of them be shooting at the rest of us? One of this killer's partners got to them." Turning to level his gaze at Sol, Cam asked, "How many more of you are out there?"

"I don't know how many more there are," a third man said from somewhere outside the camp, "but there ain't nobody around here no more."

Cam's face brightened when he got a look at the man approaching from behind Sol. He smiled and asked, "Did you put the rest of them down, Wayne?"

The third man walked into Sol's field of vision. Actually, he staggered into view. When Sol looked over to the new arrival, he saw plenty of dirt on the man's face, blood on his clothes and wariness in his eyes. A dented badge hung from his shirt pocket. Slowly, Wayne shook his head. "I think I hit him, but I didn't kill him. I went to check, but there weren't no body. At least . . . not no outlaw's body."

Gritting his teeth, Cam asked, "You found Andy?"

"Yeah. Looks like someone gutted him."

Cam stared at Sol as if he meant to set a fire. "You killed my friend?"

Sol shook his head, but didn't put much into it. He knew it wouldn't do him any good. "I snuck in here and was caught. Do you think I could have gotten close enough to your friend to kill him?"

Glancing at the knife that was still hanging from Sol's belt, Cam reached out to pull it from its sheath. He looked at the blade and then ran his finger along the flat portion of it.

"Where's everyone else?" Wayne asked. "I heard a lot of shooting."

"They took the wagons and moved on," Cam replied. "That dandy didn't want to risk getting his suit dirty along with the rest of us."

"Mr. Oberlee paid you to keep his shipment safe," the man without the badge said. "If you don't hold your end up, I'll see to it he finds out and you won't get the rest of your money." Even as Wayne turned and stalked toward him, the gunman held his ground. "And if . . . anything happens to me," he gulped, "the sheriff will find out about this extra work you agreed to do."

Sol watched the men stare each other down as if he were watching two dogs fight at the bottom of a pit.

"And if you're inclined to be so difficult," Cam replied, "maybe Mr. Oberlee should be told you were killed along with the others when all the shooting was going on."

The gunman didn't back down as such, but those words had obviously shaken him down to the core. His concern grew when he realized he was the only one left in the camp who wasn't a lawman or a prisoner. "I was just saying you got a job to do," the gunman said. "We all do."

Cam nodded and shifted his eyes back toward Sol. "You're right about that." As he said those words, Cam aimed his pistol at Sol's head.

When he heard the metallic click of that hammer being thumbed back, Sol closed his eyes and waited for the inevitable.

"Wait," Wayne said. "You can't do that."

Cam's voice was cold as ice. "He killed Andy."

"It might have been one of his partners."

For a moment, Sol felt a faint whisper of hope brush through his head.

"But he killed at least one man in this camp," Cam replied.

"And Bill," the gunman added. "He was one of Mr. Oberlee's men. That man there shot Bill dead and ran off with Charlie Lowell's money."

"You know that for a fact?" Wayne asked.

The gunman kept his voice steady and nodded solemnly. "There's a price on his head for it," the gunman explained. "Twenty-five hundred dollars."

"You hear that, Wayne?" Cam asked. "Anyone can kill this man and they'll collect a reward. After all the blood this animal's spilt, I won't even accept the reward. That make you feel any better?"

Without missing a beat, Wayne said, "The only money you accept is your wages."

"Sure, but don't forget the money we took from Mr. Oberlee. You think the sheriff would take too kindly to that?"

"It wasn't a bribe."

"Maybe not, but we was bought and paid for," Cam told him. "The sheriff ain't around and we're taking orders from someone who paid us plenty to do what he tells us to do. You can call it what you want, but that's what it is."

"We were hired to protect that shipment," Wayne said sternly. "The wagons have moved on and the shooting's stopped. We're not Oberlee's killers."

Sol watched the two lawmen argue and was careful not to move or make a sound. The scales might not be tipped in his favor just yet, but things were looking a whole lot better than they had a few minutes ago.

Although the fire in Cam's eyes wasn't as intense as it had been before, it was still burning when he said, "This man's a killer, Wayne. He's wanted and he fired at damn near everyone in this camp. The only reason he didn't kill more was because he missed."

"If I wanted to be another one of Oberlee's hired killers, I would have asked for a lot more money," Wayne said. "No matter what jobs we took on the side, we're still lawmen."

"Last time I checked," Cam growled as he once again stared at Sol, "we were still doing our duty by putting down mad dog killers like this one here."

"True, but we need to do it the proper way."

Sol was beginning to see a prison cell and courthouse in his future instead of a bullet through his skull. He felt even better when he caught sight of Nester creeping through the camp to get a good spot behind the lawmen and remaining gun hand.

Nester crouched on the front half of one of the small, half-collapsed tents left behind by one of the wagon drivers. With the other half of the little tent still propped up, Nester's silhouette could hardly be seen.

"What's the proper way to deal with someone who killed one of our own?" Cam asked.

Wayne looked over his shoulder and back toward the direction from which he'd approached the camp. "There are some sturdy trees over there. I say we hang him. That way, if the sheriff wants to check up on what happened here, they can find Andy's body up on that rise and this one's swinging from a branch. We've done our jobs and it'll all be done by the letter of the law."

"And if any more of those robbers come along, they can get a real good look at what's in store for them," Cam added as he eased the hammer of his pistol back down. "Sounds just fine to me."

"And why the hell don't we just shoot this one and be done with it?" the gunman asked.

"Because the sheriff would hang him," Cam replied. "We're deputies of the sheriff, so we'll follow his way. You ever seen a man hung?"

The gunman shrugged and shook his head. "No."

"Then you should watch this one and you'll see we're not doing him any favors. Once that rope starts tightening, he'll wish we would'a shot him and been done with it."

Sol felt a cold sweat push its way out of his face and hands. That chill rolled all the way through him and seeped down to the marrow in his bones when he got a look at Wayne's face. Only a few moments ago, it had seemed the other lawman was fighting to keep Sol from being cut down like a dog. Instead, Sol was going to be strung up like a man.

Frantically looking in the spot where he'd seen Nester, Sol didn't find the sight he wanted. Rather than take aim with his rifle to give Sol the chance to run, Nester was backing away so as not to draw any attention. Apparently, he was more than happy to have Sol take the fall for both of them.

In the blink of an eye, all of the warning signs flooded through Sol's mind. Nester had told him more than once not to trust another outlaw. Nester had even harped on how dangerous it was to ride with men who were too stupid to shoot when the time came to do so. He'd said those things so many times that Sol had stopped listening. Now it looked as if Sol would be taught this lesson the hard way and Nester could take a shot at all that money himself.

Sol didn't want to get Nester killed, but he wasn't about to let the old man slink away. If Nester meant to let Sol hang, then the old man deserved to be chased down as well.

Just as Sol opened his mouth to say his piece to the lawmen, he was cut short by a sharp punch to the jaw. Before he could pull in another breath, Sol felt a dirty piece of cloth being stuffed into his mouth.

Chapter 26

For Sol, the next few minutes were more of a jumble than the failed attempt to escape that camp. He kept trying to speak, but could only mumble and grunt into the bandana that filled his mouth. He was dragged away from the camp and dropped next to a tree. When Sol rolled onto his side and squirmed to get a look at where the other men had gone, he found one of them standing directly beside him.

Wayne knocked Sol out with one well-placed kick to the temple.

Once Sol opened his eyes again, he thought he might already be dead.

He was blind. His head ached so badly that Sol feared his skull had been cracked open. Soon, he realized he was breathing. After that, Sol realized he was sitting upright in a saddle. His hands were still tied behind his back and he could still taste the filthy cotton that had been stuffed into his mouth. Every breath smelled like a mix of rust and dirt. The one thing he could hear above everything else was the rush of blood through his veins and the slamming of his heart in his chest.

He was alive. At least, he was alive for the moment.

". . . like he's awake," someone said from nearby.

Although Sol could hear the voices, they were muffled and distorted. Every beat of his heart sent a wave of sound through Sol's aching head. It reminded him of when he'd gotten knocked on the head by a piece of falling rock while working in Charlie's mine. Sol fought to keep listening, but couldn't shake the feeling that his head was at the bottom of a bucket of water.

"He's awake all right. I can see him squirming," someone else replied. It might have been Cam.

"That noose tight?"

"Let me check."

It was tight, all right. Sol could feel the rope scratching against his neck as it was twisted around and cinched in to squeeze even tighter across his throat. Once that adjustment was made, the pounding rush in Sol's ears grew even louder. As the horse beneath him shifted its weight, Sol could feel the rope digging even deeper into his neck. That woke him up, but only so he could wonder if his head was going to pop.

"That branch gonna hold?"

Since the other man was a bit farther away, Sol couldn't quite hear the response. He forced himself to swallow, straightened his back and lifted his chin. The blood flowed a bit easier through him, but just enough to make the throbbing in his skull ease up a bit. He could feel the gentle touch of a breeze against his hands. Since he couldn't see and couldn't feel anything on his face or neck, Sol guessed there was something covering his head.

"Looks official," Cam said. "Get that horse moving and let's be done with this."

In the space of the next few seconds, Sol reflected upon his entire life. Every moment rushed through him like a cascade of photographs and he could somehow see every single one as they went by. Beneath that rush of memory, Sol thought about the little things he would miss.

Coffee that was brewed just right.

A pretty lady's singing voice.

Crisp bacon.

Sleep.

Then again, Sol guessed he wouldn't miss that last one too badly. He'd be getting more than his share of sleep real soon.

With that, Sol grinned. His cheeks brushed against whatever was covering his head and he let out a tired laugh, which was soaked up by the dirty bandana in his mouth.

". . . told you to hand that man over!"

"Who the hell are you?"

Sol didn't start paying attention to the conversation until he heard Cam's distinct growl in the mix. The horse was still under him and the rope was awfully tight around his neck. Before long, Sol would no longer have the strength to keep his chin up.

"I'm one of the men doing your job! There's a posse out there getting shot to pieces and you're here fooling about with a lynching!"

Sol couldn't quite place this new voice. His own

heartbeat was thumping too loudly for him to hear more than just the words themselves.

"What posse?" Cam asked.

"The one chasing down that gang of robbers!" the new man replied. "The sheriff got wind that he was missing some deputies and sent us to check on all of you."

"Who are you?"

"I'm a deputy from Santa Roja. See for yourself."

There was a long moment of silence, during which Sol began to drift into sleep. He figured it was all for the best. If these were to be his last moments, he didn't want to spend them listening to a bunch of lawmen bickering among themselves.

After a while, Sol felt as though he were drifting downward like a falling leaf.

His heartbeat faded away and the constant pounding in his ears tapered off.

He still couldn't see.

All in all, death wasn't so bad.

Sol opened his eyes and was greeted by a bright, brilliant light. The light almost immediately blinded him, but at least he wouldn't feel any more pain.

Come to think of it . . . that wasn't exactly true.

In fact, everything above Sol's shoulders was in a lot of pain. The moment he started to move, he quickly regretted it.

"Rise and shine, lazybones," Nester said from somewhere nearby.

Sol was confused. He rubbed the back of his head where it hurt the most and struggled to sit up. The next time he tried to open his eyes, he took his time and slowly raised his eyelids. The bright light was still there, but that was only because he was facing the sun. Something drifted through the air, however, which made him feel somewhat closer to heaven.

"Is that . . . coffee?" Sol asked.

Nester was sitting on a log beside a campfire. He grinned and handed a dented cup to Sol. "Just brewed it up myself."

Sol took a sip and let it trickle down his throat. It hurt terribly, but the taste was more than worth the suffering. He drank again, let his eyes adjust to the sunny skies and then finally looked back toward the old man. "Tell me what in the blazes happened. The last thing I recall was having a noose around my neck. Some deputy came to get me." Steeling himself for the answer, Sol asked, "You shot him, didn't you?"

The old man didn't say anything. When Sol looked back to him, he found Nester grinning like the cat that ate the proverbial canary. Finally, Nester pulled open his jacket to reveal the tin star pinned to his shirt pocket. "You didn't know it was me?" Nester asked. "And here I thought I had such a distinctive singing voice."

"That was . . . that was you?"

"Sure was."

"How did you get me away from there?" Sol asked. "I didn't even hear any shots!"

Nester used his sleeve to proudly wipe off the front of his badge. "Only one of them boys laid eyes on me before I got hold of this badge He was one of them scouts I spotted. Just so's you know, I did have to put him down." Sipping his coffee, Nester leaned back and spoke as if he were telling another one of his tall tales. "I was surprised as all git out when I saw that scout was a deputy. After my tussle with him, I saw his badge and took it fer myself. A man never knows when somethin' like that will come in handy.

"I started making my way back to that camp when you must've slipped up because all hell was breaking loose. I got close enough to pick off a few of them others before they got a chance to put a bullet into yer worthless hide."

"I heard those shots," Sol said. "I recall at least one or two of them saving my life. What happened after that?"

"Well, them dandies were awful quick to get them wagons rolling as soon as they could," Nester replied. "I thought about chasing them down to get that money, but damn near every one of them hired guns went along to guard it.

"When I saw they got a hold of you," Nester sighed, "I managed to get up close before you lost too much of yer wind and talked them into handing you over. I told 'em they were needed to help the rest of those law dogs protect them wagons. From what I could hear, it seemed those boys weren't so much crooked as they were enterprising. They were mostly more loyal to their boss than to any of them dandies in that camp."

Sol nodded and sipped his coffee as his strength slowly trickled back into him. "More scouting told you all that, huh?"

Tapping his temple with one finger, Nester winked and nodded.

"All that happened when it was still dark," Sol said. "Looks to me like that was a while ago."

"Yeah. Sorry about that. My story was that I was to take you back to the sheriff so they could do a legal hanging, if there even is such a thing. Them deputies were too rattled and confused to push the matter. I think they might've had a guilty conscience on account of them stringin' you up like that. Anyway, one of 'em wanted to come along with me to bring you in. I refused, so he cracked you on the back of the skull so's you wouldn't fight me."

"That was thoughtful," Sol grumbled.

"Actually," Nester admitted, "it was. Them deputies sure stick together."

Holding his tin cup between both hands, Sol swirled the coffee around and let his eyes wander among the dark liquid and wet grounds that stuck to the sides. "Tell me something, Nester. Were you scouting when you were crouching with your rifle in that collapsed tent?"

Without so much as a twitch, Nester said, "Yeah. I was."

"So you saw me before I had that rope around my neck. You were right there when I was going to be strung up. You could have shot all those men and freed me, but you didn't."

"Killin' lawmen ain't a smart thing ta do, boy. It tends to get all the others riled up."

"You already killed one," Sol declared as he looked up from his coffee. "Or did he just hand over that badge out of kindness?"

"I did kill one. Stabbed him good too. It was a fight and only one of us was gonna walk away. I didn't know he was a lawman till it was too late."

"Would it have made a difference?" Sol asked.

Nester thought it over for a few seconds. "Probably not," he finally admitted. "We should'a known there was lawmen riding with those wagons goin' in, but we didn't."

"And even if you did know . . . would you still have fed me to them?"

"What's that supposed to mean?"

"You heard me, old man," Sol replied. "You made it to that camp. You got in a good spot to take out those lawmen. You could have scared them away or scattered them from that horse that was holding me off the ground. You could have shot the damn rope! Shot the tree! You could've done anything but just crawl away!"

Refusing to be riled up by Sol's words, Nester nodded and said, "I don't need to explain myself to you nor any man, but you needed to feel the end of that rope."

Sol was on his feet before he could think about it. He reached for his holster and was genuinely surprised to find his gun there. "I better not have heard you right. Did you just say I needed to be hung?"

Nester slowly took in the sight of the man in front of him. When he saw that Sol was about to draw his gun, the old man stood up and lowered his head so he was staring at Sol the way a wolf stares down its prey. "What I said is that you needed to feel that rope tightening around yer neck, but if you needed to hang, I would'a left you there."

"So you could take all that money for yourself, is that it? Perhaps I should see about making you feel some pain of your own. Maybe all those stories about you are just that. Stories. Right now, you just seem like a yellow—"

"You'd best watch yer tongue, boy," Nester barked. "I felt more pain than you could ever know, but you ain't felt enough. Leastways, you ain't felt enough to know what a mistake you made in tossin' everything you had out the window so you could try to be a bad man." Nester's hand remained less than an inch above his gun and his eyes remained fixed upon Sol. "That may have been the way for me and it may be the way for other men, but it ain't the way for you, Sol. You ain't a bad man. You may be angry and you may have gotten yer feathers ruffled by some cheatin', lyin' bosses, but you ain't bad to the core. You ain't a killer."

"I've killed," Sol said quietly. "That makes me a killer."

"You got into some scrapes and had to take a life or two, but you didn't take to it naturally." Nester's scowl eased up a bit as he continued to speak, but his hand didn't stray too far from his gun. "I can sniff out a good killer or a good thief the way a blacksmith can sniff out a good apprentice. Bad men steal because they can. They kill because they're killers. It's in their blood. They don't get into fights and fire their guns to stay alive. They don't shoot to defend themselves. They kill. They murder. That's what a bad man does. That's what makes him bad, Sol. You ain't a bad man."

"Why didn't you tell this to me before?" Sol asked.

"I did. At least . . . I tried. Hell, I ain't no teacher, because the men I rode with didn't need to be taught.

What would you have done if I told you that you didn't have what it took to ride with me and that you should go back to a quiet life somewhere else?"

More than anything, Sol wanted to lie. As always, however, he knew he couldn't pull that off while facing Nester Quarles. He was also too tired and rattled to be very convincing no matter who he was facing. Grudgingly, he said, "I would've gone ahead without you."

"And you would've gotten yerself killed. In case you hadn't noticed, you ain't too good at robbin'."

"What's so hard about it? Stick a gun in someone's face and take what they got."

"There's more to it, boy," Nester growled. "You can't pick a gun 'cause it's pretty. You gotta be ready to use it. You gotta be ready to kill a man just because he got in yer way. And if need be, you gotta be ready to kill anyone else that gets in yer way.

"You know what your problem is? You only wanna hurt them's that has it comin'. I killed men just to clear a path for a getaway. I gunned down plenty of folks that didn't deserve it. I even shot plenty of 'em in the back. You know how much that haunts me to this day?"

Sol shook his head.

"It don't," Nester hissed. "I don't lose one wink o' sleep over none of the widows I made or throats I slit. I don't give a damn whose money I stole. You wanna rob and kill for a livin'? That's the kinda blood that's gotta run through yer veins."

Listening to Nester's words, Sol waited for a sign that the old man was bluffing or that he was even stretching the truth. He didn't get a hint of any such thing.

"I seen you when you was a kid," Nester continued. "I know you got a real nice family who'd miss you if you became the sort of man I am. Maybe I'm gettin' soft in my old age, but that's why I decided to do you the biggest favor I could ever do by showin' you the error of yer thinkin'.

"You got blood on yer hands. You took a walk through the mud and I could tell you didn't like it. When I pulled my gun and went to work in that trading post, it was all you could do to keep from keeling over. Any other man I ridden with would'a killed that salesman just to see what he had in his pockets.

"You tried to take part in what could have been a real sweet job and damn near got yerself killed. With the idiots runnin' that caravan, we should have been able to get both of them wagons. Instead, you have a talk with some dandy until he gets a chance to turn things around on you. When the lead started to fly, you barely made it out alive."

"You weren't in there with me," Sol said. "You didn't see how it all happened."

Nester smirked and cocked his head a bit. "I saw plenty. You tryin' to tell me you were runnin' that show?"

"No. There were too many of them."

Shaking his head, Nester replied, "You got into that camp. I was proud of you for that. If you would'a killed a few of them, the rest would'a scattered or fallen into line. The least you could'a done was drop some of them hired guns. But you lost yer wits and bolted like a spooked horse."

Seeing the look in Sol's eyes, Nester held up one hand as if to hold back the torrent he knew was coming. "I ain't saying you're a coward. Ye're just biting off a whole lot more'n you can chew. The only way you'd know for certain is for you to get a real good look at what happens to men who sit in on a game like this when they ain't ready to play. Men like that get shot or hung. The first didn't wake you up, so I thought the second might. That's why I crawled away and let you dangle for a bit. Hanging like that, it takes a real long time for you to die. At the very least, you got a good taste of what a bad man's death is like."

"And what if you didn't get to me in time?" Sol asked. "What then?"

Nester's response was quick and succinct. "I would've had to watch you die," he said. "The way you were goin', I would've had to watch that sooner or later anyhow. Since you held back on some of that money you were supposedly bringing along to fund our travels, I might've been forced to kill you myself."

When Sol tried to laugh that off, he only saw Nester's scowl become darker.

"I know you stashed them other saddlebags in that mine near my place in Leadville. Didn't I tell you I could watch anyone making their way up that mountain from up there?"

"Yes. You did."

"And I know I told you I've killed partners for holding out on me."

Sol's fingers trembled as if to remind him that he was still an inch or so away from his gun. Noticing that Nester was in a similar spot, Sol asked, "Is that where things lie now?"

"Only if you push me, boy."

The next few moments passed in utter silence. During those moments, Sol couldn't help but feel that noose tightening around his neck one more time.

"Don't make another mistake, Solomon. We had a good run. You got some stories of yer own to tell. Don't dig in any deeper than that."

"It's too late to turn back . . . isn't it?" Sol asked.

"You can head north. If you go through Leadville, you can pick up that money you stashed away. Keep headin' north from there and put that money to use. Maybe open up an assayer's office. Ain't that the men who pay for gold?"

Sol nodded. "Among other things."

"An honest man could stand to make a good livin' in that line o' work. Once word spreads, you'll have miners seekin' you out to do business with ya."

"Won't the law be coming after me for what I've done?" Sol asked. "Won't men still be coming for that reward money?"

"That's why you keep heading north until ye're so far away that nobody ain't never heard'a you or them men you killed. Believe me, it's possible to run far enough to pull that off. As for the men you killed . . . that's on yer shoulders. Just be glad you stopped before you piled any more on there. That's the best advice I got, but I don't know how much it's worth."

Sol's arms dropped until they hung limply from his shoulders. Although he was still within easy reach of his gun, he clearly wasn't going to draw. "I could've done without the noose around my neck," he said, "but I see your point."

"Good."

Without another word, Nester turned and walked back to where his horse was waiting. He climbed into the saddle and said, "You can get to Leadville on yer own."

Eyeing the set of saddlebags that hung across the back of Nester's horse, Sol asked, "So you're robbing me, after all?"

"You can keep them fancy clothes you haul around in that carpetbag, but this money's comin' with me. Since I'd still be in my cozy little house on my own stretch of mountain if not for you, I figure I'm owed enough to get me goin' again."

Sol took another look at the set of saddlebags containing a healthy portion of Charlie's money. "You've earned it," he said with a nod. "Put it to good use."

"I will. In fact, I may give it some company. I reckon them wagons can't be too far ahead. After all the hell we put 'em through, them dandies are ripe for the pickin'."

"You're loco, old man."

Nester smirked and tipped his hat. "*Gracias*, amigo. When you get settled, do me a favor, would ya?"

"That depends on the favor."

"I got a story I'd like you to pass along. It'd sure help make things easier for me since I'm on the move again and all."

Nester told his story, shook Sol's hand and steered toward the trail that Oberlee's wagons had been using.

Sol watched him go, rubbed the raw skin around his neck and wondered how the hell he could make it back to Leadville in one piece.

Chapter 27

Beckett, Oregon, one year later

Abner Brakefield had never been to southern Oregon and he'd certainly never heard of a town called Beckett. The fact that he was in Beckett at the moment had only come about through a complete convolution of circumstance. When he'd stepped into Sloane's Trading Post, however, he'd had a single purpose in mind. Abner walked to the counter next to the front door, knocked on the wooden surface and waited for the man behind that counter to acknowledge his presence.

"Help you, sir?" the man asked.

Abner stared at the man's face and smiled. "You sure can. I'm looking for a runt kid named Solomon Brakefield."

The man behind the counter scowled a bit and started to reach for the gun that was kept in a rig beneath the apron tied around his waist. Once he got a better look at the fellow who'd spoken, Sol made it look as if he was merely drying off his hands. "Is that you, Abner?"

"It sure is!" Abner declared as he reached out to shake Sol's hand. "How in the world are you and what in the world are you doing in some trading post in the middle of the woods?"

"I own the place."

"That a fact? Great news! Looks like you're prospering."

Sol nodded. "For now. There's just enough miners about to keep me afloat. What are you doing?'

"Eh, just on my way to California. I'm sure you hear that a lot around here."

"I sure do."

"We need to have some dinner," Abner said. "Catch up on old times."

Slipping into an eager smile and casual tone made Sol feel like he was pulling on an old shirt that had been forgotten at the bottom of a trunk. It may have been a bit frayed and a little thin, but it was sure comfortable. "There's a place across the street that makes some fine pork chops."

"Sounds great! By the way," Abner added as he leaned forward and dropped his voice to a conspiratorial whisper, "I heard tell that ol' Nester Quarles is out and about. Seems the old dog is up to his tricks and causing quite a stir around Texas and New Mexico. Have you heard about that mining company he was supposed to have robbed single-handedly?"

Reluctantly, Sol shook his head. "I doubt that's true."

"How can you be so certain? You heard anything different?"

"Nester Quarles is dead," Sol said as he recited a bit of the story Nester had asked him to spread a year ago. "He was buried in Colorado some time ago. There's records to prove it."

"Really?" Abner said with a bit of surprise wrapped around an even bigger portion of disappointment. "Then who's the old devil ripping through the southern part of our great country?"

"I don't know, but it's not Quarles."

After considering that for a few seconds, Abner shrugged and said, "I suppose I'll pass that along."

"Be sure and do that. Oh, and do me a favor," Sol added. "Folks around here know me as Ed Sloane. It's a long story, but don't toss about that other name. It'll just confuse my customers."

"A long story, huh? So long as you tell it to me over a plate of them pork chops, I'll play along."

Sol walked around the counter and started getting the place ready to be locked up. "That's a deal. Don't expect too much, though. It was just easier to take that name than change the sign at the top of this old store."

"Didn't I hear something about you being chased out of some silver mining town a while ago?" Abner asked. "With wild times like that, you must have some good stories to tell."

"Not really," Sol said with a contented smile. "Not anymore."